THE APE CAVE HORROR

BOOKS BY CLINT ROMAG

CHRONICLES OF A WEREWOLF:
The Werewolf Manuscript
Search For The Werewolf
The Werewolf King *

THE SASQUATCH ENCOUNTERS:
The Unleashing
The Ape Cave Horror

A Spreading Madness

* Forthcoming

The Ape Cave Horror

The Sasquatch Encounters Two

Clint Romag

iUniverse, Inc.
New York Lincoln Shanghai

The Ape Cave Horror
The Sasquatch Encounters Two

Copyright © 2008 by Clint Romag

All rights reserved. No part of this book may be used or reproduced by any means, graphic, electronic, or mechanical, including photocopying, recording, taping or by any information storage retrieval system without the written permission of the publisher except in the case of brief quotations embodied in critical articles and reviews.

iUniverse books may be ordered through booksellers or by contacting:

iUniverse
2021 Pine Lake Road, Suite 100
Lincoln, NE 68512
www.iuniverse.com
1-800-Authors (1-800-288-4677)

Because of the dynamic nature of the Internet, any Web addresses or links contained in this book may have changed since publication and may no longer be valid.

This is a work of fiction. All of the characters, names, incidents, organizations, and dialogue in this novel are either the products of the author's imagination or are used fictitiously.

Cover art and illustrations by Jahrome Youngker

ISBN: 978-0-595-48376-1 (pbk)
ISBN: 978-0-595-60467-8 (ebk)

Printed in the United States of America

For my little, big sister Natalie Jude

AUTHOR'S NOTE

While finishing the final edits to this book, Bigfoot made national headlines a couple times, which was exciting. The first was in Pennsylvania. A man set up a camera in the forest in hopes of getting pictures of deer. Instead he got a picture of some hairy creature sprawled out next to a tree at night. Some said it was a juvenile Bigfoot, while others said it was a mangy bear with a skin disease. Whatever it was, the picture was freaky looking.

A couple weeks later, there were news reports in Florida of some ape-like beast with orange hair spotted in the trees. People were calling it a baby Bigfoot, but it turned out to be a fox squirrel.

Rest assured, the Bigfoot in this book aren't squirrels or bears.

With "The Ape Cave Horror" I wanted to capture the energy of the first book and at the same time expand on what we learned about Bigfoot. The character of Andrew Bridgeston was originally going to be in "The Unleashing" until I moved the location to Canada and then he didn't fit into the story. He finally gets to make his debut.

Virus SD5E is mentioned in this book. The virus comes from the pages of "A Spreading Madness." In that story, the virus spreads through the deer and elk population around Mount Saint Helens making them go crazy.

Most of the animals were slaughtered to stop the virus. The Ape Cave Horror takes place about two years after the events that take place in that book.

A word of warning: The Ape Caves are dangerous, so be very, very careful once you turn this page. I hope you can run fast and if you can't, I hope you have a big gun to protect yourself. Step quietly and don't make any loud noises. If you see a Bigfoot up ahead in the shadows, you might want to turn around and check your back, because there's a good chance that you'll probably already be surrounded. If you get to that point, make your peace with God quickly.

I wish you luck and be courageous as you start turning these pages.

Clint Romag
November 27, 2007

ACKNOWLEDGEMENTS

A very heartfelt thanks goes to my Mom who spent a lot of time editing this book. I learned that my Mom's red pen is just as stinging as her wooden spoon from days of old.

A very big thank you goes to Jahrome Youngker who did an awesome job with all of the art. The cover, the map and the illustrations are fantastic.

A thanks goes to Virginia "Kerley" Franken and her English eyes for doing a final proofread.

A thanks goes to Cameron Zeidler who helped me explore The Ape Caves, Lava Canyon and The Trail of Two Forests, while researching this book.

And a final thank you goes to Enrique and his machines.

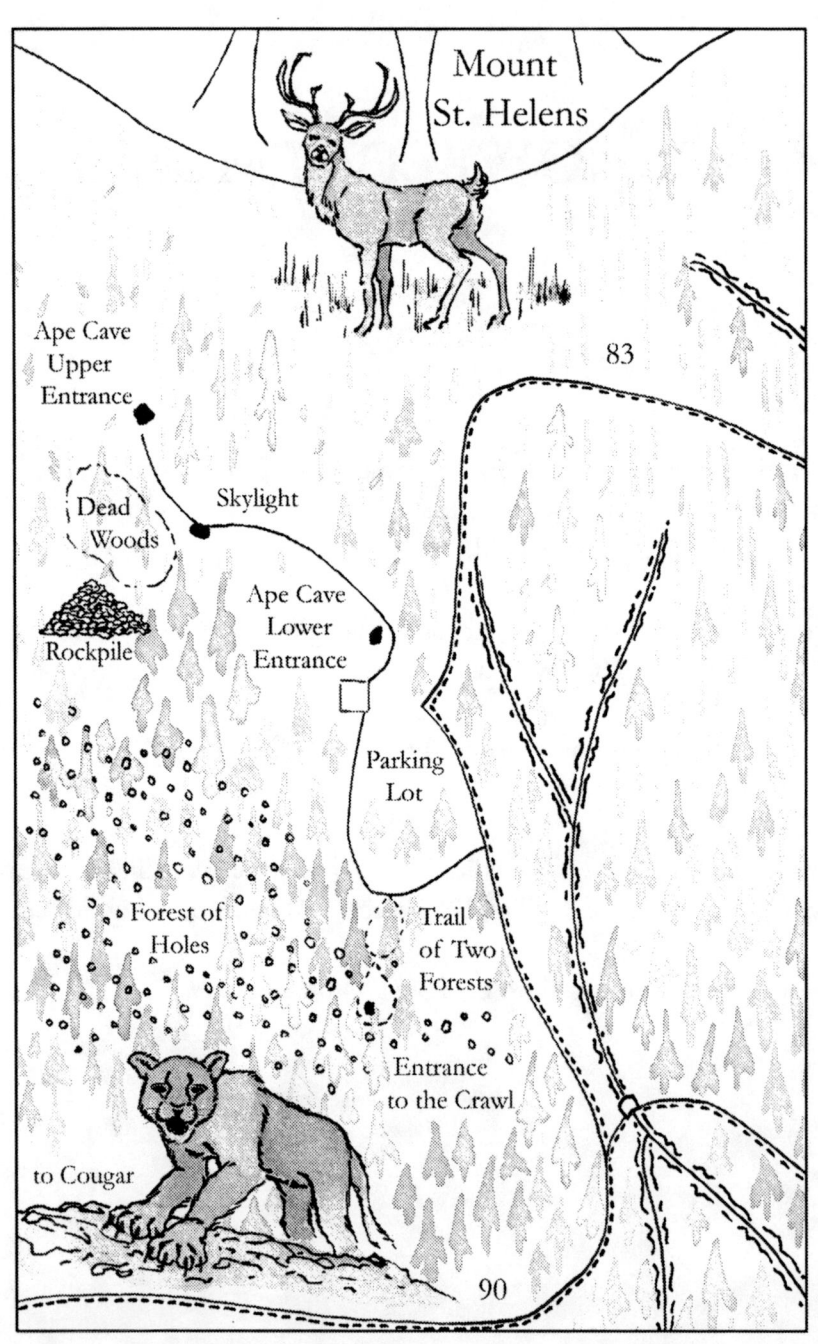

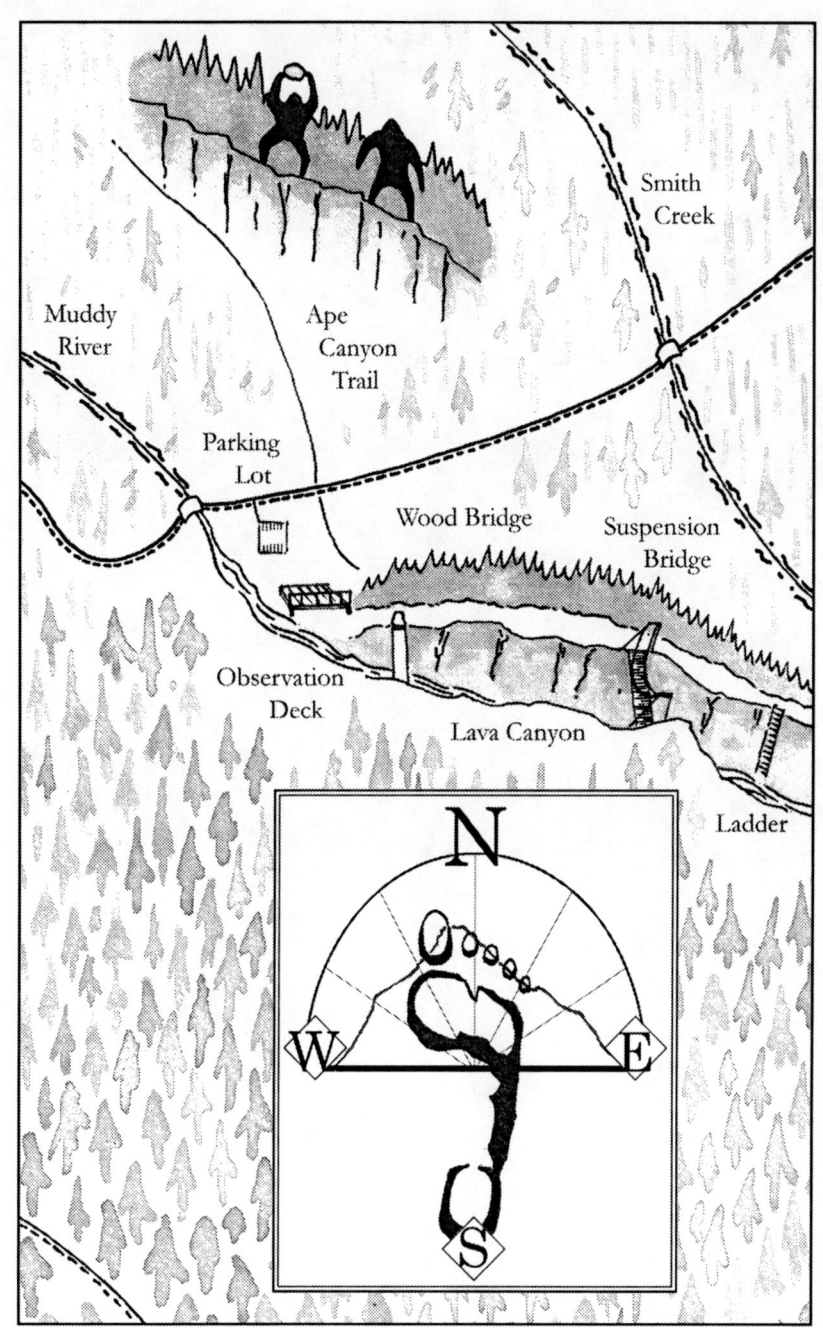

Chapter 1

▼

Rain spilled heavily from the dark gray clouds that were covering the entire sky, pressing down against the small town of Longview, Washington threatening to drown it. The rain lashed hard over the pointed rooftops of the houses, onto the muddy lawns, adding to the streams of water that rushed down the gutters along most of the roads. Many of the drains were clogged creating growing pools of water over sections of neighborhood streets. The rain roared in every direction, consuming all other sounds in its powerful presence. Even though it was mid-morning, there was not a single hint of the sun above as if the bright orb was hiding from the onslaught. The light was dim and dusk-like, draining away any color and making everything dreary and dark. Most people were in their homes or at work, not wanting or daring to go outside.

Chad Gamin glanced up at the black sky and smiled as the heavy raindrops pummeled his face. To him, it was just an ordinary November day and the rain made him feel alive. He breathed in the cold air as he gazed at the brownish, green waters of Lake Sacagawea. He still found the park beautiful even in the stormy weather. The gravel softly crunched underneath his steps as he walked along a muddy path spotted with puddles. The rain beat steadily against the hood of his blue jacket.

Most of the trees had lost their leaves, revealing bare, wet branches twisting and turning up towards the gloomy sky. The wind stirred in random gusts pelting him with rain. The ducks and geese were huddled in groups along the banks keeping warm, quacking amongst themselves. Chad spotted a squirrel running across the grassy lawns that covered the banks of the lake. It darted around a bush and scrambled up the thick trunk of a gnarled oak tree.

Ever since Chad had moved back to Longview, he had walked the lake nearly everyday whether in rain, sun, snow or wind. It was his way of relaxing and getting his mind off the dark memories that continually plagued him. The gravel path went down a slope and underneath a two-lane bridge giving Chad a momentary relief from the rain that roared overhead. He stopped for a moment and gazed into the narrow waterway that flowed under the bridge. Wet, slimy rocks lined the shallow banks, poking out from the brown surface of the water. The cement bridge was about thirty feet long and ten feet over the lake. Chad placed his hands on the wooden rail that ran along the bank beneath the bridge as his wary eyes were drawn into the dark shadows. A sudden anxious feeling fell upon him causing him to back away from the water, take a deep breath and continue walking again.

A solitary jogger, a woman dressed only in shorts and a T-shirt, smiled briefly as she jogged by Chad. Startled, he nodded and smiled. No matter what the weather, there were always people at the park. In the summer the trees were full of leaves with countless shades of green that almost glowed in the sunshine, while daisies and buttercups dotted the lawns with color. It was a beautiful sight, but the winter months had their own beauty. Chad stepped out from under the bridge into a wall of rain and moved up the path that meandered along the bank towards three Redwood trees that towered ahead of him. He was still amazed at the variety of trees that grew around the lake.

"Must be hundreds," he was thinking when he noticed a lone figure standing in the path with an umbrella in one hand and a cane in the other; a dark silhouette in the rain. Chad had passed several people during his walk and all of them had been on the move, jogging, walking or bicycling, but none of them had been standing still in the rain and cold. The figure remained stationary facing him as he approached. The stranger turned out to be an old man, wearing a long tan overcoat and an African Safari hat with one side tied up. The stranger's face was leathery and deeply creased as if he had spent most of his life outdoors. The man stared at him with intense, gray eyes, his thick, white eyebrows arching up. Chad nodded briefly and would have walked by, but the man stepped into the middle of the path blocking his way.

"Good morning Chad Gamin," he greeted in a deep, booming voice. "Are you ready for an adventure?"

Chad stopped and gave them man an amused look, before asking, "What? What do you mean?"

"Andrew Bridgeston." The man raised his weathered hand to shake. They shook hands as Andrew's gray eyes studied Chad trying to gather in every detail. "I've been wanting to meet you for a very long time."

"What for?" Chad asked

"Come let's get out of the rain," Andrew said in a loud, eager voice, his eyes beaming, motioning him to follow. Andrew moved under the three towering Redwood trees with branches that were intertwined creating a relatively dry shelter for them. They stood on a blanket of needles that had fallen onto the soggy ground. Andrew turned to Chad with excitement flaring in his gray eyes. "You saw the Sasquatch, a whole community of them in Canada. I have been hunting this creature for almost forty years and have never once seen it. Over the years, I've found many footprints and hair samples, but never the actual animal, not even a glimpse."

"Feel fortunate," Chad said. "That community of Sasquatch killed thirty people including my father and best friend."

"I've seen the news reports, documentaries, read your book and even saw the movie." Andrew nodded and smiled, his face creased deeply.

"The movie sucked," Chad said. "They made stuff up, filled the movie with models and the computer generated Bigfoot looked so cheesy."

"The documentary was much better," Andrew said as he leaned on his cane, his knuckles white with a hint of blue from the cold.

"Yes, at least the documentary reported accurately on what happened and they filmed on the actual locations," Chad said as a chill coursed through his body.

"Now for the adventure," Andrew stated loudly. "There are Sasquatch by Mount Saint Helens and I need your help capturing one."

"Sasquatch?" Chad asked, hoping he had not heard right.

Andrew nodded, his gray eyes gleaming.

"No way," Chad said, shaking his head. "If there are Bigfoot up there, I'm not going anywhere near the place. I haven't gone into the forest for three years now. The last time was in Canada and you know what happened up there."

"A tragedy," Andrew said. "I am sorry about your father's death and for all the others, but we have an opportunity here that we must seize. I've been waiting for this for decades."

"You don't want it," Chad warned, shaking his head in disbelief.

A frown settled on Andrew's wrinkled face as his eyes beaded up. "To be honest, I am extremely envious of you. You got to see these legendary creatures with your own eyes, while I've spent most of my life hoping to see one face to face. I've even gone on four expeditions to Camp Elizabeth searching for your community of Sasquatch."

"You and everyone else," Chad snapped.

"And no one has found them," Andrew said with dismay.

"Good," Chad said, "so they can't kill anyone else."

Andrew sighed. "This meeting is not going how I thought it would. At least do me a favor and hear me out."

Chad looked at Andrew's passionate face. Strangers had been approaching him for the last three years asking questions about Bigfoot, but this man in an African safari hat sparked some deep curiosity. "Okay, let's hear it."

Andrew tapped his cane in the needle-covered mud. "We have been monitoring the Mount Saint Helens area for about a year now, ever since a group of hikers vanished near the south face of the mountain close to the Ape Caves."

"Yes." Chad nodded. "I remember."

"Around the same time," Andrew continued, "a group of teenagers found some rather large footprints claiming that they were from a Sasquatch."

"Most thought it was a joke," Chad said.

"It was no joke, Chad." Andrew shook his head and stamped his cane hard into the mud. "We did our own investigation in the same area and found more footprints, 16 inches in length. There is a Sasquatch up there. I would bet my life on it."

"I wouldn't do that," Chad warned, slowly shaking his head back and forth as a sense of foreboding settled upon him.

Andrew smiled briefly and then his stern, creased expression returned. "There have been five disappearances or attacks since then, the most recent occurring at Lava Canyon."

"I heard about that too," Chad said.

"Yes," Andrew nodded. "A young man and lady were found dead at the bottom of the canyon, which isn't out of the ordinary since many have slipped to their deaths in that area. Have you ever been to Lava Canyon?"

Chad shook his head. "No I haven't."

"It's about a twenty minute drive from the Ape Caves," Andrew explained. "Lava Canyon is a very beautiful place with waterfalls, ancient rock outcropping and steep cliffs that give a history of the volcanic eruptions of the mountain through the centuries. Some of the paths are dangerous and if one isn't careful, it would be very easy to slip and fall. Several people have over the years, but most of them died going off the paths where one wrong step can send you plummeting down into a rocky crevice."

"What's that got to do with Bigfoot?" Chad asked, shivering again in the cold.

"I prefer the term Sasquatch," Andrew said in an annoyed voice.

"Whatever you call it," Chad snapped. "The big hairy monster that kills people in the woods."

"I also contest that point but we are getting sidetracked. The young lady and man were found at the bottom of Lava Canyon with bite marks. Rather substantial chunks of flesh were missing."

"It could've been a bear or some other animal," Chad remarked.

"That was what the authorities finally concluded. They even killed a bear about a week ago claiming that it was the one, but I beg to differ. My assistant, Javier, scouted the area and found Sasquatch prints. The size of the prints were about 15 inches in length, smaller than the ones we found near the Ape Caves meaning that there are at least two of them up in the area, maybe more."

"But why do you want my help?" Chad asked.

"You were in the thick of them," Andrew said. "I want your experience and expertise, plus I need another man. I run a small team and could use your help. I would like to talk to you in more detail. It's rather cold and the rain doesn't look like it is going to stop."

"Let me think about it." Chad said as a giant drop of water fell from a branch, smacking the hood of his coat. He had grown much colder standing in one place under the Redwood trees and felt an ache in his stomach as well as a tightening in his throat with all of the talk of a Bigfoot so close to his hometown. It was a scary, unbelievable thought to think these monsters might be so near. Part of him wanted to flee to his apartment immediately and lock all the doors and hide.

Andrew handed him his card. "This is my cell phone number. I was hoping we could meet tonight. Dinner's on me."

"I'll think about it, but I can't guarantee anything." Chad stuffed the card into his coat pocket.

"Yes, yes," Andrew said and smiled, his whole face wrinkling in a satisfied expression. They shook hands and said goodbye. Chad started walking back to his car, disturbed by the conversation. For three years there had been people coming up to him asking him questions, trying to buy the rights to his story and even lecturing him. He hated being reminded of the events in Canada, which still haunted him nearly every night. Even during his waking hours, it was hard to forget as he was assailed by anxiety and panic attacks. He finally reached his silver Audi A4 and drove to his apartment near the old downtown area close to Commerce Avenue. He walked into his cold, dark apartment, locked the door and flipped on the light. Dark rooms made him uncomfortable so he turned on another light next to his leather couch and sat down. His mind raced over every part of his conversation with Andrew as unwanted memories returned to the forefront of his mind. Mount Saint Helens was only a forty-five minute drive away. "Much too close," Chad whispered.

"How could a Bigfoot live in an area filled with thousands of tourists, hikers and hunters?" Chad wondered, hoping that Andrew's whole story was nothing more than a lot of B.S. He stood up and looked out the window at the falling rain. For some reason, he felt vulnerable. A sense of dread fell upon him as he walked into the hallway, where he flipped on a light. He entered his bedroom and turned on another light.

"There's no way in hell I'm going up there," Chad decided as he stripped off his wet clothing and took a long, hot shower.

Chapter 2

Chad's cell phone rang in the afternoon with the name Stephen Denmin flashing on it. He hesitated for a moment contemplating if he should answer. A Bigfoot had killed Stephen's late wife Claire in Canada. Chad could still remember that horrifying night like it was yesterday. After his best friend Shane had mistakenly shot a baby Bigfoot, a horde of them attacked Camp Elizabeth killing close to thirty people. Chad, Meredith and Jay were the only survivors of the initial attack. They had tried escaping by hiking through the forest to a lakeside cabin. Jay had been killed before they even reached the cabin, where they found Claire. Stephen had left his wife at the cabin for an emergency business meeting promising to return the next day. Claire had been very nice, inviting them in, feeding them and calling her husband, who immediately started flying back to help. By the time Stephen had returned to the cabin, Chad was the only one left alive. The Bigfoot had killed all the others, including Claire. Even the cabin had been burned down.

The phone continued to ring. "What the hell," Chad muttered as he answered.

"Chad," Stephen greeted in his usual loud, aggressive voice. "It's Stephen."

"How are you?" Chad asked as he sat down on his couch.

"Andrew Bridgeston called me and said you didn't sound like you wanted to join him."

"You know Andrew?" Chad asked.

"I've been financing his organization for the last two and a half years," Stephen said in his terse, no-nonsense way. "And I want you to join him."

"I really don't want to go," Chad replied.

"Listen Chad," Stephen blared in a loud, annoyed voice. "You're going to go or I'll stop paying your stipend every month."

"If there is a Bigfoot up there I don't want to go," Chad snapped back.

"If there's a Bigfoot up there walking around, I want it dead," Stephen yelled. "And I would think you would want the same thing."

"Of course I do," Chad replied defensively.

"Good," Stephen huffed, "You're going. It's settled. I've been paying you for two years now as a consultant and I haven't asked much from you, only a few phone calls now and then asking for your opinion. For three years I've been looking for these monsters that murdered my wife and I've found nothing. They disappeared which is incredible. How could so many hide from us, from everyone? We've gone into caves, up mountains, into the deep forest and nothing. I don't like failure. Andrew says that it is very likely a Bigfoot is up there and if so, I want it killed. My patience is at an end. If we kill the one at Mount Saint Helens, maybe we'll learn something that will help us track the ones in Canada. I've invested all of my time, money and life into this, so I am asking you as an employer, but more importantly as a friend to go with Andrew and find this fucking monster."

Chad's mind raced. He didn't want to lose the money, which was a nice sum for basically doing nothing. It was enough to cover rent each month. He also doubted that there were Bigfoot so close to civilization. The chances of him ever running into one were so low that a trip up to the mountain would probably be safe. Chad felt sick to his stomach with indecision.

"We need to be avenged," Stephen cried.

Chad glanced anxiously around his living room. He hated feeling pressured into something. He shook his head, his eyes stopping on a picture of his father. Feelings of anger and guilt surfaced about his father's death. Sometimes he wondered if he had only been a little quicker, he could have stopped the Bigfoot from ambushing his father. He stared at the picture for a moment, his mind made up. "I'll go."

"That's what I wanted to hear my boy," Stephen said.

"But if it gets crazy, I'm out of there."

"You'll be fine," Stephen assured. "Andrew and his team are professionals with a lot of experience out in the forest. If you need help, just give me a call and I'll send as many armed men as you need to get the job done. Mount Saint Helens is a lot closer to civilization than Camp Elizabeth. We can always get you out of the area quickly and come back with enough firepower to decimate a small town. Keep me updated and give Andrew a call."

"Talk to you soon." Chad set the phone down and stood up and looked around his apartment taking deep breaths and exhaling slowly. The pit of his stomach seemed to drop a foot with anxiety. "What am I getting myself into?" he asked himself and began pacing back and forth in the living room. He stopped at the same picture of his father and him posing with their rifles at Camp Elizabeth. It was the last picture of his father alive. The camera had been found among the ruins of the camp and the authorities had given it to Chad months later. It was like one last goodbye from his father.

"I'll do this for you Dad," he said and touched the picture. The last three years had been hard to get through and he missed his father dearly. He went into the bedroom and pulled out a rifle and a handgun, which he examined thoroughly. "I will be needing these," he thought and placed the weapons on his bed. He opened up his closet and pulled out a cardboard box full of junk, setting it on the floor. He fished through the box and pulled out ammo. Setting all the shells and clips on the bed, next to the weapons, Chad felt a little safer although a sense of foreboding filled the back of his mind. Before meeting Andrew for dinner, he would make a stop by the gun shop and buy more ammo.

He walked over to his desk and opened a drawer, pulling out his knife named Vengeance. It had a wide 7-inch blade, with a slight curve and a square, wooden handle lined with silver metal. Gripping it with his right hand, he flashed it in front of his face and sliced the air several times. It felt good to hold the weapon. Last 4th of July Chad had purchased it from a knife dealer at a booth at Lake Sacagewea. Thousands of people crowded the Lake during the fourth enjoying live music, contests, food and the hundreds of booths that sold everything from old comics to arts and crafts. The knife had immediately caught his eye under the glass casing and he bought it right on the spot. From all the fantasy books he had read, the heroes' weapons always had names so he decided to do likewise. Vengeance seemed to be a perfect name. A few weeks after buying the blade, he got the words "Vengeance" carved on one side of the hilt and "Chad Gamin" on the other side. It came with a brown leather sheath, which attached nicely to his belt.

Chad called Andrew to meet at a Mexican restaurant by the Three Rivers Mall. In the meantime, Chad surfed the net reading up on Lava Canyon, The Ape Caves and the recent deaths and disappearances as the pit of his stomach began to ache even more as the minutes passed. It seemed all too much as pictures of the forest popped up on his screen. He hadn't gone out into the wilderness for three years. Glancing over at the guns on the bed for reassurance, Chad slammed his fist on the desk frustrated with himself. "I'm stronger than this," he said as he read some of the articles about the Ape Caves. He nervously began tapping his fingers on the desk and knocking his feet together.

"It's just dinner," Chad said. "I can always tell him that I don't want to go." Chad took a deep breath and then a determined expression settled on his face. "I will at least hear Andrew out."

At the Mexican restaurant, Andrew greeted him with a firm handshake and an enthused smile. "So glad you decided to join me. Adventure awaits."

"More like a bloodbath," Chad thought as he shook Andrew's hand. They sat down and ordered their food and drank Coronas.

"So tell me about Canada," Andrew said as he placed his African Safari hat on the seat next to him, revealing a full head of white hair with shades of brown. Deep crease lines, sunspots and an inch long scar marked his forehead. His gray eyes were fierce and quick as they examined Chad, taking in every detail.

"I really don't want to talk about it," Chad said, shaking his head. "It was a nightmare, which I'm still trying to get over. Plus I've said all I can in the documentaries and in the book, not to mention the countless interviews."

"Let's get down to business then," Andrew said and opened a black briefcase. He pulled out several pieces of paper, which he spread across the table. There were charts representing each decade from the 1940s to the present, which he spread across the table. "This is a computer print out of Sasquatch migration patterns. We have documented every sighting in the last sixty years in North America, throwing out the probable hoaxes. As you can see, each decade the Sasquatch sightings in the south such as California and Nevada have decreased while the sightings in the north such as Washington, Idaho and Canada have increased. The Sasquatch have been migrating north over the last few decades probably trying to find new places to live as mankind has encroached into their territory. From this data, the main group has moved deep into Canada and I would guess Alaska as well.

"Of course the journey north grows more difficult as the years go by because the cities are bigger, forests are cut down, roads are built, the suburbs spread out and so on. My theory is that the main group has already migrated into the Canadian wilderness, while pockets of Sasquatch have been left behind and in essence trapped. That's why there is still the occasional sighting in the lower 48. One of these pockets of Sasquatch has been living by Mount Saint Helens and I think I know where." Andrew pulled a map of the Gifford Pinchot National Forest and Vicinity, which starts out just above the Columbia River covering Mount Saint Helens and all the way north to the Mount Rainer National Park.

"As I told you earlier today, in the last year there have been five incidents of hikers who have gone missing, most were never found and none found alive. I think all of these incidents have involved a Sasquatch." Andrew began marking the map with a red pen. "These are the areas where the hikers vanished including the couple who were found dead in Lava Canyon." Andrew moved the map across the table to Chad. "Tell me Chad, what is in the center."

Chad looked at the map and said, "The Ape Caves."

"Yes, and we have been searching the surrounding area, including making trips into the caves."

"You can't be serious," Chad said. "The Ape Caves are a major tourist attraction. Thousands of people visit the caves each year. They go hiking and sightseeing all over that area. The Bigfoot would've been spotted by someone after all these years."

"The Sasquatch," Andrew said emphasizing the word Sasquatch. "They do not live in what you know as the Ape Caves. First of all, what do you know of the Caves?"

"It's the longest lava tube in North America discovered in the 1940s and explored in the early 1950s by a Boy Scout group that named them The Ape Caves. People like to say, as a joke, that Bigfoot lives there. I've never been to them," Chad said.

The waitress walked over and served them their dinner. Chad got a chicken burrito and Andrew got steak fajitas, which he covered in hot sauce and salsa. After a few bites, Andrew continued the conversation. "Let me tell you my theories on why the Sasquatch have never been caught. First of all, they are intelligent."

"I know that … they destroyed a camp full of armed hunters and then tracked us for miles through the forest," Chad said in between bites of his burrito.

"And then they vanished into thin air." Andrew snapped his fingers for emphasis and took a long drink of his Corona. "The Sasquatch live underground in caves and caverns, only coming to the surface to hunt. They most likely hunt at night, rarely going out during the daylight."

"Most sightings have occurred during the day," Chad said.

"Yes." Andrew nodded. "I think the majority of those sightings are of Sasquatch attempting to migrate north. They leave their caves and hunting grounds and quickly become more vulnerable as they move through unfamiliar territory. They have to cross over roads and move through areas populated with people."

"Interesting," Chad mused as he tapped his finger on his chin. "But if they don't live in the Ape Caves, where do they live?"

"The Ape caves are vaster than most people realize," Andrew explained. "The lower cave, the easiest to navigate takes an hour to go round trip. Part of the cave collapsed centuries ago, closing off the remainder of the lava tube. There are caves down there that have never been explored or discovered, inaccessible from what we know as the Ape Caves. There might be an entrance to the hidden caves out in the forest that has remained undiscovered. My men have been scouting the area for the last three months and have found many small tunnels, holes in the sides of rock walls that lead to chambers, big enough for something to live in. Mount Saint Helens erupted two thousand years ago, covering the whole area in lava, so the terrain is very rocky with lots of dark holes where something could hide."

"This still doesn't explain, if the Bigfoot have been living there for centuries, why people have been vanishing only in the last year or so. Why haven't people been attacked in the last few decades," Chad said, finishing off his Corona.

"A change in behavior," Andrew said and tapped his rough-looking finger on the table. "What major event happened around the Mount Saint Helens area two years ago?"

Chad thought a moment and then said, "The crazy deer disease."

"Yes," Andrew said. "Virus SD5E originated in the Mount Saint Helens area in Spirit Lake infecting the deer population and making them rabid. The virus spread throughout southwest Washington, but Mount Saint Helens was hit the hardest. As you know the deer population was nearly wiped out."

"You're right," Chad said. "It will take years before the deer population returns to its former levels. All of them were slaughtered to stop the virus."

"Correct, as well as the elk and other animals removing the main source of the Sasquatch food supply, causing a change in behavior. They now have to leave their caves and walk even farther to find food."

"People," Chad said, his eyes growing wide with a horrifying realization.

"Yes," Andrew nodded. "The Sasquatch are feeding on humans."

CHAPTER 3

Early the next morning, Chad packed a duffle bag, deciding not to call his mother to tell her what he was doing, knowing that she would disapprove and be stressed about his safety for the entire time. She had just started dating again since his father's death. He thought it was strange, but he wanted his mother to be happy and he definitely didn't want her to worry while he was out tramping through the woods with Andrew. Chad's sister was now living in Bellingham, pursuing a degree in education at Western Washington University. His sister had taken their father's death the best, always the strong one, keeping herself busy working full time while getting her associates degree in Longview.

Chad finished packing and zipped up his blue rain jacket, picked up his rifle and looked in the mirror. "What am I doing?" He shook his head and rolled his eyes, taking a deep breath to relax his nerves. Picking up his duffel bag, he stepped outside into the cold morning air. Rain steadily fell from the dark gray sky with no hint of stopping. The sun was nowhere to be seen, making everything a dismal color. "Sometimes I do miss the warm weather and beaches in Los Angeles," he thought as he took a deep breath of the cold, fresh air. "I would never move back though." Chad had lived in Los Angeles for five years trying to become a successful screenwriter. He failed to sell one script and returned to Longview to be with his family after his father's death. He actually liked the seasons in the Northwest, thankful for the fresh air, something that L.A. was lacking. He even enjoyed the rain and found it refreshing and peaceful.

A green van was parked along the street in front of his apartment complex. Andrew stepped out of the van wearing a long trench coat and his African safari hat folded up on one side. He leaned on a cane and smiled. "Good morning Chad," he called out loudly in a cheerful voice. His friendly demeanor suddenly turned when Andrew noticed the rifle Chad was carrying. Andrew's gray eyes beaded up and a frown descended upon his face. "No guns," he said in a stern, terse voice, stamping his cane on the cement for emphasis.

"What?" Chad asked. "You've got to be joking."

"I am not joking," Andrew said angrily. "I intend to capture a Sasquatch, not kill one."

"They are dangerous," Chad cried.

"Misunderstood," Andrew shot back.

"What are you talking about? Are you crazy?" Chad asked, finding the whole conversation ludicrous. How could anyone think that the Sasquatch weren't dangerous after what had happened in Canada?

Andrew pointed his rough finger at Chad. "The Sasquatch only attacked your group after one of your comrades shot and killed their child. They are peaceful by nature, hiding from us through the centuries, keeping to themselves."

"They slaughtered thirty people," Chad yelled. "You even said the ones up by Mount Saint Helens are feeding on people."

"I did," Andrew said with a curt nod. "They have no choice. Their food supply is gone."

"I am taking the rifle," Chad said as he glared at Andrew.

"We will use tranquilizer guns," Andrew countered.

"Fine, but I am still taking my rifle." Chad gripped the weapon in his hand and locked eyes with Andrew, who shook his head in disgust. "Either that or I am not going."

"It is against the law to shoot a Sasquatch in Washington State. They are protected by the law," Andrew stated smugly.

"Fuck the law," Chad yelled. "I am taking my rifle."

Andrew sighed, flabbergasted, his cane wobbling underneath his white knuckles. "Let's compromise. You can take the rifle, but you have to leave it in the van. I'm not going to have you hiking around like Rambo. Instead, we will be armed with very strong tranquilizer guns."

"Deal," Chad agreed as he briefly touched the handgun that was hidden inside his coat. "Although you are making a very big mistake."

"I disagree. I know what I'm doing." Andrew glowered at Chad for a moment and then the anger dissipated. "Let's be off."

Chad nodded and thought, "What a nut job." They got into the van and there was a very long, uncomfortable silence as they headed out of Longview taking I-5 south. Chad shook his head as he looked out the passenger side window. How could someone not take guns with them while hunting Bigfoot? Those monsters had slaughtered thirty hunters. Was Andrew crazy? That question kept repeating in Chad's mind. He finally couldn't take the silence, so he asked, "What made you decide to hunt for Bigfoot for all of these years?"

"Sasquatch," Andrew corrected him in an annoyed voice.

"Yes, Sasquatch," Chad said, holding back laughter at his situation.

"The idea of the Sasquatch has intrigued me since I was a young man. I inherited a lot of money after my parent's untimely death and was trying to decide what I wanted to do with my life. I didn't want or need a 9 to 5 job. I wanted to do something extraordinary and then I saw the Patterson film and my life changed. You've seen it I presume?"

"Yes, I think everyone has," Chad said.

"Until you crossed paths with the Sasquatch in Canada, the Patterson film was the best evidence of the existence of the creature. As I was saying, when I saw the footage, my life changed. I decided to dedicate my life to searching for and capturing this legendary creature. I've spent years following leads, hiking through the Northwest, Canada and almost all the other states. I had the money and the time and this ultimate hunt has been exciting and exhilarating to this very day. I don't regret one minute of it. Most of the money is gone now because of my divorce and years on the hunt, but thankfully Stephen is financing some of our operations. I even spent four years off and on hiking through the Himalayans searching for the Yeti, a close relative to the Sasquatch."

"How was that?" Chad asked.

"Magnificent, awe inspiring and damn cold. I found a few hair samples that turned out to be yak hair, but I did find a trail of footprints across a glacier. It was the best evidence I found of the Yeti. I'll show you the pictures later. My team is waiting for us in Cougar."

They turned off the freeway at Woodland and took the 503 east. It was a two-lane road that twisted and turned up into the forest-covered hills. Occasionally they passed a house or a driveway that led to a home in the woods. Chad locked his door and took slow deep breaths as the growing anxiety threatened to turn into panic. He hadn't been in the forest for three years since Canada.

"Nothing's going to happen," Chad thought and touched his handgun for assurance. The van rattled each time a log truck rumbled down the hill. To his right, the slope dropped steeply and occasionally through the trees he caught a glimpse of Lake Merwin in the valley below. It was a giant reservoir of water held back by the Merwin Dam. The rain fell steadily from the dark sky with no hint of stopping. They continued driving for another twenty minutes and then passed by another large body of water called Yale Lake.

"We're almost there," Andrew said. "You'll get to meet the rest of the team. This damn rain will make it almost impossible to find anymore footprints."

Chad looked out at the trees racing by and shuddered. A shiver shot through his body as the gruesome memory that had haunted him for three years returned. An image flashed through his mind of a Bigfoot erupting from a brake of ferns, all hair and muscle, grabbing his father, snapping his neck and then throwing him through the air. Chad turned his head away from the trees and looked at Andrew. "Where do you live?" Chad asked randomly to get his mind off the memory.

"My ex-wife got our house in Portland years ago and sold it, so I've rented ever since. Currently I live in a condo in downtown Portland. Most of the time my home is whatever hotel I am staying at. I travel year round investigating as many leads as possible. Here we are … Cougar."

The road led into a small town with a few houses and a couple two-story buildings lining the road. They slowed down and Andrew pointed out the statue of a cougar. "These animals are dangerous, quick and big," Andrew remarked.

"I've never seen one," Chad said as they pulled into the parking lot of a motel next to another green van. A short while later, they all met up at the local diner and Andrew introduced everyone.

"This is my youngest daughter Sherrie," Andrew said.

Sherrie, who looked to be in her early 30s had long, slightly wavy, red hair and was tall and slender like her father. She smiled and said, "It's so good to meet you Chad. You're a celebrity to us. How does it feel to be famous?"

Chad smiled. "Considering the circumstances, I'd rather not be, since it cost the lives of my Father and friends. People are always asking me about Bigfoot."

"Sasquatch," Andrew corrected.

Sherrie laughed. "Don't mind my father; that's one of his pet peeves. If you call it a Yeti, he'll get even angrier."

Chad laughed.

Andrew introduced Javier, a short man in his late 40s originally from Costa Rica. He had bushy, black hair with lots of gray.

"Nice to meet you," Javier said quietly. "I've worked with Andrew for 18 years, longer than anyone."

"Yes," Andrew said. "Javier has been through thick and thin with me. He even went with me to the Himalayans. And this is Javier's nephew Enrique who grew up in Miami and decided to join our band of merry men a year ago."

"And women," Sherrie added.

"Of course," Andrew said, patting Sherrie on the back. "My daughter is as stubborn as a mule."

"Just like my Father," Sherrie laughed.

Enrique was in his early 20s, with, short, black hair and a handsome, mischievous face. "Nice to meet you," Enrique said with a big grin. "I saw the Bigfoot movie. It was so good."

Chad smiled and nodded. "Thanks."

"I love working for Andrew but the Northwest is so damn cold. I'm use to the Miami heat. It's 85 degrees there right now. I haven't seen the sun in weeks. How do people survive up here?" Enrique asked.

"Lots of coats, hats and gloves," Chad said.

"And last but not least, this is Donald our technical guru," Andrew said.

"Good to meet you," Donald greeted with a handshake. He was in his late 40s, overweight with a beer belly and a deep receding hairline, which he combed over.

"Tell Chad what you've been doing up here," Andrew said.

"We've set up various cameras at potential hot spots throughout the area which I have been monitoring. If there are Sasquatch up here, they'll have to come out of their caves at some point and when they do my cameras will catch them."

"You'll need more than cameras," Chad said, praying that the monsters would stay in their caves and never come out.

"And now that our team is complete," Andrew said. "The Sasquatch will be ours."

Everyone cheered except for Chad who shuddered as the ferocious shrieks and growls of the Sasquatch were forever branded in his mind.

Chapter 4

After breakfast, Sherrie walked up to her father as they were leaving the diner and asked, "Can I go with you and Chad today?"

"Not today my dear," Andrew said as he put on his hat.

"My Dad can be grumpy," Sherrie warned and winked at Chad. "You guys be careful."

"We shall," Andrew replied and gave his daughter a kiss on the cheek.

Sherrie, Javier, Enrique and Donald got into one of the green vans and drove off.

"Where are they going?" Chad asked, wishing he could go with them.

"They're going to scout the area east of the Ape Caves."

"What are we going to do?" Chad asked.

"First, I want to show you a few of the prints," Andrew said. They walked into Andrew's motel room, where on a table, there were several cardboard boxes. Andrew opened one of the boxes, unwrapped the paper and pulled out a white cast of a giant footprint. He set it on the table. "This one we found up in Lava Canyon about a week ago … it's 15 inches long."

Chad touched it and chills shot through his body as memories of Canada returned. "I've seen a lot of these up in Canada … Too many."

Andrew opened another box. "I have some from Camp Elizabeth. I was one of the first groups of people allowed up there." Andrew pulled out three prints of various sizes.

Chad looked warily at the prints and took a step back from them. "Those prints come from the same creatures that killed my Dad and friends at the camp."

"Yes," Andrew said, putting them back in the box. He opened another box and took out the largest print yet. "This one we found near the Ape Caves. Shortly after we found the print, it started raining and hasn't let up since. It's hard to find tracks in the mud. The water distorts the prints."

Chad picked up the big print with both hands, amazed at the size and fearful at the same time. "This is huge. Are you sure it's not a fake?"

"Yes," Andrew said. "It's a rather large one and it's not a fake. The footprint is 20 inches long, one of the biggest I've seen. We found it by what we call the Dead Woods underneath the branches of a tree. I think it was hunched down waiting in one spot for a while before it moved off. We tried following the tracks, but we lost the trail. It's too detailed to be a fake. I doubt there's any prankster out here in the cold and rain of November making false tracks that no one would likely see."

Chad placed the giant print down on the table. "I don't want to run into this one."

"If we do, we have these," Andrew opened a trunk near the side of his bed and pulled out a dart gun. "Very simple to use, with strong tranquilizers. You just click the dart into here, point and pull the trigger. Make sure the safety is on when not in use. These darts could take down a bear. Here is yours," Andrew said.

Chad took the gun and a clip of darts. "I hope they work."

"They will my young man. You have nothing to worry about," Andrew promised. "We should be off. The morning is getting late."

They got into the van and Andrew drove out of Cougar towards the Ape Caves. The rain poured heavily from the sky, which grew darker from low-hanging clouds. The wipers were on at full speed as the rain rattled against the roof of the van. The road moved into the forest, lined by tall fir and Western Hemlock trees. With wary eyes, Chad looked out the passenger window expecting a Bigfoot to step from behind a tree trunk and charge the van at any moment. He closed his eyes for a second and gripped the handgun hidden in his coat, pushing back the dark thoughts.

"Today, I want to check out an area south of the Ape Caves," Andrew said as he pulled off to the side of the road. Chad zipped up his coat and put on his hood, before he stepped outside. The air was cold as he glanced around the deep shadows of the forest. Under the canopy of branches and the gray sky, the forest floor was very dark. Chad nervously looked around as he gripped the dart gun with his right hand while his left hand touched the handgun inside his coat. The steady down pour caused an occasional branch to creak, startling him.

Andrew stepped out of the van with a backpack and his cane gripped in his weathered hand. "Ready to do some exploring?" he asked in a jovial voice, his gray eyes bright with excitement.

"Where's your gun?" Chad asked worriedly, not sharing in Andrew's apparent joy to be outside in the pouring, cold rain in a forest where there might be a Bigfoot.

"In my backpack," Andrew said and motioned him to follow. Andrew stepped down into a ditch alongside the road and then up into the undergrowth. Chad followed surprised at how fast Andrew moved. Chad pushed through the undergrowth, his clothes becoming immediately wet. He followed Andrew weaving in and out around the tall trees. Chad's entire body became tense; he kept glancing back as images of a Bigfoot grabbing him terrorized his mind. He clenched his teeth and gripped the dart gun, his hand trembling slightly.

A branch cracked behind him and Chad twirled and raised the dart gun. "I think I heard something," he yelled.

"What?" Andrew asked, walking back over. "I don't see anything."

For several seconds Chad looked at a thicket of thorn and tall, leafy bushes that were twisted together. There was bramble, long grass, saplings and rotten logs that covering the forest floor around the trunks of the trees, creating thick undergrowth. "There are too many damn places for it to hide," Chad said, his fearful eyes darting back and forth searching the area.

"Nothing to be alarmed about," Andrew assured.

"You don't understand," Chad said frantically. "When it killed my father it was lying flat on the ground concealed by a bunch of ferns. It's crafty and dangerous." Chad glanced around an area covered in moss and thick grass. "It could be hiding so close to us and we wouldn't even know."

"Chad," Andrew yelled. "Calm down. There isn't anything here, but us. Now come on." Andrew started walking, pushing through the branches of a tall bush.

Chad pointed the dart gun ahead of him, his finger on the trigger. He then noticed that Andrew had walked off so he chased after him, scared to be alone. Andrew climbed over a rotten log and dropped down five feet to the muddy ground on the other side. Chad followed and slipped to his knees in the mud. He stood up, anxiously glanced around the area as he wiped the mud off of the dart gun. Andrew seemed to get even farther ahead, so Chad ran after until he was caught up.

Andrew continued at a decent clip, leaning heavily on his cane. They circled around a knot of trees growing so close together that it would have been possible to cut across. They hiked through deep mud and splashed through clearings of standing water. The rush of a creek rumbled ahead and a short while later they reached the low muddy banks. The creek was about eight feet wide, tumbling swiftly over mossy rocks and around mounds of mud and water soaked branches. Andrew stepped out onto a rock and then onto a small island of muddy grass and then to the other side, pulling himself up the bank using branches. Chad followed close behind.

Andrew moved along the creek bank down stream and stopped a couple minutes later. He knelt down with a grunt. "Look," he said. "Deer tracks."

Chad examined the markings in the mud. "I guess they didn't all die from the virus."

"The government has introduced vaccinated deer back into this area, but it will be some time before their numbers are replenished. Deer hunting has been banned for the next several years in southwest Washington, which has made many hunters angry," Andrew explained. "I was out of the state when the outbreak occurred."

"I was too," Chad said. "One of the guys my sister knew from high school was killed by the mad deer. His name was Eddy."

"Tragic event," Andrew said, veering off from the creek into the trees. They reached a clearing of tall grass. The rain poured even harder overhead now that they were temporarily out from under the protection of the tree branches. Andrew stopped and looked around. "Any advice Chad? Any particular behavior patterns of the Sasquatch that you witnessed?"

Chad looked around the clearing as an image entered his mind of several Sasquatch suddenly standing up surrounding them in a circle of death. He took a deep breath, gripping the dart gun. "They know how to hide … they are relentless. They followed us for miles trying to kill us. That's about it … the only times I witnessed any behavior was when they jumped out from behind a tree and killed someone."

"It's almost like trying to find a needle in a haystack," Andrew said. "A needle I've been searching for during the last four decades. You know after I saw the Patterson film, it took three years before I found my first footprint. I knew it was going to be difficult but I thought I would find a Sasquatch in the first year. It was discouraging when I didn't, but when I found my first print in central Oregon, I was ecstatic. I have it framed in my home. At that time, I thought finding the Sasquatch was so near. Little did I know almost forty years later I would still be looking for it."

"That's a long time," Chad said.

"It is, but it goes by fast," Andrew said. "Remember that … it is such a truth. People spin their wheels and then one day they wake up and ten or twenty years have gone by before they even know it. Take advantage of the short time you have on this planet Chad. It will be gone before you know it. I also don't have any regrets. People have thought me foolhardy, but I've enjoyed my life out in the wilderness, instead of being behind a desk in an office building."

"I hear you. I can already feel it happening. Not too long ago, I was a naïve, fresh-eyed young man moving to Los Angeles to pursue my dreams of stardom. Now, I'm a scarred wreck who has lost a lot in life." Chad looked around the clearing, gripping the dart gun tightly. "Where to now?"

"This way." Andrew motioned with his cane to follow. They hiked out of the clearing and back into the trees where it was darker, but more protected from the rain. Instead, the water would bunch up on the branches and then suddenly fall sending big drops splashing against their coats. They hiked down a hill where a wide, muddy stream filled with debris flowed swiftly by them. Andrew stopped and watched the water churn and rush past for a few minutes.

"I love it out here in the forest," Andrew said. "Isn't it invigorating?"

"It is," Chad agreed, "but I don't feel very safe out here."

"I will protect you," Andrew said with a grin the creased his entire face.

"I feel so much safer now." Chad laughed.

"I've been hiking in the forest for forty years and nothing has ever happened to me. The attack in Canada was a fluke, a rare event that has never happened before. Lightning won't strike you twice." Andrew assured.

"Let's hope not," Chad said as he suspiciously glanced around at the trees surrounding him, wondering what was lurking in the shadows.

They spent the next several hours hiking through the forest and by the end of the day Chad was cold, wet, exhausted and his nerves shot. It was such a relief when they finally reached the van and drove off with the heater blasting on full. "One day down, who knows how many more to go?" Chad thought.

It wasn't until Chad took a long, hot shower that his body finally rid itself of the chill from the cold day in the woods. He met the team at the diner for dinner. Everyone seemed to be in good cheer, laughing, telling jokes and stories. For the most part, Chad was silent answering questions posed to him, but not joining in on the revelry. He was in a retrospective mood and thought about Canada and the last three years. He felt like his life was coming to a crossroads and he would have to make a decision soon on what to do with the rest of it.

"Want to grab a beer?" Sherrie asked after dinner.

Chad looked at her for a moment and smiled. "Sure."

"For a second I thought you were going to say no," Sherrie said and laughed. "You seemed quiet at dinner."

"Oh, I just have a lot on my mind," Chad said.

"Did my Father drive you crazy with his non stop talk about the Sasquatch?"

Chad chuckled. "No … being out here in the forest is just bringing back a lot of memories from when I was in Canada. A lot of crap which I've been avoiding that I need to face eventually."

"I understand," Sherrie said as they walked to the bar next door. They sat down and ordered a couple beers.

"So how was today beside reminding you of Canada?" Sherrie asked.

"It was filled with rain, mud, more rain, more mud and more rain," Chad said in a tired voice.

"Welcome to my life." Sherrie smiled warmly and then laughed. "How was my Father?"

"He has so much energy," Chad said. "He kept walking up hills and then down hills, climbing over logs and rocks. I could barely keep up."

"That's him," Sherrie said with a proud smile. "He's been doing this for four decades. Most people half his age can't keep up. I'm in the best shape of my life since I started working for my Father."

They talked for a while and after Chad finished off his second beer, he said, "Well I guess I should go to bed. We have to be up early tomorrow."

"Goodnight Chad," Sherrie said and smiled.

"Goodnight." Chad walked back to his motel room dreading the coming day.

CHAPTER 5

▼

Four days later, Chad woke early in the morning in his motel room in Cougar to the patter of a steady rainfall. He yawned and stretched his arms and legs, which were sore and aching. The room was drafty and cold so he turned up the heater in the wall. They had been hiking through the woods for several days now and they had found no sign of a Sasquatch. The first day had been a harrowing experience for Chad as he had been on the verge of panic the whole time that they had spent out in the forest. The fear of a Bigfoot behind every tree would not leave him. The proceeding days had been no better, but Chad was determined to continue helping out Andrew for at least a few more days.

Chad took a long, hot shower knowing for the rest of the day he would be out in the cold and the rain. It was his one comfort. He turned the shower off and dried himself off. He dressed slowly, zipping up his blue jacket, tying his muddy hiking boots and then walking outside, meeting the group in the diner.

"Good morning Chad," Andrew greeted in his usual early morning, cheerful voice, full of enthusiasm as if today would be the day that he would make his big discovery and find a Bigfoot. He was dressed in his long coat and wore his African Safari hat.

"Morning," Chad said and sat down. Javier sipped on a cup of coffee while Donald ate a donut he had bought from the gas station store. Sherrie smiled and sat down next to Chad. "Where's Enrique?" Chad asked.

"He'll be here," Javier said. "He's not a morning person."

A few minutes later, Enrique showed up in a heavy, red rain jacket and hat. "Good morning everyone. I didn't want to get out of my warm bed." He grinned.

They ordered breakfast and then Andrew began his daily briefing. "Today, Javier, Enrique and I will explore that rock pile thoroughly. Donald will monitor the video equipment in the van as usual. Any updates Don?"

Donald shook his head, his hair was a mess and the comb over didn't hide his bald spot. He finished the donut in one bite. "A couple hikers walked by one of the cameras but that's about it, not even a deer."

"Do deer exist or do they not exist just because we haven't seen one yet?" Andrew asked.

"They do exist," Donald answered enthusiastically. "I do believe they exist."

Everyone laughed.

"And so does the Sasquatch," Andrew said and then turned to Chad. "Sherrie and Chad, I want you to take the van and drive to Lava Canyon and explore it. It has been closed to the public due to the recent accident and bad weather so be careful. A lot of those trails alongside the cliffs can be very perilous in the rain."

"Alrighty Daddy-0," Sherrie said and then turned to Chad. "Have you ever been to Lava Canyon before?"

"No." Chad shook his head. "This whole area is new to me. I rarely go out of Longview's city limits since my infamous Canadian trip."

"The canyon is beautiful," Sherrie said.

"I'm sure it is." Chad smiled, dreading going out into the woods again.

After breakfast, Chad and Sherrie took one of the vans, while the others took Donald's van with all of the video monitoring equipment in it. Sherrie drove, taking 81 East heading for Lava Canyon. The narrow road was lined with a wall of trees. Chad began tapping his foot anxiously. He breathed slowly trying to relax as thoughts of Bigfoot filled his mind. His nervous eyes looked out at the blur of green trees rushing by the window.

"Do you like working for your father?" Chad asked trying to relax.

"He can be difficult at times and as stubborn as a moose, but I love him and what we do … it's very exciting. My father's 67 year's old and is so full of life and energy. He's been hunting the Sasquatch for forty years since his mid twenties and hasn't lost any of his passion or enthusiasm. I really admire him. A lot of people his age are retired and sitting at home watching television, while he's out in the world pursuing his dream," Sherrie said.

"I think it is cool that you work with your father." Chad smiled as a jealous feeling fell upon him. His father had been dead for three years. Chad tried not to think about it.

"My sister thinks I'm crazy." Sherrie sighed. "She doesn't have the best relationship with him and probably blames him for the divorce. My mother divorced him when we were little and she never has anything nice to say about him."

"That's too bad," Chad said.

"Yes," Sherrie agreed. "My father is consumed with finding the Sasquatch so he was gone most of the time while we were growing up."

"Life is short," Chad mused. "Enjoy your parents while you have them."

"Amen to that," Sherrie said. "I rarely saw my Dad until I joined him on his quest. I am so happy that I did. He's not such a bad guy like my mother always told me. So what do you do for a living?"

Chad shrugged his shoulders and smiled. "Not a lot. I moved back to Longview after my father's death, worked at an insurance agency briefly and then I got a book deal, sold the movie rights to my story, the documentary, and ended up with a lot of cash all at once. Plus, I get a monthly stipend as a consultant from Stephen Denmin. I had always wanted to be a writer and I now have a successful book about Bigfoot, but it was at the cost of my father's life and all the others. So, the last couple years, I've been wandering aimlessly with no motivation. I don't feel passionate about anything anymore. I think I've grown numb to life."

"Do you like living in Longview?" Sherrie asked.

"It's quiet and slow, which I prefer right now. I lived in Los Angeles for five years so I've been from one extreme to the other."

"I've lived in Portland all of my life," Sherrie said.

"How's that?" Chad asked.

"Great ... I love it." Sherrie nodded enthusiastically. "Portland is such an awesome place to live and is in the midst of a resurgence. They're building beautiful condos and houses all along the waterfront. A lot of the scummy areas have been revamped with upscale restaurants, retailers and grocery stores."

"I like Powell's bookstore and the whole downtown shopping area," Chad said.

"Portland has a lot of character ... lots of trees and parks and all of the bridges," Sherrie said. The road veered to the right and the forest suddenly ceased as they entered a grassy hilly area with only a few trees. Sherrie pointed to their left at a massive gray area in the dark, cloud-covered sky along the horizon. "On a clear day you would have a majestic view of Mount Saint Helens right now. When the mountain erupted, it melted the glaciers on this side sending water, mud, trees and boulders crashing through the area, knocking down the old growth. Muddy River filled with debris and flooded Lava Canyon eroding away the dirt, revealing amazing rock formations from ancient lava flows of eruptions that happened two thousand years ago."

Chad looked at the dark gray horizon unable to see the mountain. He had never been on this side of Mount Saint Helens before, which was spared from the massive 1980 explosion. He had gone to the north side several times to the visitor centers where the eruption blasted over miles of forest, tearing it down and turning it into a muddy, desolate wasteland. Chad wondered what it would've been like to be on this side of the mountain during the eruption and see the massive black ash cloud cover the sky.

"Do you have a girlfriend?" Sherrie asked.

"Nah ... well nothing serious," Chad said. "I date occasionally, go out to the bars, but nothing long term. How about you?"

"Well, I was married for four years," Sherrie said and grinned.

"You were?" Chad asked.

"I got hitched when I was eighteen, which was a mistake. It didn't work out and we were divorced four years later. I haven't talked to the asshole since. I think I was trying to be independent from my mother. Since then I've had a few relationships, but at the moment I'm single. I don't have time really with all the traveling I do with my father."

They entered a turn off and stopped in the empty parking lot where a sign said that Lava Canyon was closed. The rain continued to pour steadily as they got out and zipped up their jackets and put on their hoods. Chad attached Vengeance to his belt and touched the handgun hidden in his jacket. He grimaced as he looked at the wall of trees in front of them.

Sherrie grabbed a camera and a dart gun. She put on a backpack that had bottled water, a ruler, knife, rope and a flashlight in it. "Do you want a dart gun?" Sherrie asked.

"Of course," Chad said, deciding that if they did run into a Bigfoot that he would use the bullets first.

"Here you go," Sherrie said, handing him the dart gun. "These should do the trick."

"I doubt that," Chad said under his breath.

They walked around a sign that said no trespassing and down a paved pathway into the forest. The wind stirred in sudden gusts sending the treetops swaying and creaking, causing Chad to jump and look frantically about with a startled expression on his face. They walked for half a mile and reached a wooden platform overlooking the beginning of Lava Canyon with a view of a wide bed of rock thirty feet below where a stream flowed down the middle. From this location Chad could still see the devastation of the 1980 eruption. The remaining tall trees were spaced apart as if many had been knocked down. Much of the bark and limbs were missing twenty to thirty feet up on the surviving tall trees, which was caused by the mudflow that came crashing through the canyon. There were a lot of younger trees ten to twenty feet tall, growing around the trunks of the older trees. On the platform were several signs that gave the history of the canyon. They walked to the end of it and reached a muddy trail that disappeared into the woods.

"This is where it gets difficult," Sherrie warned and stepped into the mud.

The trail led through the trees and opened up occasionally revealing the canyon as it grew deeper and narrower with steep cliffs edged by overhangs. The sound of rushing water grew louder. They reached an opening in the trees where white water rushed through a narrow gorge, crashing down a twenty-foot waterfall into a churning dark pool of water.

"I love it out here," Sherrie said as she gazed at the waterfall. "Isn't it beautiful?"

"Yes." Chad nodded. "But I rather visit in the summer." He glanced around at all of the trees, bushes and rock outcroppings. "So many damn places to hide," he thought. The trail sloped down into the canyon where a twenty-foot long wooden bridge spanned black, buttresses of rock. The narrow river roared 15 feet below the bridge. They stopped on the bridge and looked over the rail. The water crashed into a swirling pool hedged in by rock walls before it shot down a narrow gorge that cut through the steep rocks. Instead of crossing the bridge to the other side of the canyon, they backtracked up to the top of the chasm. The trail led into the trees and followed along the edge of the canyon that grew steeper with sheer cliffs made of dark basalt. The cliffs had rock-hewn, vertical columns down the sides twenty to thirty feet long creating amazing shapes and giving a visual geological history of the area.

"Let me get your picture," Sherrie said.

Chad stood near the edge of the cliff where it dropped a hundred feet down to the roaring rapids. Behind him, the opposite cliff face was composed of jagged crumbled rock at the top and vertical columns in the middle section.

"Cheese," Sherrie said and then took the picture. Chad took a picture of Sherrie and then both of them together holding the camera out in front of their faces. The trail went up the slope into the trees and then came back out to reveal a hundred-foot-long suspension bridge in the distance supported by a tower on each side of the cliff with steel cables. On the other side of the bridge, the trail opened up to a fenced off outlook area where a sixty foot waterfall shot over a sheer chasm into a spray of white.

"Cool," Chad said as he approached the bridge. "Looks like something in the movies. Are we going to cross it?"

"On the way back," Sherrie said. "We still have a ways to go. When we come back, we'll cross the bridge and hike up to the car following the trail on the other side. That way we'll cover more of the canyon and my father will be pleased. I gotta please Pops," she said and then laughed. The rumble of the waterfall was deafening. They had to yell so they could hear each other. "Lava Canyon falls is right past the bridge," Sherry said. They followed the muddy path into the trees again and walked by the bridge. The Lava Canyon falls was the biggest and most dramatic as it crashed down for a hundred feet, making a spectacular view. The trail reached an open cliff face where one wrong move would send someone tumbling down the side.

"Be careful," Sherrie warned.

Chad heeded Sherrie's advice as he glanced nervously over the side of the cliff. He walked slowly and took his time stepping over the wet rock. They reached a rocky wall where the water streamed over the trail. A cable grab-line was bolted in the side of the rock wall for twenty feet. Sherrie held onto the cable and stepped through the flowing water, which was several inches deep making the rocks on the trail slippery. Chad went next gripping the cable tightly. His foot slipped slightly halfway through the water but he held himself up and continued forward.

"It's like an obstacle course," Chad yelled to Sherrie.

"A deadly one, with giant Sasquatch walking about and rickety bridges." Sherrie turned back around and raised her hands like claws.

Chad laughed and shook his head.

A few minutes later the trail went over the side of a cliff. Sherrie motioned Chad to the cliff's edge and pointed down at a thirty-foot metal ladder bolted to the side. It led to the rocky floor of the canyon where the river rushed down the center over jagged basalt. "We'll climb down and look around for a bit and then head back. I'm already getting hungry and most of the hike back will be uphill."

"I'll go first," Chad said. The metal of the ladder was cold, wet and slippery. "No wonder this place is closed during the winter. We've hiked over so many places where one wrong step could have sent us falling to our deaths."

"I know," Sherrie said and started down the ladder after Chad. "The canyon has taken too many lives. We just have to be careful."

Chad reached the bottom of the ladder and stepped down, slipping as a rock shifted under his weight. He landed on top of a boulder stopping his fall.

Sherrie reached the bottom and took a picture of Chad. "No sign of a Sasquatch." The rain fell harder in a sudden rush pounding against their rain jackets, drenching everything.

"Thank God," Chad said. "I'm ready to go back to the motel. My clothes are soaked and I'm cold."

"Same here." Sherrie rubbed her hands together. "I wish the motel had a hot tub."

"A hot shower will do just fine." Chad gazed at the river that rushed nearby.

Suddenly, a boulder hurtled down the cliff, crashing in front of Sherrie who screamed and fell back, falling to the ground. Chad slipped on a wet rock as a familiar, monstrous, shrill roar pierced the gray sky above them and echoed off the canyon walls.

Chapter 6

▼

The green van pulled into the empty Ape Cave parking lot as the rain rattled loudly on the roof.

"Will this infernal rain ever stop?" Andrew asked as he put on his hat and grabbed his cane, which had a carving of a Sasquatch head on it. The rain had been falling for nearly two weeks. Andrew couldn't remember the last time he had seen the sun. Everyday had been the same dismal gray and gloom. Usually the rain didn't bother him, but with the Sasquatch within his reach, he wanted the best weather conditions as possible to help him in his search.

Enrique buttoned his red jacket. "In Miami we get brief showers that last for a few minutes almost everyday, but it doesn't rain non-stop for weeks."

"Welcome to the Northwest," Donald said from the back of the van. "I grew up in Olympia and the rain doesn't bother me. Washington is called the evergreen state. The reason why it's so green is because it rains all the time."

"At least you get to stay in the warm van," Enrique said.

Donald smiled smugly and shrugged his shoulders. "Someone has to monitor the video cameras." He opened up a cooler and pulled out a diet cola and a box of donuts, which he planned to munch on for the rest of the morning.

Javier was the first out of the van, opening the back door and grabbing a backpack full of equipment. He handed another backpack to Enrique.

"Keep me updated Donald," Andrew said. "You are my ears and eyes."

"Of course." Donald bit into a donut. "Please shut the door, it's getting chilly in here."

Andrew stepped out of the van and glowered up at the gray sky as rain splattered against his face. The weather was making his job harder. He tapped his cane on the asphalt and said. "Let's catch us a Sasquatch today boys." The others gave a half-hearted cheer. Javier shut the back door of the van and met Andrew and Enrique in the front. Andrew frowned in frustration, his brow furrowed as the rain splattered against his face as if taunting him that it would never end. "Footprints will be hard to find in the rain, but keep your eyes open ... also hair samples, broken branches, the usual. Enrique, do you remember how to get to the rock pile?"

"Yes." Enrique nodded.

"Then lead the way," Andrew said and pointed with his cane in the direction they were supposed to go.

Enrique tied his hood and walked across the parking lot to the beginning of the muddy Ape Cave trail, which led up a slope into the trees. Andrew followed behind walking briskly with his cane while Javier took to the rear. Under the branches of fir and western hemlock trees, the rain was partially blunted. The ground was muddy and wet with puddles from the constant rain. Enrique led them up the path for about thirty minutes until they reached a crop of dead, burnt trees still standing, most of the limbs and bark had been burned off.

"The Dead Woods," Andrew said as he looked at the burnt trunks. Other trees were white and weathered as if missed by the fire, but were killed when ash fell from one of the eruptions in 1983.

"Looks haunted," Javier said.

"Indeed," Andrew said.

Enrique turned left off the trail and moved into the Dead Woods where the ground became more treacherous and rocky. Pale green moss covered much of the forest floor making it even more slippery. They had to navigate around broken rock outcroppings, trenches, holes and uneven ground.

"Slow down Enrique, my knee is acting up," Andrew yelled as he took his time, making sure he braced himself with each step. He had a bad left knee from an accident at his home and didn't want to hurt it again. He had spent enough time and money on surgery for the knee. He had been having good days with it for the last few weeks, but today was a bad day. Enrique slowed down as he climbed over a fallen tree. Andrew climbed over grunting loudly and refusing Enrique's help. Javier slipped, scrapping his knee.

"Be careful," Andrew said.

"I'm fine boss." Javier stood up and tried wiping the mud off his pant legs.

They moved down a slope leaving the dead woods behind and stopping in front of a black, gaping hole in the rocky ground. Enrique knelt down and shined his flashlight inside the manhole-size opening.

"See anything?" Andrew asked.

"Empty," Enrique said. "It goes in about ten feet and stops."

"We'll check every hole, nook and cranny until we find the entrance to their lair," Andrew said as he walked to another black hole about three feet high in the side of a rock wall. Andrew gazed in and to his dismay found that it was only a few feet deep. He stood up and said. "We get closer with every step." For the next hour they stopped at twelve more holes in the ground all of them empty.

"Why are there so many holes?" Enrique asked.

"Two thousand years ago Mount Saint Helens erupted sending lava flowing down the mountain burning the forest. As it cooled it left a layer of basalt with tunnels, caves, holes and interesting rock structures. That's why it's so damn rocky around here."

"What about the 1980 eruption?" Enrique asked.

"No lava flows, just magma building in the crater after the initial blast," Andrew said. They crossed a loud brook that flowed twisting and turning around rock outcroppings. It was about a foot deep.

"Almost there," Enrique said as they entered a clearing where a pile of dark basalt rose up to twenty feet in places and was large enough in diameter to fill a gymnasium. Some of the boulders were the size of an automobile.

"Amazing," Andrew said as he gazed at the rock pile. "We didn't get a chance to fully investigate this area so let's be thorough about it today. Enrique, I want you to climb up on top looking for any trace of our Sasquatch. Be careful, the rocks will be very slippery."

"Harry won't be able to hide from me," Enrique said with a smirk on his face.

A scowl burst onto Andrew's face, his eyes beading. "Sasquatch," he yelled as Enrique laughed. Andrew shook his head in frustration and turned to Javier, who had been quiet for most of the hike. "Javier, you and I will walk along the perimeter. I'll go to the right and you go to the left and we will meet on the other side."

"Okay boss," Javier said.

Walking along the base of the rock pile was much more difficult than Andrew had envisioned. Trees and undergrowth with low hanging branches that touched the ground ringed the whole perimeter. Andrew had to duck and push under water-laden branches that drenched him, step through thick bushes, and navigate over slippery rocks and mud. Andrew gritted his teeth and continued on with a determined, serious expression over his leathery, creased face. At one point, Andrew had to get on his hands and knees and crawl through the thick undergrowth. He took a deep breath, already winded, and sat down on a wet rock. Occasionally he saw Enrique scrambling over the top of the rock pile.

Enrique smiled and waved. "Nothing yet sir," he yelled.

"Oh to be young again," Andrew muttered and stood up with a groan as a sharp pain shot through his bad knee. He whacked a bush with his cane and pushed through wondering how Javier was doing. When over half way around one side, Andrew reached a clump of trees with thick, low hanging branches. He sighed, dropped to his knees and started crawling again. A few feet in he stopped and gasped. In front of him, the branches were broken and the foliage on the ground was pressed into the mud creating a short path from the base of the rock pile, under the clump of trees, to a rock about ten feet away, which led into the forest. Andrew traced his fingers around a water-filled indention that was the shape of a large footprint. His gray eyes grew wide as he noticed the clumps of brown coarse hair in the mud. He picked up a few strands and rubbed them in between his fingers. He sniffed them and then saw that there was hair all along the hidden trail. He pulled out a plastic bag and gathered samples of the muddy hair. He studied the broken branches and what could be three different sets of footprints.

Andrew crawled down the path and moved to the lone rock that led to the forest. He stood up and pushed through the boughs of a fir tree to examine the ground on the other side of the rock. He touched with the tip of his cane what looked liked more footprints, which led into the forest. He ducked back down and followed the hidden trail to the base of the rock pile. He examined a large rock and found white streaks on the dark basalt that may have been claw marks. He grabbed the rock and with a groan he pulled finding it was loose. He also noticed deep indentions in the mud around the rock as if a heavy weight had landed there.

"This is it," Andrew whispered as an excited smile touched his lips, his gray eyes beaming. "This is it," he yelled. "After all this time, I am so close." Andrew stood up and pushed through the wet branches. "Enrique," he called. "Enrique."

A moment later, Enrique popped his head over a rock near the top of the pile and waved.

"Get Javier," Andrew yelled. "I think I found something. Hurry."

"Be there in a second," Enrique said and began calling out for Javier. A few minutes later all three of them were on their hands and knees underneath the low branches looking at the secret path.

"See here," Andrew said, showing them the hair that was pressed into the mud all along the path. "And the footprints," he pointed. "The hair is similar to the hair we found near Camp Elizabeth. I guarantee this is Sasquatch hair."

"So is this where they sleep?" Enrique asked.

"This is the entrance to their lair," Andrew said.

"Where?" Javier asked.

"Behind this rock ... it's loose," Andrew tapped the boulder with his cane. "I guarantee on the other side of this rock is a tunnel that leads to their chambers. No wonder they've remained hidden for so long. Most people that visit the Ape Caves stay on the trails and if someone did happen to wander off the path, they would walk by this rock pile and never in a million years see this secret little trail. If someone did crawl under here, they might not even notice the trail and if they did, they might think a deer slept here and not even pay attention to this boulder. They would climb over this loose rock and not even know what they had just walked over."

"So you're saying a cave is behind this boulder that the Sasquatch move when they enter or leave their lair?" Enrique asked.

"Yes." Andrew nodded. "They move the rock ... see the mud on it. Also look at the deep indentions in the ground caused when the rock is pushed opened. They crawl along the path up the lone rock over there and into the forest to hunt, most likely at night. They kill a deer or a bear or some other animal, pull it into their lair, move the rock back and remain hidden from mankind for all of this time. The only problem they have now is that the virus has killed most of the deer so they have to travel much farther for food. They may be starving."

"Well, let's see if there's a tunnel." Enrique crawled over to the rock.

"I tried moving it earlier but it was too heavy." Andrew scooted out of the way.

"Javier and I will try," Enrique said excitedly. They both gripped the top of the boulder and pulled. The boulder started to budge and then suddenly toppled over into the mud. On the other side was a gaping black hole about three feet high and four feet across.

"A tunnel," Enrique yelled excitedly and pulled a flashlight out of his backpack. He shined it in revealing a tunnel that went about ten feet, before turning a corner.

"Well done men," Andrew congratulated. "We are about to make history."

Javier patted Andrew on the back. "We did it boss after all these years."

Andrew gave Javier a hug. "We did it," he said and smiled. "Alright team, we need the dart guns, cameras and flashlights. We should explore this tunnel immediately. Javier and I will go into the tunnel."

"I want to go," Enrique said.

"He can take my place," Javier said. "I don't like tight places."

"Are you sure?" Andrew asked.

"Yes, just be careful," Javier said.

"Javier, I want you to give Donald a call letting him know of our discovery. If we don't come back within an hour, you know something is wrong. Call Sherrie and Chad and tell them to meet us here. Also, while you're waiting you could set up one of the cameras to monitor the entrance. Coordinate and organize with Donald," Andrew said as he holstered the dart gun on his belt.

"Will do boss," Javier said. "Good luck and bring back a Sasquatch."

"I intend to." Andrew's face creased with excitement as a smile appeared. "Oh and grab the rope Enrique."

Enrique holstered his dart gun and pulled a rope out of his backpack. "Can I go first?"

"All right Enrique." Andrew nodded. "You are much more nimble then me, but go slow and be very careful."

"Okay." Enrique set his backpack on the ground next to Javier. "See you soon Uncle."

"Be careful and don't do anything crazy," Javier warned. "I don't want to use the belt on you like your father use to do." He then turned to Andrew and they shook hands. "Congratulations."

"Congratulations to both of us." Andrew smiled. "All of our time and hard work is finally paying off."

"Yell if you need me," Javier said. "We're going to drink beer tonight and celebrate."

"So we shall." Andrew turned to the black entrance of the tunnel.

Enrique clicked on his flashlight and crawled into the cave mouth. Andrew kneeled down slowly and groaned; his knees ached as they pressed down against the rocky ground. With thoughts of glory and burning curiosity, Andrew flipped on his flashlight and crawled into the tunnel disappearing into the darkness behind Enrique.

Chapter 7

Chad scrambled to his feet as a Sasquatch roared somewhere above them. He fumbled in his pocket, pulled out his handgun, clicked off the safety and fired at the top of the cliff as rain splattered against his face. The loud gunfire echoed in the canyon; Chad shot blindly unable to catch a glimpse of the beast. "Sherrie," Chad yelled as he wiped rain out of his eyes. "Get over to the ladder."

Sherrie, white in the face, cowering on the ground and gripping a rock with trembling hands as her frantic eyes darted back and forth, stood up and ran behind the ladder, where there was a shallow cleft at the base of the cliff. Chad rushed over and joined her seconds later, both of them looking up as the rain continued to fall.

"What was that?" Sherrie asked gasping in fear, gripping Chad by the shoulder.

"Bigfoot," Chad whispered. Another boulder the size of a television crashed twenty feet away, bouncing down the bank into the rapids. Sherrie cried out and pressed back against the cliff wall as Chad raised his gun. "We're sitting ducks," Chad warned.

A loud, punctuated roar that sounded like a mix between a man, ape and monster shrieked overhead. Sherrie dropped to her feet trying to hide as Chad pointed his gun up, his eyes squinting in an attempt to spot their attacker. He wiped the rain out of his face and fired once, the gunfire deafening as it echoed through the canyon. Sherri pulled out her dart gun and stood up.

"What's down the river?" Chad whispered.

"The canyon goes on for another mile or so until it reaches the Smith Creek trailhead which circles back up around the canyon. It's a four or five mile hike."

"We'd be exposed in the canyon for a mile." Chad grimaced and shook his head. "Not good."

"What are we going to do?" Sherrie asked, her face aghast.

"We're protected behind the ladder for now. It can't hit us with boulders. Do you have a cell phone?" Chad asked.

Sherrie frantically fished through her pockets and then shrugged her shoulders with a frustrated expression filling her face. "I left it in the van."

Chad pulled out his cell phone and looked at it for a few seconds. "No reception."

Sherrie sat on a rotted log against the cliff wall. Suddenly a boulder slammed into the bottom of the ladder, causing it to rattle violently. The rock bounded off the ladder and smashed into the muddy ground five feet from where they sat. Sherrie screamed and fell to the ground. Chad jumped back, slipped and crashed down next to Sherrie.

"We're trapped," Sherrie cried as she desperately glanced around for a way to escape.

Chad scooted close to Sherrie, grabbed her hand and whispered. "Don't panic. These monsters are intelligent and we can't fuck up. It can't reach us at the moment."

Sherrie nodded and squeezed Chad's hand. "Okay."

They sat huddled against the cliff holding each other in the cold as the rain poured and the river rumbled loudly. They kept looking up, but from within the cleft they could only see part of the ladder as they waited, saying nothing as they listened for any signs of the creature. Time seemed to stop, both of them growing anxious. Chad gripped his handgun, assuring himself that the Sasquatch could not get them while behind the ladder. If one tried, he would have time to shoot it, he hoped. The monster's roar kept replaying in Chad's mind sending chills through his body, bringing back memories of Canada when there had been dozens of these creatures making the same sound.

"Maybe it's gone?" Sherrie whispered.

Chad shook his head. "It's up there waiting for us. They are relentless."

"Should we wait here for help?" Sherrie asked.

"It would be hours until they even knew we were missing and by then it would be close to dusk. We would be sitting ducks in the dark," Chad said. "And if it decides to come down here, we won't have any place to run. If there's more than one, our chances of escape grow even worse. We have no choice, but to climb up that damn ladder and hike back to the van."

Sherrie shook her head. "I don't want to go. I want to stay here."

"If we get caught out here at night we're dead," Chad said. "We don't know how many there are. The longer we linger in one place, the more chance of being surrounded. Believe me, I've been through this. We have to keep moving and not get caught."

Sherrie nodded reluctantly. "Okay … I wish I had a gun instead of this pathetic thing."

"There's a rifle in the van," Chad said. "Your father didn't know I brought my hand gun."

"Thank God you did," Sherrie said. In an instant, her eyes grew wider and her mouth dropped open as terror filled her face. "Listen."

Muffled grunting could be heard over the rainfall and then it stopped. Both of them sat still, not moving a muscle as they listened. Moments later the same grunting started again for just a few seconds before becoming quiet again. Sherrie moved closer to the cliff until her back was pressing against the rock. She held her dart gun with both of her hands, white knuckled and trembling.

Chad took deep, slow breaths as he looked up at the curtain of rain pouring down in front of them across the cleft opening. They waited for what seemed like an eternity listening and nothing until finally Chad whispered. "Let's try for the ladder."

Sherrie shook her head, dismayed and frightened. "It's up there. I know it."

Chad nodded and sat close to Sherrie on the rotted log against the wall of the cliff. More time passed as both of them began to shiver from the cold. "All right, let's do this. I'll go first, follow close behind and be quiet," Chad whispered and gave Sherrie a quick hug. Chad stepped through the long grass that jutted up between the rock and the ladder and peered up to find a shadowy man-like creature standing at the top of the cliff holding a large rock over its head. The monster roared. Chad dove back pushing Sherrie with him as the rock slammed into the ground next to them.

Chad took a deep breath, jumped up and yelled, "Come on." He leaped over to the ladder, looked up and saw no creature. He fired his gun once and started up the ladder. He fired every few rungs yelling until he reached the top where he quickly scanned the empty perimeter. "It's clear," Chad yelled and noticed the large footprints all along the cliff edge. Sherrie climbed up after Chad and reached the top seconds later. The rocky ground was open along the cliff for 15 feet before it reached a wall of trees and thick green undergrowth. Chad stood in one place searching the area as he aimed the gun at the trees. "Do you see it?" Chad asked.

Sherrie shook her head. "My gun is gone. It slipped out of my hand while I was climbing. Should I go back and get it?"

"We're not going back for it," Chad said and motioned for her to step closer. "Listen," Chad whispered. "These things are big but they can hide in the smallest of places. They blend into the forest like a chameleon. The one that got my father was lying on its back in the middle of a bunch of ferns. We didn't even see it until it was too late. Stay close to me and keep your eyes open. Yell if you see anything."

"Okay," Sherrie said.

A branch snapped nearby and they both tensed. Chad shot his gun in the general direction of the noise and then his gun clicked. He fished into his pocket grabbed an extra clip and replaced it. They glanced around for several long seconds and saw no sign of the monster. They started up the path walking as fast as they dared, Chad leading the way.

In front of him next to the path was a large fir tree with a wide trunk. Chad slowed down as he approached it and came to a halt. He stared at the trunk pointing his gun and then took a quiet step forward. He forced his hands to stop shaking and took another step as his breathing quickened almost to a pant. Sherrie stepped behind him quietly, glancing frantically around with eyes wide and bursting with fear.

"Be strong," Chad thought as he took another step now only three feet from the front of the tree. Chad jumped forward and fired, the gun blasting loudly through the canyon. Chad lowered his gun and sighed with relief. "Nothing." Chad motioned Sherrie around to the other side of the tree. They continued on, as the thunderous roar of the waterfall grew louder as they hiked up the trail, drowning out all other sound. They caught a glimpse of the Lava Canyon Falls through the trees.

"We're getting closer," Sherrie said, her voice muffled by the loud sound of the waterfall.

"What?" Chad asked.

"We're getting closer to the bridge," Sherrie said into his ear.

"Good." Chad nodded and hastened up the path. They reached a point in the trail that veered along the edge of the cliff. Chad stopped and pointed. "Look," he said. In front of them were the giant tracks of the Bigfoot moving up the trail towards the bridge. "It's already ahead of us." Chad shook his head, frustrated and angry.

"Should we go back?" Sherrie asked as she scanned the trees in front of them.

"No, we have to get to the van. We don't know how many of them are here. The one that attacked us could still be behind us."

Sherrie turned and looked behind her. "I'm scared," she said as she gripped Chad's shoulder.

"Me too," Chad said and then unsheathed Vengeance and handed it to Sherrie. "Take Vengeance."

Sherrie grabbed the brown hilt of the knife, the blade seven inches long. "Vengeance?"

"I named it," Chad said and winked.

Sherrie nodded. "This is better than nothing."

They started up the treacherous part of the trail that was muddy, narrow and on the side of a steep slope, giving them only about two feet to maneuver. Chad walked slowly, watching where he stepped as well as the terrain ahead of him. They would be defenseless if the Bigfoot attacked them now. The rain blew in on hard gusts of wind spraying them as the thunder of the waterfall grew deafening. Chad stepped into the footprint of the Bigfoot. It had begun filling with water. Both of Chad's feet could fit into it. The trail led them around a bend where they reached safer ground.

"The bridge," Sherrie said, pointing.

The Lava Canyon Bridge was suspended with cables 100 feet across the canyon, where the rapids rushed white in a narrow gorge before shooting off into the falls. They reached the 17-foot tall tower of Douglas Fir wood, which supported the bridge.

"Should we cross?" Chad asked. "Or keep going on this side?"

"Let's cross," Sherrie yelled over the roar of the waterfall. "I doubt it would cross the bridge. We should be safer with the canyon between us."

"Okay, you go first," Chad, said. "I'll watch your back."

Sherrie stepped on the first plank, which was about three feet wide, and grabbed onto the cold wet cable and started across. The planks bounced and creaked under her weight. Chad followed behind making the bridge bounce even more like a trampoline. He held onto the cable with his left hand, gripped his gun with his right and kept glancing behind him as he moved over the slick planks. Chad gazed down in between the wood to see the rapids shoot through dark, jagged rocks. About half way across the bridge Chad turned to look behind him and gasped.

A tall, dark man-like figure, covered in shaggy, wet matted brown hair stood fifty feet away at the entrance to the bridge staring at him underneath the tower. It was holding a boulder over its thick, wide head. At least seven feet tall and over four hundred pounds, the Bigfoot glared with black eyes, growled and then heaved the rock, sending it crashing in front of Chad. The planks cracked and snapped as the rock crashed through sending the whole bridge shaking wildly. Sherrie cried out and lost her footing, falling flat on her stomach. She reached for Vengeance, which bounced to the end of a plank and tottered at the edge. It started to fall, but she grabbed it at the last moment.

Chad stumbled back trying to dodge the boulder as he tripped and fell on his side. The whole bridge bounced up and down. His handgun slipped from his hands and skidded across a plank and started to fall, but Chad lunged forward and grabbed the weapon. The Bigfoot roared revealing sharp, jagged teeth and started across the bridge causing it to shake even more underneath its weight. The Bigfoot moved steadily across, hunched over to balance as the bridge shook.

"It's coming," Sherrie screamed as she tried to stand up, stumbling and falling to her knees.

Chad sat up, and braced one hand on the plank and raised the gun with the other. He fired, missing as the bridge shook harder. The Bigfoot growled viciously and moved faster, closing the distance. Chad grabbed onto the cable trying to steady himself and fired a second and third time missing. Sherrie screamed as Chad clenched his teeth, and fired again, clipping the Bigfoot in the leg. The creature cried out and stumbled forward, crashing through the cracked planks and plummeting into the rapids below.

Chapter 8

Enrique reached a turn in the tunnel and came to a halt shining his flashlight around the corner. "Looks like it keeps going," Enrique called back to Andrew.

"Onwards Enrique," Andrew said, grimacing as his bad knee ached from the cold, hard rocky floor of the tunnel. They crawled around the turn, as the tunnel grew steeper. Only the scrapes of their shoes on the cave floor broke the still of the dark. Andrew noted all of the coarse hair that was caught on the sharp edges of the rocks. "This is a well traveled passageway."

"What?" Enrique asked and turned back.

"Notice all the hair in the tunnel." Andrew shined his light on some of it and picked up a few of the strands. "Several different colors, even a few gray hairs, meaning they age just like us and there's more than one."

"It's gross," Enrique said. "It looks like my sister's hairbrush."

"This appears to be a main thoroughfare of the Sasquatch," Andrew said.

"A Bigfoot highway." Enrique smirked and started crawling again.

Andrew frowned and would have corrected Enrique, but excitement and curiosity were consuming him. They crawled down the tunnel, which slowly curved right and then made a sharp turn to the left. The dark rock showed no mercy on Andrew's knees and he groaned periodically. When they had first entered the tunnel, the rain pounded loudly against the rock but now all was silent and dark.

"Looks like it stops up ahead," Enrique said as he shined his light, revealing a dead end. They neared the wall and Enrique stopped and found a black gaping hole about four feet wide in the cave floor. Enrique peered over it, flashing his light. "It drops down about six feet into a big tunnel."

Andrew crawled over and examined the hole. "It's not too deep. We'll be able to climb out afterwards. Are you up for it Enrique?"

"I'm not scared," Enrique said and laughed. He put his legs into the hole and eased himself over the side and then dropped down, smacking the floor hard. "Owww," Enrique yelled. "It's slippery."

"Help me boy," Andrew called down.

Enrique held onto Andrew as he slowly descended into the hole. Once at the bottom they shined their lights, illuminating a tunnel that ranged from six to ten feet in height and about twelve feet across.

"A lava tube," Andrew said as he examined the flow marks on the rock walls. "Undiscovered until now."

"We'll be famous," Enrique said.

Andrew leaned heavily on his cane. Now that he could stand up, he would be able to use it and take some pressure off of his bad knee. They followed the lava tube, which had a relatively smooth floor except for the occasional ridge or the deep groove that ran down the center as it went deeper into the ground. The air was dank, cold and stale. The tunnel began to narrow and the ceiling dropped down until Andrew had to hunch over so as not to hit his head. They turned a corner and Enrique coughed.

"It stinks," Enrique said.

Andrew took a deep breath, cleared his throat and put his hand to his nose. "The stink of a Sasquatch." He remembered all of the interviews and the countless reports of a stench associated with the creature. It smelled like putrid rot and body odor.

Enrique waved his hand in front of his nose. "Disgusting."

"We're getting closer," Andrew announced excitedly as his cane clicked on the rocks.

Enrique ducked under a low area of the ceiling. On the other side, the tunnel opened up so they could stand without knocking their heads. Enrique suddenly stopped and flashed his light towards the top of the cave wall. "Did you hear that?" Enrique asked.

"No," Andrew said. "What did you hear?"

"Sounded like something was moving." Enrique flashed his light twelve feet up and saw a black crevice at the top of the cave wall.

"Be alert," Andrew cautioned.

"No shit." Enrique pulled out his dart gun.

"Be careful with the gun," Andrew said. "We are entering their home and we do not want to do anything to provoke them. They have been hiding away from mankind for centuries, living peacefully. We don't want to upset them."

"What about Canada?" Enrique asked.

"A man shot and killed one of their children. Of course they would attack out of anger and revenge," Andrew said.

"Aren't we going to capture one?" Enrique asked.

"Of course," Andrew said, his gray eyes gleaming in the dim light. "I want to bring the first one back alive or dead if we have too."

"Sounds good," Enrique said.

A few minutes later they reached the entrance to a vast cavernous room concealed by darkness. They could tell that it was big from the change in air and sound quality. Their lights, consumed by the vast darkness, were doing little to illuminate the chamber. The sound of water dripping could be heard somewhere up ahead to their left. There was a twelve-foot tall rock pile in the center of the room concealing whatever was behind it. The ceiling, jagged with stalagmites, was a good thirty feet above them. The walls had ledges, recesses and dark entrances to possible other tunnels giving countless places to hide.

They heard a scraping noise above them and flashed their lights up to a ledge over their heads unable to see what was in the deep shadows. A rock rattled down on the far side of the room, beyond the rock pile. They turned and flashed their lights in that direction. Enrique pointed his dart gun with his finger on the trigger and Andrew gripped his cane tightly. An apish grunt burst loudly somewhere on the ledge of the cave wall and then went silent.

"What the hell is it?" Enrique asked flashing his light up.

"The Sasquatch," Andrew stated with a grin.

To their left, towards the dripping water, a low muffled moaning pierced the silence followed by hard coughing.

"Hello," Enrique called out flashing his light towards the sound of the dripping water. The coughing stopped for a moment and then the moaning began again sounding throaty and almost human as if someone was in extreme pain.

"Let's check it out," Enrique said. "Sounds like someone is hurt."

"Be careful," Andrew warned and followed Enrique to the left side of the cavern around a ten-foot tall rock outcropping. On the other side was a dark pond where a hairy, humanoid figure sat near the edge of the water with its back turned. The creature began moaning again unaware of their presence. It started coughing loud and deep and began spitting into the pool. They stepped closer to the creature, which seemed oblivious to their presence even though their lights were aimed on it. The back of the beast was covered in wet, matted hair and its breathing was slow and wheezy. They stopped about seven feet away and noticed the fat rolls around its sides and back.

Suddenly the creature turned and began sniffing and staring in their direction with white, cataract-covered eyes. Its face was covered in coarse hair that was pressed to its skin with mucus that oozed and bubbled out of its nose. Hairy, hanging breasts shook as they hung over its bloated, fat stomach.

"A female," Andrew said with wonder.

The creature's nostrils flared and its white eyes bulged. Its mouth opened wide revealing yellow, rotted teeth as it began screeching like a demon. They both stepped back as Enrique fired his gun, sending a dart sticking into the female's blubbery stomach. The female Sasquatch screeched even louder and pulled out the dart.

Suddenly they heard heavy breathing behind them. Startled, both Andrew and Enrique turned and found a tall, shadowy figure standing ten feet away, covered in thin grayish white, hair. This new Sasquatch was seven feet tall, hunched over and skinny. Its wrinkled faced creased as it raised its hand and pointed at them with a gnarled claw. The Sasquatch opened its mouth making a short loud rasping, threatening sound. Apish grunts and howls arose somewhere in the distance in the great darkness of the cavern as if in reply.

"Let's get the hell out of here," Enrique cried out and ran, dodging by the tall, gray Sasquatch, which swiped clumsily at him, but missed. In a panic, Enrique fled around the rock outcropping and caught movement to his left. A dark shape grunted loudly leaping from the top of the rock knocking Enrique to the ground, his flashlight rolling across the floor. Enrique twisted out of his attacker's grip and stood up. The third Sasquatch, short and squat, jumped to its feet, only five feet in height, thick and stocky, weighing over two hundred pounds. The Bigfoot beat its chest like an ape and sprang through the air knocking Enrique on his back. The Sasquatch's strength was unbelievable as Enrique fought back with all of his might hitting and kicking. The Bigfoot growled slashing with its sharp, black claws and biting with its pointed teeth. Enrique cried out and then went silent, when the Bigfoot smashed his head against a rock and tore open his throat. The short Bigfoot raised its head and howled victoriously, beating its chest in celebratory movements.

Andrew had started to follow Enrique when the tall, gray Sasquatch blocked his way.

"Back off," Andrew commanded in a steadfast voice and raised his cane. The elder Bigfoot stepped forward and Andrew whacked it, knocking its hairy hand back. Andrew struck a second and third time, causing the Sasquatch to retreat two steps.

Suddenly a sharp pain exploded in the back of Andrew's head as an unseen attacker struck him. Andrew collapsed as darkness took him, his cane rattling to the ground.

Chapter 9

Sherrie and Chad reached the end of the suspension bridge, both trembling as they stepped onto solid ground. Chad gazed over the edge of the cliff down into the gorge, but there was no sign of the Bigfoot in the rapids or on the jagged rocks. The waterfall rumbled loudly and the rain poured hard, the sky a dark gray with heavy, thick clouds. A wind stirred in the treetops causing them to sway.

"Do you see it?" Sherrie yelled as she stood near the base of a tree away from the edge of the cliff. "Is it dead?"

"It's gone," Chad said as he gazed down into the gorge. "Maybe it went over the falls."

Sherrie gripped Vengeance as she looked nervously up the path that slipped around a twenty-foot tall rock outcropping before disappearing into the trees.

"Are you okay?" Chad asked as he walked over to her.

Sherrie nodded, breathing hard, her face pale. "I'm fine. I don't want to see one of those damn things ever again. We have to tell my father."

"We need to get back to the van. There could be more out here," Chad said.

They started up the muddy trail, walking under the treetops where the forest floor was dark with deep shadows. The wind gusted causing the branches to sway and creak. Heavy drops of water fell from the branches splattering hard against their jackets. They hiked around the rock wall and up a slope. The trail began to descend into the wide-open area of the canyon. They reached the wooden bridge that they had crossed earlier and walked over it as the river rushed underneath with a loud rumble. The trail ascended the rocky side of the canyon and then went back into the trees. After a few minutes they reached the wooden platform viewpoint.

Sherrie smiled. "We're almost there."

"About time," Chad said. "I hope your father invests in some guns if he plans to come here to hunt the Bigfoot."

"I won't let him unless he's armed with several guns and grenades and missiles," Sherrie said. "My father always told me how Sasquatch is a peaceful, quiet creature living in the forest in harmony with nature. Fuck that … that thing is a monster."

"I'm ready to go back to Longview where it's safe," Chad said. "I've had enough encounters with Bigfoot to last a lifetime."

They walked across the platform and then onto the paved trail. Minutes later, they emerged from the woods and entered the parking lot, both stopping in their tracks with faces aghast. The van was knocked over on its side.

"Shit," Sherrie said in shock, tightly gripping the square hilt of Vengeance.

Chad raised his handgun, scanning their perimeter. They stood in one spot searching for any sign of the Sasquatch. Sherrie glanced back at the paved trail that led into the woods as she started breathing hard from fear. Behind the trunks and branches of the first trees were deep, black shadows and thick foliage.

"It could be anywhere," she whispered and looked desperately at Chad. "I need to get the cell phone." Sherrie rushed over to the van and opened the back door crawling inside. Chad followed and shut the door behind him.

"At least we'll be out of the rain in here," Chad said.

Sherrie rummaged through all the supplies that had fallen over and finally found her cell phone. She dialed her father's number and it went to voice mail. "Father, it's Sherrie. There's a Sasquatch in Lava Canyon. It attacked us. Chad shot it and it fell into the river. It knocked over our van please call me as soon as you get this. I love you. Goodbye." Sherrie sighed and looked at Chad. "Where is he?" Sherrie called Donald who answered after a few rings. Sherrie told him everything. "Get your ass over here ASAP," she said and hung up. Sherrie smiled at Chad. "Donald's on his way." She sat down next to Chad against the wall and gave him a hug and a kiss. "I am so thankful that you brought that gun."

Chad shrugged his shoulders and smiled. They took off their wet jackets as it continued to rain, rattling against the van.

"While we're waiting, want a pop?" Sherrie asked, opening up a cooler. She handed one to Chad. "Cheers," she said as they clicked their cola cans together. "To finding a Sasquatch and surviving." She took a long drink and then retrieved sandwiches and a bag of chips from another cooler. They ate lunch quickly, both of them tired and hungry. Outside the rain fell steadily, rattling against the van while the wind blew eerily in whistling gusts.

Chad clicked the safety on and handed the gun to Sherrie. "Take it," he said.

"I've never shot a real gun before, except for those stupid dart guns," Sherrie said as she took the gun and looked at it.

"Simple to use, click the safety off right here, point and pull the trigger. It only has a few shots left. I don't have any more clips. I left them back at the motel. At least keep it with you until we get back to Cougar. I'll feel better."

"Okay," Sherrie said and smiled. "Here's Vengeance back."

Chad sheathed the knife and then rummaged through the mess in the van until he found his rifle. He stuffed a handful of shells into his pocket. "I'll use this," Chad said. "I had little experience with a gun until recently. Growing up, I wasn't interested in hunting with my father, who loved it and went every year. As soon as it was hunting season, he would be out in the woods every weekend. I finally decided to go with him to Canada and you know what happened next."

"Yes," she said and squeezed his shoulder. "It must have been terrible … unthinkable."

"It was more than terrible," Chad said. "I can't even describe it. I'm the only survivor out of thirty people. Sometimes I feel guilty for living while all the others died. There was this woman, Meredith. She and her husband Frank ran the camp. Meredith, a guy named Jay, who was about to get married, and I were the only ones to survive the first assault. We hiked through miles of forest to escape and found a cabin. By then it was just me and Meredith left. A huge freaky looking one had just ambushed Jay. Meredith should have made it. All we had to do was wait a few hours at the cabin until help arrived by airplane. At least she was able to call her son in Portland before it happened. Shortly after dinner, the Bigfoot attacked the cabin and by the next morning I was the only survivor."

"I'm so sorry," Sherrie said.

"It's been a hard three years," Chad said. "I've been going to an indoor firing range to become a better marksman. I felt so useless around all those experienced hunters in Canada while I could barely use a gun. I swore I would never be helpless like that again."

"It worked," Sherrie said. "You kept your cool and shot it, while I was in near hysterics."

"I guess," Chad said, grabbing some more potato chips. "When did Donald say he would get here?"

"Any minute," Sherrie answered. "He was going to call Javier. He said my Father had discovered some cave. Javier was trying to set up some camera but it wasn't working. Donald said he had nearly gotten out of the van to bring Javier a new camera."

"Donald getting out of the van? Amazing," Chad said.

"I don't think I've ever seen him get out of the van unless he's setting up camera equipment," Sherrie said. "He told me he was about to but then he said I had called. Likely excuse ... I think I'll call him again." Sherrie leaned over to pick up her phone when suddenly the back window shattered, sending glass flying as two giant, hairy arms shot forward into the van, seizing Sherrie by her hair and shirt. Sherrie screamed and Chad fell back, gasping in surprise. Loud snarls erupted; Sherrie was jerked towards the back of the van. Chad grabbed Sherrie's waist, as she struggled madly, hitting the monstrous hands that now gripped her by the shoulders and arm. Both Sherrie and Chad were dragged closer towards the broken window despite their best efforts.

Chad unsheathed Vengeance and started hacking the monster's thick, muscular arms. He sliced deep; the Bigfoot roared releasing Sherrie. Its arms swung wildly smacking Chad in the chest, knocking him to the floor. Sherrie twisted free of the other arm and jumped to the front of the van. The hands shot forward trying to grab her as Chad crawled out of the way next to Sherrie. The beastly hands withdrew quickly and the whole top of the van, which was on its side, dented inwards, creaking and snapping. Sherrie dropped down to the floor looking for the handgun that had slipped out of her hand in the confusion. The entire van shook violently and then the ceiling dented deeper. Chad grabbed his rifle.

A hairy, massive hand broke through the passenger side window, which was now part of the ceiling. The hand clawed at the air, missing Sherrie by inches. She yelled and fell back into Chad, both of them scooting out of reach. The beast snarled viciously and withdrew its hand.

With a violent jerk, one side of the van was lifted up and the entire vehicle flipped over. Chad rolled and fell back losing his grip on the rifle when a cooler, boxes of supplies and backpacks slammed into him. Sherrie cried out as falling containers pelted her. The vehicle turned over and came to a stop on its other side. Chad pushed the cooler off the top of him and sat up glancing fearfully over at Sherrie, who crawled out from under two backpacks and a blanket. Chad grabbed his rifle. The snarling abruptly stopped and all went silent except for the rain rattling against the van.

Both of them were breathing heavily, looking at each other with terrified eyes. Chad moved away from the back window and sat near Sherrie who was rummaging through the pile of stuff searching for the handgun. Chad kept glancing out of the windows expecting the nightmarish hand to reach in at any moment. In the distance, the hum of a car engine started, slowly growing louder.

"Someone's here," Sherrie whispered. A car horn began honking. "What if its Donald?" Sherrie asked.

Chad sat still saying nothing, looking out the shattered, back window. The honking continued. They both sat where they were huddled together in the van.

"What if it's still there, waiting for us to get out?" Chad whispered.

"I have to warn Donald," Sherrie said. "Come on. We'll go out the back."

Chad took a deep breath, and exhaled slowly. He gritted his teeth and nodded. Sherrie moved as quietly as she could to the back of the van. Chad followed behind with his rifle when he spotted the handgun. He grabbed it and handed it to Sherrie, who slowly raised her head to the window and quickly peeked out.

"One, two three," she whispered and opened the back door and stepped out. Chad jumped out and scanned the area. There was no sign of the Bigfoot. In front of them was the other green van, with Donald waving at them through the windshield.

Chapter 10

Andrew woke to the sounds of chomping and grunting as he slowly opened his eyes to darkness. He was lying on his stomach facing a black rock. His head ached and his body shivered in the cold air. He turned his head in the other direction, his gray eyes growing wide in shock. A short, husky Sasquatch no more than five feet tall and over two hundred pounds in weight, squatted over Enrique's corpse, tearing and biting. Horrified, Andrew watched in the dim light. "A child," he thought. "At least three Sasquatch are in the cave."

The Sasquatch child chewed into Enrique's left arm, bones crunching and cracking. Andrew had to close his eyes in revulsion for a moment. Near Enrique's body, was his flashlight, lying on the ground, illuminating the immediate area. A few feet behind Enrique, the black pond of water reflected the light. Next to the water's edge was the unconscious fat female, snoring and coughing. To his left, on the other side of the rock outcropping, a dim light shined in the utter blackness that surrounded it.

"It must be the other flashlight, the one Enrique dropped when he tried to escape," Andrew thought as he watched the child eat his former employee. "They must have killed him over by the other flashlight and then dragged him back to the pond." Andrew clenched his teeth. He had only lost one person during all of the years he had hunted the Sasquatch. "Eighteen years ago," he thought. "Foo," he remembered the name of their Chinese guide who took them up in the Himalayans. Eight days into their hike Foo had slipped into a hidden ice crevasse and fell to his death. After the accident, Andrew had called off the expedition.

"And now Enrique," Andrew thought in dismay, shaking his head in disgust as he watched the child feast on the young man only fifteen feet away. Andrew's keen eyes examined every detail as he lay there trying to gather as much information as possible. The child Sasquatch was muscular with short, brown hair covering its body. The female had long, shaggy hair, much of it pressed against her flesh, most likely from sweat and grime. The tall, old Sasquatch had thin gray hair with many bald spots over its malnourished body. Andrew searched the darkness trying to find the old Sasquatch, but it was nowhere to be seen.

Andrew gasped quietly. A fourth Sasquatch, about six feet tall, medium build and close to three hundred pounds jumped out of the darkness near Enrique's corpse. The child Sasquatch growled and flashed its claws. The taller one replied in turn showing off its sharp teeth as it snarled. This exchange carried on for about thirty seconds and then the taller Sasquatch bit into Enrique's leg, while the child finished off the arm.

"Another adolescent," Andrew thought. "Not fully grown but a bit older than the child." The adolescent's hair was longer and shaggier than the child's. The adolescent ate the legs quickly in rapid bites devouring the chunks of flesh as if it hadn't eaten in days. After a few minutes, the adolescent walked to the edge of the pond and began drinking making loud slurping sounds. It burped, beat its chest like an ape and then scurried off into the darkness out of sight.

"How many are there?" Andrew thought amazed at what he had just witnessed. He had spent his entire life in search of these legendary creatures and to see them in the flesh up close was unbelievable. The child continued to feed gnawing on the bones, discarding bits of bloody clothing in all directions. Luckily, none of it hit Andrew. Suddenly, the female began to moan, loud and long.

"The mother awakes," Andrew thought.

The moan broke into hard coughing and then the mother began to make raspy throaty noises. For several minutes, the mother moaned and then it stopped and rolled over onto its stomach and began pulling itself over to the child and the corpse. Its nose flared while it sniffed loudly, snot bubbling out. Its white, cataract-covered eyes were wide open and darting back and forth. The child stopped eating as the mother approached. Andrew rested the side of his head on a flat rock as he watched. "If only I had Tylenol or a shot of whiskey," he thought as his head throbbed painfully from the blow.

The child moved in front of Enrique's corpse, blocking it from the mother who sniffed loudly and spit up phlegm. The child growled in warning and then the mother chomped her rotted teeth, raised her body and made a loud gasping, barking sound. The child lowered its head and scampered out of the way of the mother.

"The child defers to the mother," Andrew thought in wonder. He wanted to write down all that he had witnessed, film it, show it to the world, become famous and rich and prove to everyone that he wasn't crazy, that he wasn't wasting his life hunting a supposed imaginary creature.

The child began to circle the flashlight, staring curiously into the light. It cautiously touched it with a finger and then jumped back as if it was dangerous. The child growled in a low tone and touched the light again. This time the flashlight rolled a foot down a slight slope making a clattering noise. The child leaped away and ran off into the darkness.

The mother scooted over to the corpse and began sniffing, its wide nose flaring. The mother was obviously crippled in the legs.

"She's a disgusting sight," Andrew thought. The mother's face was bloated, splotchy and covered in crusty yellowish material. Snot dripped out of its nose and its eyes were puffy, with dark, black circles underneath them. Its eyes were white and blood shot. The mother weighed close to five hundred pounds, much of it in fat rolled around its hairy, saggy stomach and breasts. The mother picked at Enrique's corpse trying to find meat, sniffing and swaying its head. There wasn't much left, since the child and the adolescent had gotten to it first. The mother slammed its fists angrily against the corpse and made a gasping roar. It snapped its rotted teeth as its eyes bulged wide.

"If that's the mother, where is the father?" Andrew thought suppressing a cough. He relaxed for a moment and then coughed quietly putting his hand to his mouth to muffle the sound.

The mother stopped hitting the corpse and looked in Andrew's direction with its cataract, white eyes. It stared at him sniffing and then began to growl loudly. Pushing Enrique's corpse to the side, the mother began pulling itself over the rocky floor towards Andrew. It moved rather quickly with powerful muscles in the arms that had been built up over the years of dragging its heavy weight across the cavern. The mother's sagging hairy breasts and fat stomach flapped over the rocks as it moved.

Andrew gasped and tried to stand up, but a dizzy spell hit him and his bad knee gave out causing him to collapse. The mother growled louder and pulled its heavy mass towards him. Andrew pushed himself to his knees and cried out in pain. His cane was by Enrique's body and of no use to him, so he began to crawl over the rocky ground scraping his legs in the process. The mother closed the distance quickly. Andrew crawled faster despite his knee and dizziness, scrambling over the rocky floor as best he could away from the pond and the flashlights into the darkness.

The mother reached out nicking the sole of his boot with her claw. Growling in excitement the mother lunged forward with one arm, clawing for him. The hairy hand missed Andrew's leg three inches to the right of his calf, hitting the rock instead. The mother began coughing up phlegm as Andrew climbed down a two-foot drop, scraping his hands on the sharp rock. He slipped hitting his elbow. The mother dropped down a few seconds later and seized his right ankle with her powerful hand. Andrew kicked and wiggled to break free, but the mother held on with surprising strength. Yelling, Andrew kicked the mother in the face with the heel of his boot. Enraged the mother roared and bit into his leg below his knee tearing his pant leg and making a shallow cut in his skin. Andrew cried out.

"Get off of him you cow," Javier yelled as he emerged from the shadows and jumped on the mother's back, stabbing it with a hunting knife. The mother screamed and jerked swatting Javier with one of its muscular arms, sending him crashing to the ground.

The mother screamed loudly, punctuated with her hard coughing as it tried pulling the knife out of its back.

Javier stood up. "Boss, you okay?" he said and moved around the mother.

"Thank you my friend," Andrew said. "I feel light-headed. It bit me." Andrew gripped his bleeding leg.

Suddenly a loud roar erupted as the adolescent leaped from the darkness slamming into Javier sending him tumbling to the floor. The adolescent picked up a rock and tried smashing Javier as he rolled out of the way and jumped to his feet. The adolescent charged as Javier backed up and then they collided against the top of a rock outcropping. Both of them fell back, grappling together. The adolescent knocked into Javier knocking them down the bank into the dark waters of the pool with a loud splash. Javier yelled and then tackled the adolescent, submerging them under the water.

Andrew felt faint and with his remaining energy, he began to crawl away from the mother who was still screaming and writhing on the ground. He moved deeper into the darkness. He heard Javier cry out and then his friend went silent. The adolescent emerged from the pool, pulling the limp body of Javier onto the bank.

Andrew spotted two large boulders leaning against each other forming a crawl space underneath. He pulled himself into the dark shelter, his whole body trembling. There was barely enough room for him to fit lying on his stomach.

"This will have to do," he thought as his head grew light and vision began to fade. "Don't come down here Sherrie," he thought as he slipped into unconsciousness, while the mother cried out in agony and the adolescent began to feed on Javier.

Chapter 11

"For the tenth time, I didn't see anything," Donald said as he pulled out of the Lava Canyon parking lot, glancing back at the tree line in hopes of catching a glimpse of the Sasquatch. "All I saw was the overturned van."

"It must've heard you coming and ran back into the woods," Sherrie said as she looked back at their wrecked van. She locked the passenger door and took a deep breath, wiping her eyes as the reality of what just happened hit her. She shuddered and sat back in the chair, glad to be out of the cold and rain, but she didn't feel safe. She crossed her arms and pressed them against her stomach.

Donald slowed the van and came to a stop. "Maybe we should stay here until we contact your father. We don't want the Sasquatch to escape. We have plenty of dart guns."

"Drive," Chad yelled angrily from the back of the van.

"Go," Sherrie cried in a panic. "We're not safe. You saw what it did to the van, now drive us the hell out of here."

Donald stepped on the gas and turned the windshield wipers on swiping the torrent of rain. "Ok, ok … did you get any pictures?"

"None." Sherrie shook her head glancing warily out of the passenger side window. "The last thing on my mind was taking pictures while it was throwing boulders at us."

"Unbelievable," Donald said. "I wish I had set up some cameras out here. I want some video of it. Did you provoke it somehow? Your father always said that the Sasquatch are peaceful creatures."

"They're fucking monsters," Sherrie snapped. "It attacked us for no reason."

"Well your father did say that their food supply is gone because of Virus SD5E, which caused them to change their behavior and become more erratic."

"It wanted to eat us for lunch." Sherrie shuddered as she stared out the window. "It was the scariest freaking thing I ever saw."

Chad sat in the back of the van rubbing his hands together trying to get warm. His clothes were muddy and wet and his skin pale. He was exhausted, both physically and emotionally and felt like he was back in the Canadian wilderness reliving his nightmare. "At least no one has died this time," he thought with relief. The event in Canada had scarred him for most likely the rest of his life. This new attack was almost too much for him, although he was proud of himself for not panicking. He had been much more useful today then when he had been up in Canada. He still had no idea how he survived while experienced hunters, who had spent years out in the forest, were killed.

Chad thought of Meredith, the lady who had nearly escaped with him. They had survived the initial attack and fled into the forest hoping to find a cabin on a lake that her husband had spotted while flying his airplane. Meredith had complained about her knees the whole time, but managed to hike several miles to the cabin. Chad remembered feeling safe and relieved to be in the warm cabin after spending days out in the woods being hunted by Bigfoot. They had just eaten dinner and Meredith volunteered to do the dishes. The next thing Chad had heard was glass shattering and Meredith's scream. He had rushed to the kitchen just in time to see her being pulled through the window by two giant hairy hands. Her body was never found which made Chad cringe at the thought of what had happened to her. At least if they had found her body, there would have been some closure. Instead, Meredith had vanished along with the horde of Sasquatch somewhere in the Canadian Wilderness.

"Thank God we're closer to civilization this time," Chad thought wrapping his arms around his knees as he sat on the floor of the van near the back door.

"What took you so long to get here?" Sherrie asked.

Donald took a deep breath and sighed. "I was on the phone with Javier. Your father found a tunnel at the rock pile and decided to explore it with Enrique. They were supposed to be back after one hour, but they never came back, so Javier went in after them. I tried talking him out of it until I picked you guys up but he can be stubborn. He's worked for your father a long time and didn't want to stand around if his boss and nephew needed help."

"What kind of tunnel?" Sherrie asked.

"A possible entrance to a Sasquatch lair. It could be the secret cave system that your father always talked about, one where they could live hidden away from mankind for all of these years."

"Shit," Sherrie said. "When did Javier go into the tunnel?"

"Thirty minutes ago," Donald said.

Sherrie tried calling Javier, his father and Enrique but all the calls went to voice mail. "Step on it," Sherrie yelled. "If Sasquatch are really down in those caves, they are all in danger."

Donald drove the van drove through the flat, mud flow where the trees and saplings were few and spread apart in between fields of tall green grass and thick foliage. To their right Mount Saint Helens stood concealed behind a rainy, dark mass of clouds, filling the horizon and the entire sky. They drove along I-83 and a few minutes later they entered the forest. The rain continued to pour, rumbling against the van. Chad sat stoically in the back, enjoying the warmth and protection of the moving vehicle. He rubbed his numb hands together trying to get the circulation going.

"You okay?" Sherrie asked as she glanced back at him.

Chad nodded and smiled. "I'm fine, just tired and my nerves are fried."

"Mine too," Sherrie said. "I'll feel better once I find my father."

"Maybe we should call the police," Chad suggested.

"Not yet." Sherrie shook her head. "Most likely my father lost track of time. If he found anything of interest, he'll spend hours studying it. I just want to break the news of the Sasquatch to him first before we go to the authorities. My father can decide what to do next. I'm sure he doesn't want the police finding the Sasquatch before him."

They pulled into the Ape Cave parking lot and found three other cars parked.

"These cars weren't here when I left," Donald said. "Must be some people that decided to hike through the Ape Caves."

"It's open year round," Sherrie said as she opened the passenger door and was greeted by a gust of cold, wet air. "I'm going in the tunnel to find my father."

"You know where the rock pile is?" Donald asked.

"Yes." Sherrie stepped out and zipped up her jacket as the rain continued to pelt her with heavy, cold drops.

"Javier has left his backpack by the entrance to mark the location of the tunnel. He said it was at the base of the rock pile." Donald turned the heat up to high as all the warm air was quickly being sucked out of the van.

Sherrie nodded. "Okay, I'll be back. If you don't hear from me, call the police."

Donald smiled, although he could not conceal the worry in his eyes. "Be careful and call me when you reach the tunnel."

"I will," Sherrie said.

"I'm going with you," Chad called from the back of the van after quietly contemplating his next course of action for the past several minutes. He couldn't let Sherrie go by herself, even though he had no desire to hike into the woods again. If it were up to him, he would have Donald drive them back to Cougar and call the police. He knew Sherrie would protest his suggestion.

"You don't have too, especially with what we've just been through. This is a pretty safe, well-traveled area." Sherrie smiled. "I can take care of myself."

"I'm going with you, period." Chad grabbed his rifle and opened the back door, stepping out into the cold rain. He zipped up his wet jacket and met Sherrie at the front of the vehicle. "I hope your Dad didn't find anything."

"Me too, although I can't believe I'm saying that," Sherrie said. "He's been looking for the Sasquatch for forty years thinking that they were peaceful creatures instead of blood thirsty monsters."

"I tried telling him that in Longview, but he wouldn't listen," Chad said as he strapped the rifle around his back. He put on his hood and glanced around the parking lot at the wall of trees that they would be entering shortly. He took a deep breath as the thought of jumping back into the van filled his mind.

"My father's set in his ways," Sherrie said and offered him the handgun. "Can you hold this for now? You're a much better shot than me."

"Okay." Chad took the gun and checked to see if the safety was on. He placed Vengeance in the knife sheath clipped to his belt and gulped with anxiety.

They hiked up the Ape Cave Trail, which was a wet muddy path covered with fallen needles from the trees that towered overhead. Ferns and tall bushes lined the trail and behind them were deep shadows; the forest floor was dark on this stormy day. Chad shuddered as he glanced around apprehensively. He breathed slowly assuring himself that the Bigfoot that had attacked them was at least 10 to 20 miles away in Lava Canyon. What if it followed us? Chad shook his head at the absurdity. "Impossible," he thought as doubts began to creep into his mind. The image of the monster running through the forest towards them settled uncomfortably in the front of his mind.

They reached the main entrance to the Ape Caves where stone steps descended into a rocky, dark sinkhole in the ground. "What if a Bigfoot was down in the caves?" Chad thought. He hastened past the entrance following the trail as it continued to rise up a muddy slope. At one point, Sherrie slipped and slid down the path. She stood up and laughed, covered in mud.

They crossed over a crude, wooden bridge that went over a narrow creek in a gully, overflowing with rainwater. They hiked for another twenty minutes and then turned left off the trail when they reached the Dead Woods. They navigated through the skeleton-like trees missing most of their branches and bark. The uneven, rocky ground was treacherous and covered with thick grass, ferns and bushes. At one point, they reached a thicket of tall thorn and blackberry bushes, which they had to circle around. In the Dead Woods they didn't have the cover of tree branches so the rain fell hard pelting their jackets, soaking them.

They reached the end of the Dead Woods and entered a line of trees that were green with life. They hiked down a slope and found the rock pile, a giant mass of basalt rocks, black and slick with rain. They moved along the perimeter until they spotted Javier's backpack near a group of trees. There was a bottle of water right where the boughs of one tree touched the muddy ground next to a lone rock.

"Donald said the entrance was at the base of the rock pile," Sherrie said as she lifted up some of the branches and looked under to find a short pathway leading to the cave mouth. Javier left a camera in the middle of the trail and a glove as a guide. "He wanted to make sure we saw it," Sherrie said as she called Donald on her cell phone. "If you don't hear from us in one hour, call the police." Sherrie turned to Chad who was on his knees shining his flashlight into the three-foot-tall entrance.

"Ready to go?" Sherrie asked.

Chad sighed and shook his head. "I don't like the look of this. Maybe we should call the police now."

Sherrie frowned. "No way. If you don't want to go, wait here. If my father needs help, then I'm going to find him and help him."

"I'm going with you," Chad said. "I'll go first since I have the guns."

"Okay and thanks." Sherrie gave him a quick hug. "I'm so worried about my father. I pray that there aren't Sasquatch down here. One was enough."

"And that one is miles away, thank God." Chad held a flashlight in his left hand, the handgun in the other and had the rifle strapped to his back. He crawled into the tunnel and Sherrie followed close behind holding her own flashlight with a climbing rope looped to her belt. Getting out of the rain was about the only positive factor of the tunnel. The floor was composed of rough basalt, which was hard on the knees and hands. The sound of the rain grew faint almost immediately and then went silent as they journeyed farther into the tunnel, which descended and curved back and forth. Chad slowed down at each turn of the tunnel praying that there wasn't a Bigfoot waiting for them on the other side. A while later, they reached the end of the tunnel where there was a hole in the cave floor.

Chad looked into the hole with his flashlight. "It drops down five or six feet into a larger cave."

"Okay," Sherrie said. "If my father can do it, we can."

Chad leaned over the edge and slowly lowered himself down into the hole. He dropped to the ground and then helped Sherrie. They were both able to stand up in the circular tunnel.

"This is a lava tube," Sherrie said as she studied the curved sides. "Most likely 2000 years old, created at the same time as the Ape Caves."

"It's cold," Chad said, breathing in the damp, stale air and glancing into the deep blackness.

"The Ape Caves stay 42 degrees year round no matter what the weather is above ground," Sherrie said.

They moved down the lava tube and at one point it began to stink.

"It smells," Chad said as memories of Canada returned. He had smelled the same odor in Canada, usually right before a Bigfoot attacked.

"It's putrid," Sherrie said and covered her nose.

"How far do you think your father would have continued on?" Chad asked with a frustrated scowl, having seen no sign of Andrew. He wanted to go back to the warm, security of the van and have Donald drive them to safety before it was too late. He kept picturing the Sasquatch that had attacked them in Lava Canyon running through the woods tracking them, getting closer and closer with every minute they wasted down here in the cave.

"He would've gone to the very end," Sherrie said as she stepped around a rock.

"Figures," Chad said under his breath. They continued down the lava tube, which opened up into an immense, cavernous chamber where their lights were unable to penetrate the darkness.

"Wow," Sherrie said as she flashed her light up at the stalagmites hanging from the ceiling.

A sudden, loud moaning pierced the silence of the cavern, emanating somewhere to the left of a rock pile that filled the center of the cavern. They both looked at each other with wide, nervous eyes. Chad raised his handgun and motioned for Sherrie to follow. They moved to the left over the uneven floor towards a tall, rock outcropping. Their boots clattered on the rock despite their best efforts of trying to be quiet. The moaning grew louder and was punctuated with hard, throaty coughing. Near the rock outcropping a shining flashlight laid on the ground. Chad moved over to examine it and whispered, "It's one of ours."

Sherrie nodded, her worried eyes filled with fear. Chad gripped his handgun as tightly as he could to reassure himself that they weren't helpless. They walked around the rock outcropping where a dark pool of water spread out into the shadowy recesses. Another shining flashlight lay close to the pool revealing the hairy, fat mass of a Sasquatch lying on its stomach, trembling on the ground grabbing at its back where a knife was stuck up to its hilt. Chad took a step closer and then the rock he was standing on shifted and clattered loudly.

The fat Sasquatch lifted its head in their direction staring at them with white eyes, snapping with discolored teeth as it began growling. It clawed at them with one of its hands as its hairy breasts jiggled.

Chad aimed the gun and fired three times sending bullets tearing into its chest. The Sasquatch screamed, went silent and collapsed. The gunfire echoed loudly in the cavern. Chad's breathing quickened as he moved the flashlight around in search of other Bigfoot. His light stopped on two bodies sprawled on the ground. Chad and Sherrie rushed over to the bodies and found them mutilated, with most of the flesh gone from the bones. Chad stepped back and had to look away feeling sick to his stomach. Sherrie knelt down and examined the bodies.

"It's Javier and Enrique," she cried.

Chad shook his head in disgust, as his stomach grew more nauseous. "Not again," he whispered.

"Shit," Sherrie yelled angrily, standing up. "God bless their souls. Those fucking Sasquatch killed them and then ate them." Sherrie rushed over to

Chad and hugged him, tears streaming down her face. They stood for a moment, holding each other.

"Where's my father?" Sherrie whispered frantically. She sighed, let go and walked over to the mother. "That's Javier's knife. It's a female. Look at those breasts."

"Where's your father?" Chad asked, moving his flashlight back and forth, hoping he would see another body.

Sherrie shook her head, waving her flashlight around the perimeter. "Father," she called out. "Daddy." Her light stopped at her Father's cane stuck between two rocks. "Oh my word," she muttered and then rushed over to the cane, lifting it up. "Where is he?" she asked.

A ferocious roar filled the cavern as the adolescent jumped down from the top of the rock outcropping, knocking Chad to the ground. Chad cried out and dropped his gun as the beast raised its fist to strike and swung down with a roar. Chad raised his arms deflecting much of the blow, but the adolescent pinned him to the ground with its knees. The Sasquatch growled and snapped its sharp, long teeth. It grabbed Chad by the throat with its left hand and raised its right hand, revealing pointed black claws.

The adolescent was about to stab Chad when Sherrie screamed and cracked her Father's cane over the back of the Sasquatch's head. The adolescent fell over in a daze as Sherrie picked up a rock and threw it, screaming crazily. The rock smashed into its shoulder. The adolescent recovered quickly and growled, snapping its teeth. It twirled on all fours, preparing to lunge at Sherrie.

Chad grabbed the handgun and fired striking the beast twice in the shoulder and the chest. He kept clicking the trigger but the clip was spent. The adolescent fell to the floor clutching its chest and moaning loudly. Chad dropped the handgun, unhooked the rifle and pointed it at the beast. "This is for my Dad," he said and fired striking the beast at the base of the neck. The adolescent clutched its throat, made a gasping sound and collapsed. "This is for Meredith, Shane, Jay and all the others," he yelled angrily and fired striking the beast in stomach. The Sasquatch became limp and motionless. Chad lowered the rifle and touched the back of his head and felt blood.

Sherrie rushed over. "Are you okay?" she asked examining him. "Your arm." She touched Chad's bleeding right arm.

"My back and head hurt," Chad said. "I hit the rocks hard when it jumped on me. I'll be okay."

Sherrie kissed him on the cheek. "Thank you for coming."

"Thank you," Chad said. "That thing would've had me if it wasn't for you."

"My father's cane came in handy." She glanced down at the cane, which was broken in two.

"Listen," Chad said. "We have to get out of here. There is no telling how many more are down here."

"But my father." Sherrie frowned.

"We'll call the cops and come down here with armed men. We can't stay here. That thing nearly killed me."

Sherrie nodded. "You're right. The best way to help my Father is to get more people down here."

They started hurrying back across the cavern to the entrance of the tunnel which led to the surface when a loud, shrill screech erupted somewhere ahead of them.

"More are coming from the surface," Chad said, his eyes growing wide with fear, as deep roars echoed down the tunnel.

Sherrie took a step back and cried, "We're trapped!"

Chapter 12

▼

Chad and Sherrie stumbled back from the entrance to the tunnel as the roars grew closer and louder. They stood at the edge of the massive cavern, both of them glancing fearfully around in the cold and dark.

"What now?" Sherrie asked on the verge of panic. Terror touched her wide eyes as she glanced back and forth, flashing her light all around. "Is there another exit?"

Above them they heard a clattering noise and then a rock the size of a softball crashed at Sherrie's feet. She yelled and jumped back as something began growling in the darkness over their heads. Chad's flashlight revealed a short, squat Bigfoot kneeling over a ledge twenty feet up, its black eyes glaring down at them, snapping its teeth as it snarled. Chad aimed his rifle and fired but the young Bigfoot, jumped back into the shadows out of sight. The roars coming from the tunnel grew louder.

"Come on Sherrie," Chad said in a desperate voice and waved her over to follow. "We're sitting ducks here."

They scrambled over the rocky floor and headed left towards the pond. Moments later, they reached the bodies of Javier and Enrique and stopped in their tracks as they flashed their lights around, exploring the area. A tall rock pile stood ahead of them, filling the entire center of the cavern, concealing what was beyond it. They moved along the edge of the pond and passed the fat corpse of the mother. Chad kept his eyes away from the bodies of Enrique and Javier. They started climbing over the jagged, damp rocks covered in cave slime, a sticky residue that he had read online was caused by bacteria. They quickly circled around the base of the rock pile. Loud, beastly growling and fierce roars filled the cavern behind them.

"They've reached the cavern," Sherrie whispered in a panicked voice, pointing her flashlight ahead. Her eyes grew wide with horror and dismay as she pursed her lips. The back of the cavern was filled with bones and carcasses of deer, elk, bear, cougars and humans. Both Chad and Sherrie stopped and moved their lights over the floor of bones, which was at least forty feet wide.

"What now?" Sherrie said. "Maybe we can circle around the rock pile and make a run for the surface."

"We'd have no chance," Chad said and pointed his light at the back wall, revealing a three-foot tall entrance to what appeared to be the mouth of a tunnel. "Look," Chad said. "We can hide in there against the wall."

"Hurry," Sherrie cried and rushed down the rocks to the cave floor. She stepped onto the bones, which crunched and shifted under her weight. Chad followed behind Sherrie as the sounds of pursuit grew louder. Chad stepped around the obvious remains of a human and continued across the floor of bones. Something dark and small scampered over his foot. Chad stopped and looked down in fright as several black creatures scrambled underneath the bones.

"Rats," Sherrie cried out in revulsion.

Chad grimaced, shaking his right leg wildly, knocking a rat off his ankle. He took a step back and crunched one underneath his heel. The rat squealed and then there was a grotesque popping sound. "This is sick," Chad said trying to remain calm. Sherrie kicked at the rats as the bones rattled and cracked.

"They're everywhere." Sherrie jumped up and down, screaming loudly.

"Keep going," Chad yelled, dodging a rat only to crush another one under his hiking boot. It squealed and wiggled underneath his foot. Chad jumped off of it and nearly tripped as his foot got caught underneath the bones of what may have been a deer at one point. He steadied himself and pulled his foot out and continued forward.

Sherrie moved her flashlight back and forth in front of her trying to avoid the rats. Even so, she stepped on the tail of a rat causing it to screech and snap at her foot. She side stepped the creature and tripped, falling on top of the rotting carcass of an elk. "Ahhhhhhh," she screamed as her arm jammed into the rib cage. She struggled to break free, her arm pinned in between two ribs. A rat inside the skeleton started squeaking and nipping at her hand. "Help," she yelled struggling madly to break free, the whole carcass shaking. Chad rushed over and pulled the ribs back so she could pull her hand free.

Sherrie raised her small hunting knife and began hacking frantically at the rats by her feet. "Die you son of a bitch," she yelled stabbing one of them in the back. She flicked the wiggling rat off her knife and sliced at another one.

Suddenly, a shrill, high-pitched shrieking filled the cavern. Chad looked back and at the top of the rock pile was the massive, dark shape of a Bigfoot over seven feet tall staring at them. The beast raised its arms over its head and screamed like some demonic harpy from Greek mythology. It jumped off the rock it was perched on and moved down the pile in quick, fluid movements leaping from rock to rock.

Chad raised his rifle and fired, missing his target, the shot echoing through the cavern. The Bigfoot reached the bottom of the rock pile seconds later. Chad fired again missing a second time.

"Hit it," Sherrie screamed, flashing her light on the approaching beast, which by now was charging over the floor of bones making loud cracking and snapping noises under its steps. Rats squealed and squeaked, as they were smashed underneath the behemoth's giant feet.

Despite the cold, sweat dripped down Chad's forehead as he aimed, trying to keep a steady hand. Part of him wanted to flee as the monstrous creature drew closer, but he knew he couldn't outrun it. He focused a moment and pulled the trigger. The bullet clipped the Bigfoot in the shoulder, which caused it to stumble forward and crash into the bones, sliding several feet. The Bigfoot roared angrily and immediately struggled to get up, knocking bones and rats off of its body. A chorus of roars and shrieks rumbled through the room as several Bigfoot reached the top of the rock pile, dark silhouettes in the dim light.

"Run," Sherrie cried as she rushed over the bones towards the back wall ignoring the rats, the stink of rotten flesh and the fact that she was stepping over the bodies of dead animals and humans. Chad turned and followed as the other Bigfoot began climbing down the rock pile. The one that Chad had shot stood up and began to pursue them. They reached the back wall of the cavern where the tunnel mouth stood, a black gaping hole. Sherrie knelt down and shined her light into the entrance, "Come on … it looks like it goes in a ways."

Sherrie crawled in and then Chad dropped to his knees and rushed in after her. The wounded Bigfoot reached the entrance seconds later and roared, sticking its head in as it clawed at them, missing Chad's foot by inches. He gasped and quickly twisted around and fired his rifle, sending the bullet bursting through the monster's chest. Chad fired again, blasting the beast in the top of its skull. The Bigfoot shuddered a moment and collapsed, temporarily blocking the entrance.

"Go, go," Chad yelled, turning back around.

Sherrie crawled frantically as a rat scurried past her. The tunnel turned sharply to the right and as she approached the corner she slowed down. She raised her hunting knife and peeked around. "Clear," she said and started crawling again.

Chad took quick, shallow breaths, close to hyperventilating. "Why didn't I stay in Longview," he thought. "I have to keep calm." His chest ached from where the Bigfoot had tackled him, his arm was bloody and his whole body was sore. His head throbbed, his hair damp with blood. Images of the Bigfoot lunging at him from the darkness began replaying in his mind as older memories emerged of his Father, Shane, Jay and Meredith all murdered by these monsters. "I won't let you down Dad," Chad whispered to himself. "I won't let any of you down."

Sherrie reached another corner and slowed her pace. Behind them the shrieks of the Bigfoot filled the tunnel.

"Move," Chad yelled.

Sherrie turned the corner and said, "It keeps going." They crawled faster scraping their knees and palms on the rocky floor. The tunnel sloped down making it harder on their hands. "Are they following us?" Sherrie asked.

"I don't know. I don't see anything." Chad flashed his light behind him fearful of what he would see, but the tunnel was empty.

"Maybe they gave up," Sherrie said.

Chad shook his head. "They never give up. They will hunt us down unless we find a way out of here."

"Maybe my Father went this way," Sherrie said.

"I hope … Keep going."

They followed the tunnel as it steadily sloped down, turn after turn until Sherrie stopped and said, "Shit."

"What?" Chad asked.

"A dead end," Sherrie cried. "It's a dead end."

Chad looked ahead and saw a dark rock wall, as any hope of escape began to vanish.

Back in the cavern, a massive Bigfoot nearly nine feet tall, thick and muscular, covered in scars and who could only be the Father, grabbed the dead Bigfoot that blocked the tunnel and flung the corpse across the floor of bones in an effortless motion. The Father bent over and sniffed, its black eyes bulged with rage as its sharp, thick claws clicked on the rocky floor. It stood up and roared in a deep, powerful, voice, which echoed through the cavern.

Shrill cries answered the Father's call a few seconds later as Bigfoot emerged from every dark recess of the chamber, crawling out of tunnels and appearing from connecting caves. They gathered around the Father who stood in the midst of the floor of bones. The Father looked at them with fierce, dark eyes making deep grunting sounds. It suddenly pointed at the entrance to the tunnel and several of the smaller Bigfoot, mostly adolescents charged into the hole shrieking excitedly.

Once the final adolescent disappeared into the tunnel, the Father moved across the floor of bones, each step making a loud crunching sound underneath its great weight. Other full-grown Bigfoot followed the Father, making submissive, grunting noises. The Father and the others climbed over the rock pile towards the pond. The Father reached the corpse of the Mother and kneeled down sniffing loudly. The Father began to growl deep and low as the other Bigfoot stepped away, heads lowered as if in fear. The Father touched the Mother on the head with its large hand for a moment. It then grabbed a breast and squeezed as its growling grew deeper. With both hands it shook the lifeless body of the Mother as a dark madness filled the Father's eye. It touched the knife in the Mother's back and then pulled it gently out. It sniffed the knife a moment and then flung it into the black pool of water, its growling growing ever louder. The other Bigfoot stepped back as if to put as much distance between them and the Father.

The Father, trembling with rage and aggression, suddenly raised its head and roared long, deep and hard, causing the other Bigfoot to drop their heads and step into the shadows. It stood up and stared at the other Bigfoot as it flashed its dark claws. The other Bigfoot stepped back fearfully, eyes downcast. The Father glared at them and grunted, before it started walking quickly across the cavern. The others followed behind keeping their distance. The Father entered the tunnel that led to the surface.

Chapter 13

▼

Donald sat in the back of the warm van tapping his foot and listening to loud, rocking country music as he gazed at the video screens displaying footage from various cameras placed at several points in the surrounding forest. So far, he had seen little except for the constant rain dripping down the lenses making it difficult to see. The only movement he had witnessed, was that of tree branches swaying in the wind. He wished Javier had set up a camera at the rock pile so he could monitor the situation. Everyone had gone into the tunnel making him slightly anxious. He wanted Andrew to come back as soon as possible now that Chad and Sherrie had seen an actual Sasquatch in Lava Canyon. They had to act quickly, call up more men if needed and go back to the canyon and capture it. They were about to hit the jackpot after all of these years and money and fame were just around the corner. Donald could smell it and was ready to embrace it with both of his eager arms.

Donald checked his cell phone to make sure he hadn't missed any calls and to mark the time. It had been forty-five minutes since Sherrie and Chad had gone into the tunnel. "They'll be fine," he muttered quietly. "Nothing to worry about." He had worked with Andrew for eight years and there had been many times when his boss had missed checking in at a scheduled time. Andrew was an intense, studious individual who was very thorough, but lost track of time on a regular basis.

Donald opened the cooler and grabbed a bottle of beer, which he had snuck into the van underneath the soft drinks. Andrew disapproved of drinking during a job, but Donald was feeling jittery. The whole team was in the tunnel and a feeling of foreboding settled on him as the minutes ticked by without a phone call from anyone. He took a deep drink of the cold beer, savoring the taste. When they weren't working, Donald could barely keep up with Andrew, who enjoyed vodka martinis. There had been many late nights spent drinking as Andrew told his stories, many of which Donald had heard several times. He didn't mind since the stories grew more dramatic and funny with each retelling. Javier could pound back the beers and no one could keep up with his shots of tequila. Enrique on the other hand was a lightweight and was a mess after three drinks. Sherrie could hold her own and enjoyed screwdrivers and beer. The team had many fun nights in whatever hotel bar they found themselves across the country. Donald took another drink of his beer wishing that they were all in a bar somewhere, safe and out of the rain, eating and drinking.

Donald looked at the various monitors, tapping the mouse to flip to different screens. He was slightly pissed that Javier hadn't managed to set up the camera by the rock pile. "It must have been a faulty camera," he thought. "Those damn things cost a lot of money to replace." Donald finished off the beer in one long slurp and then he burped loudly. He grabbed another bottle and started munching on a bag of barbecue potato chips. He had the best job in the group. While everyone else was out in the cold and rain tramping around in the woods, he was nice and cozy in the van, able to snack and drink beer. "What a life," he thought. Also, it was much better than working in a cubicle day after day staring at a computer screen. He hated wearing a suit and dealing with all the bullshit meetings, rules, management, annoying employees and crappy busy work. Another pet peeve of his was working for a company and watching it make lots of money while his salary rarely increased. He had worked for a software company in Seattle for several years and hated it. Although it had been a steady paycheck, he missed out on the Internet dot.com boom of the late '90s, when many people grew instantly rich. He had felt like a zombie working at that company, but his job with Andrew, each day was exciting and new and filled with the unknown. He was so glad that he had left the corporate life far behind.

"I'll let other fools slave away and give their lives as office drones," Donald said with a smug grin, sipping his beer.

Donald had always been a fan of sci-fi, fantasy, horror and the supernatural, watching the television shows, collecting comics, reading the books and scavenging the Internet for news and information about his favorite genres. A few years back, he had gone to a Bigfoot convention where Andrew was a speaker. Donald had been eager to hear Andrew who was a minor celebrity, appearing in many Bigfoot documentaries. The local networks were always interviewing him whenever there was a Bigfoot sighting.

Donald had gone to the convention and bought his first plaster of a Sasquatch footprint taken in Idaho. He still had it framed in his home in West Seattle. He had been fascinated by Andrew's lecture, which covered his theories on Sasquatch, famous sightings and his adventures in the Himalayans and across the U.S. After the seminar, Andrew had been signing autographs at one of the booths and that is where they first met. Andrew had talked about how he wanted to modernize his hunt for the Sasquatch and go hi-tech. Donald had offered his services and a few months later, he was working on Andrew's team. Ever since then, it had been one long, exciting adventure traveling across the country investigating Sasquatch sightings, interviewing eye-witnesses and spending more time out in nature rather than inside a cubicle. It didn't pay as much but his life had dramatically improved. He had been invited to speak at several Bigfoot Conferences. Strangers would come up to him and ask him all types of questions believing he was an authority on Sasquatch. It was a great feeling that people actually cared about his opinions. Donald smiled with satisfaction and said "Life is great." He took a drink of his beer and looked at his watch.

"51 minutes," he said and sighed. "Where are you guys?" he looked at his monitors, which showed the same forest scenes as they had for the last several days. He remembered back when he had first joined the organization and how impressed Andrew had been with all the technology. Donald had created databases, charts, maps and a website making it easier to gather, organize and analyze the information. There had been some lean times for the organization, but two years ago Stephen Denmin began funding it, giving them the opportunity to invest in all sorts of high-tech devices such as motion sensors, infrared cameras, wireless video and sound detectors.

Donald took another drink of his beer and realized he had to take a piss. He had been drinking soda all morning and now the beer had pushed him over the top. He looked out the window across the parking lot where there was a restroom. "More like an outhouse," Donald grumbled. It was one small room, big enough for a stall and it stunk, basically a toilet over a septic tank. Donald frowned debating if he could hold it as he looked towards the outhouse through the rain pouring in the gusty wind.

"It's so nice and dry in here," Donald thought, "but nature calls." He sighed, burped and grabbed his rain jacket. He tied the hood on tight and opened the back door. He struggled out of the van, shut the door and hurried across the parking lot as the rain pelted him. The cold wind stung his face. He reached the restroom, took a deep breath and opened the door. He stepped inside, locking it behind him. Donald started pissing as gusts of wind whistled around the restroom. The rain rattled loudly against the metal ceiling. He peered down into the black, gaping hole of the toilet catching a revolting sight. "Why can't they have a toilet with running water?" he muttered. "What are they doing with all of my tax dollars?"

Leaves crunched outside of the restroom and then seconds later, a branch snapped. Donald turned his head in the direction of the sound to listen and continued pissing. More crunching noises started as if someone was stepping through the undergrowth near the restroom. "Maybe they made it back," he thought with a relieved sigh. He finished, zipped up and opened the door taking a deep breath of the fresh, cold air. He stepped out of the restroom and found the parking lot empty of people. Donald glanced around at the undergrowth and trees nearby, but saw nothing in the deep gloom. Shrugging his shoulders, he rushed across the wet pavement to the van.

Inside, he took off his wet coat and checked his watch. "62 minutes," he said and then looked at his cell phone. "No calls." He sighed as the anxious, nervous feeling returned. "Where the hell is everyone?" He dialed Andrew's number and it went to voicemail after a few rings. He called Javier and Sherrie, but no one answered.

Out of nowhere, the van rocked with a big boom against the side. Something was violently shaking the vehicle back and forth. Donald gasped, dropped his phone and slipped out of his chair falling to the floor. A beastly, hairy arm, freakish in size, burst through the driver's side window, black claws slicing at the air. Donald cried out, his face growing pale, his mouth agape. He had been a fan of scary movies, but nothing could compare to what he was witnessing in front of him. He dropped low to the floor and crawled to the back of the van as far from the monstrous arm as possible. His laptop computer slipped off the desk and crashed to the floor, giving Donald no pause as he cowered in the back, his terror-filled eyes transfixed on the long, black claws of the hand.

The arm withdrew quickly and the van stopped rocking. Donald panted, trying to catch his breath as he glanced warily at the windows, unable to see anything from where he sat. Deep and dangerous growling broke the silence outside the van. In the distance, he heard the sounds of glass shattering as well as loud bangs as if the other vehicles in the parking lot were being attacked. Apish grunting began on one side of the van, while on the other side the low growling continued.

"There's at least two of them," Donald thought in terror and wondered if all the doors were locked. He couldn't remember if had had locked them all, but he didn't dare move to check. All he wanted to do was curl up in ball and hide. He began whimpering and trembling as he gasped for air.

A tall, dark shape ran past the front of the van. "It's huge," he thought as he scrunched down as much as he could, wishing he could disappear. His eyes were drawn to his bottle of beer, which had fallen off the desk as the remaining liquid was pouring out onto the floor.

The van began to rock again more violently than before as the growling grew louder. Donald braced himself as his equipment crashed to the floor. Another dark shape appeared in front the van and stopped this time.

Donald cringed against the back of the van, gasping as a monstrous, ape-like face covered in coarse shaggy hair with a mouth full of sharp teeth glared at him with fierce, black eyes. The beast roared and slammed a massive fist against the windshield, shattering it. Donald pressed against the back door of the van, whimpering, his face completely white.

"Go away," he whispered in a terrified, desperate voice. "Leave me alone."

The back door began to creak loudly and then it was suddenly ripped opened. Donald cried out as two hairy hands seized him and pulled him out of the van with ease as if he weighed no more than a small child instead of an overweight man close to three hundred pounds. The Father lifted Donald up off the ground, his feet dangling, until they were face to face. Its black eyes stared at him curiously for a moment. Donald closed his eyes and whimpered. The Father's eyes bulged with rage and opened its mouth, roaring like a demon burning in the deepest pits of hell, as Donald's body went limp, his face splattered with spit. The Father flung him twenty feet across the parking lot sending him crashing onto the wet asphalt, snapping his left wrist. Donald cried out and slumped down as he desperately glanced around the parking lot as his eyes grew wide in absolute terror. There were at least four Sasquatch running about, emerging from the tree line, attacking the other cars, breaking the glass, denting the sides and knocking the vehicles over.

The Father walked over to Donald, who noticed that it was the biggest one, close to nine feet tall and covered with thick scars over its muscular, body. Donald was transfixed on the Father's long, black claws. He cowered on the ground paralyzed with fright and could do nothing but watch the massive beast approach. The Father stopped within a couple feet, towering over him, staring with black eyes that burned with rage. Donald whimpered loudly when the beast roared at him. The Father raised its long claws and then swiped down slicing, stabbing and ripping into Donald who screamed and then went silent.

The Father kept tearing and cutting into the weak, pathetic human that lay in front of it, taking out its rage. Its black eyes glimmered with some form of pleasure and satisfaction as the blood spilled. After a few moments, the Father stopped, kneeled down and then sniffed the corpse. It ripped a chunk of flesh from the corpse's stomach and stuffed it into its mouth. Chomping loudly, it stood up; blood and bits of flesh were splattered across its muscular chest and arms. The Father looked at the others who were destroying the vehicles and then made a deep, loud punctuated, grunting noise. The other Sasquatch immediately stopped what they were doing and turned towards the Father who made quick grunts and motioned with one of its arms. The others rushed across the parking lot and gathered in front of the Father.

The Father glared at the three Sasquatch and then murmured low, apish grunts and pointed at the corpse. The three Sasquatch, squealing with excitement, rushed over to Donald's corpse and began devouring it. The Sasquatch looked famished, thin and unhealthy as if they hadn't had a full meal in months. The Father watched silently and then after a couple minutes, grunted deeply and started walking across the parking lot. The other Sasquatch stuffed pieces of flesh in their mouths and followed the Father up the Ape Cave Trail.

Chapter 14

▼

It took sometime before Andrew opened his eyes and when he did he found himself in complete and utter darkness. He stared into the black void unsure if he was asleep or awake as the memories slowly began to trickle into his mind. "I'm awake," he whispered with sudden realization as his body started shivering from the biting cold. He recognized the aches in his legs and arms, which grew more painful as consciousness took hold. Sharp, hard rocks pressed into his skin and then he realized he was lying on his back. He reached up into the blackness and felt a cold, damp, rocky ceiling about a foot above him. "That's right," he whispered. He had crawled underneath two rocks that were leaning against each other after witnessing the deaths of Enrique and Javier and nearly being devoured by the Mother. A stern expression creased his face, while his gray, determined eyes beaded as he came to terms with what had happened. Plans began to form in his mind.

He had to reach the surface and warn the rest of the team of the danger, especially Sherrie, who he would forbid to come down here. He would never put his daughter in harm's way and he hoped that she hadn't come looking for him. Once he escaped the tunnels, he would make a few phone calls and return with the necessary manpower and firepower. "Nothing under the heavens, except the Lord himself, will stop me from bringing back a Sasquatch dead or alive," he swore quietly. After all the long years of searching, he had finally found the elusive species. It had taken forty years, but his life long dream was now finally realized. All he had to accomplish was the difficult task of bringing back a specimen to show the world. "To hell with the laws," he whispered, remembering that Washington State law protected the Sasquatch. "And to all the fools who thought I was insane, that I had wasted my life, they can all go to hell."

Andrew moved his right leg, hit a rock and grimaced as sharp pain wracked his knee. He groaned and started to feel claustrophobic, penned in by the rocks and darkness. The smothering silence was also getting to him. It was like he was trapped in some empty, cold netherworld and the only sound was that of his own haggard breathing. He inched his way backwards out from under the two rocks until he could sit up. He glanced around and then his eyes filled with relief at the faint light of a flashlight, which shined in the distance on the cavern floor. Before attempting to stand up, he massaged his sore ankles and touched his bloody pant leg where the mother had bitten him, thankful that it hadn't been deep. After massaging his ankles, he moved to the tight muscles in his legs, wishing he was at least a decade younger. It was too cold to sit in one place for long, so he groped in the darkness and found a boulder to pull himself to his feet. He pushed himself up and braced himself against the side of a boulder testing his bad knee. He had to be careful and dreaded the thought of his knee giving out in the depths of the cave system.

"Here I go," he said quietly and began stepping across the uneven rocky floor, progressing slowly and trying not to put too much pressure on his knee. He walked towards the flashlight as he glanced at that darkness that surrounded him, knowing that a Sasquatch could be nearby and he wouldn't even see it. Moments later, he reached the dark pool where the flashlight glowed like a beacon, wedged into a groove in the rocky floor. He picked it up and flashed it around his perimeter, stopping at the horrifying sight of the corpses of Javier and Enrique. He lumbered over to them and kneeled down next to Javier's body, shaking his head in disgust and sorrow, barely able to recognize his friend. Much of the flesh had been chewed and ripped off revealing the bones, while blood stained the rocks several feet in every direction. "You won't be forgotten my friend," Andrew promised and turned his attention to Enrique's body.

"Enrique," Andrew whispered sadly. "You were too young for something like this to happen. You won't be forgotten and I promise you I will help out your family. They will be taken care of and well compensated." He looked at the bodies one last time, stood up and sighed angrily. "It wasn't supposed to be this way," he thought. "We were going to be heroes, legends in our own time for discovering the Sasquatch, not end up becoming casualties. If I had known what the Sasquatch were capable of, I would've been better prepared. If only I had heeded Chad's warning, but I was too foolhardy and gung-ho. All of my research for the last forty years gave evidence that the Sasquatch were peaceful creatures, hiding away from humanity. I thought the incident in Canada was an aberration, a fluke, something that would never happen again."

Andrew shined his light along the ground and stopped at his cane, which was broken in two. He picked up the pieces, with no memory of breaking it. "Maybe a Sasquatch did this," he said quietly. "I will purchase another one from the same person who made this one." Andrew dropped the wrecked cane to the cave floor and moved over to the bank of the dark pool, where the body of the mother lie face down with blood covering its back. Hesitating a moment, unsure if the Mother was dead, he unsheathed his knife and crept over cautiously. Seeing no signs of life, he kneeled down and examined the body. "A disgusting creature," Andrew said. "And a very sickly one." The mother's face was sticky with phlegm and spit, which oozed out the side of its mouth. Its cataract-covered eyes were puffy and lifeless. He examined the legs, which were immensely swollen at the knees and ankles. The legs were dirty and most of the hair had been scrapped off from years of being dragged over the rocky floor of the cavern. The left shin had been broken and a large scar crossed over it.

"You must have broken your leg years ago, maybe from slipping on these damn rocks in the dark, unable to support your weight. Your leg never healed properly and most likely got infected. Since then your condition has worsen. The other Sasquatch of this tribe hunt and bring back the food for you to eat. Times have been lean since the virus decimated the deer and elk population so I'm sure your diet has consisted of rats and other small rodents. Maybe the other Sasquatch gather nuts and berries from the surface and bring them to you. No matter, the feasts I'm sure you enjoyed from the abundance of deer in years past are long gone and you most likely go for days without eating. Maybe the Sasquatch make sure you are fed first out of respect since you are the Mother, which would be an example of some sort of social structure. Out of all of the Sasquatch I have seen down here, you look like the most fed. I look forward to doing an autopsy on you," Andrew said and stood up. "You will be studied and eventually displayed for all the public to see. You are mine now, my dear Mother." Andrew limped past the Mother unable to take the stink. It was a putrid rotting smell.

Andrew shined his light on the dark pool of water. The back wall was wet from water that was dripping from the ceiling. "I have to get back to the surface," Andrew said quietly, although part of him wanted to stay and gather as much information on these creatures as possible. He moved slowly towards the rock outcropping and stopped. In front of him was the body of another Sasquatch. He kneeled down. "A male, nearly full grown." And then he noticed the bullets holes and the blood, which had matted its thick hair. "Who shot you?" he asked quietly. "I don't recall Javier using a gun," he thought. "Javier wouldn't have had a gun, only the dart gun. Chad?" He looked about the cavern wondering if Chad had been down here. "Maybe they came down and didn't see me under the rocks." He quickly examined the Sasquatch noticing that it was malnourished and then forced himself to stand up. He couldn't tarry any longer and it was imperative to warn his daughter of the danger and to bring back reinforcements.

He lumbered around the rock outcropping towards the entrance to the tunnel that led to the surface as fast as he dared. His limp was growing worse as his bad knee ached with every step. In front of him on the ground was a second flashlight. He walked over to the light, noticing a dart gun a few feet away behind a rock.

"This must be Enrique's," Andrew said and picked up the weapon. He checked it over and found one loaded dart. "This will have to do." He slid the knife in his belt and held the gun and flashlight in his hands feeling more secure and protected.

He thought of his daughter Sherrie, eager to tell her of his discovery, despite the deaths of his comrades. "They will be heroes," Andrew whispered as he limped around a rather large rock. "They shall be remembered." He stumbled and fell hard to the ground, the flashlight bouncing and rolling a few feet away. He groaned deeply in pain, his legs scraped and bruised. He took several slow breaths and then forced himself to his feet. As he started to bend down to pick up the flashlight, the muscles in his lower back began to spasm and tightened up. Wincing, he slowly straightened up and massaged the muscles as best as he could with one hand while the other held the flashlight and dart gun. He stood in one place for several minutes and then sighed, hating to admit the fact that he was getting old. Andrew's face creased with a determined frown as he started limping forward again finally reaching the entrance to the tunnel a couple minutes later. Inside, the lava tube, the floor was much smoother with fewer rocks to climb over and avoid.

At one point the tunnel's ceiling became lower and lower until he had to hunch over so as not to bump his head. He groaned with each step, his back straining, growing stiffer. He finally had to stop and knelt down to rest as he rubbed his lower back. Sharp pain burned through the muscles near his spine. All the years of climbing up mountains and hiking through the forest, lifting equipment, carrying heavy backpacks had taken their toll.

"Just a couple more minutes," he whispered, thinking of his daughter. They had spent little time together during her childhood. He had always been off on his next adventure, investigating reports of the Sasquatch, traveling around the states or other countries. "They grow up so fast," he thought with regret and some guilt. His wife had divorced him almost twenty years ago, embarrassed about his career and tired of all the lonely nights.

Andrew could never explain and make his wife understand. "This is my passion," he had said to her one evening. "I feel alive when I'm out there searching for Sasquatch and just think when I do find it. We shall be famous and rich beyond our dreams."

"It doesn't exist," his wife had yelled, glaring at him with hate-filled eyes. "The Sasquatch is a myth ... a joke. It's not real. Do you know how embarrassed I am when I'm asked what my husband does for a living? Do you know how many people laugh at us behind our backs? We're a joke to everyone ... the crazy couple. You're always off in the forest, hiding away from real life, so you don't have to deal with the ridicule, while I am faced with it every damn day."

"They won't think it's a joke when I capture a Sasquatch," Andrew had said. His wife's word still stung him in the very depths of his soul, even now, years later, while he was trying to escape the actual lair of the Sasquatch. The words would hurt him until the last day of his life.

"You'll never catch one," his wife had screamed. "Because they don't exist. Get that through your thick skull. They don't EXIST."

Andrew could still clearly picture his wife's face, every detail, as she had yelled at him all those years ago, every tense muscle, angry crease, and poison-filled eyes even the timber of her voice. The image would be forever branded in his mind. Shortly after that dreadful night, his wife had divorced him, shattering his heart. How could someone who had loved him for so long, just up and leave? Andrew had been asking that question and many others for the last twenty years. Due to the nature of his job, he traveled a lot, but he was always there for her whenever she needed him. He had been there when his wife's mother had died in a car crash, when she was sick, when she had lost her job and through all the good times. He still couldn't believe that the person that had said 'I love you' almost every night, who had talked about future plans together, had changed into another person, who wanted nothing to do with him. He wasn't sure if he believed in true love anymore. Maybe some people get together out of convenience instead of love. Whatever the reason, his heart had been smashed and he had never been the same.

Andrew had thrown himself into his work after that to keep his mind off the divorce, increasing the number of trips, which grew longer and longer in duration. Sometimes he would go off for months at a time. His wife had sold their house and taken Sherrie, who was twelve at the time, and moved across town. His oldest daughter Mary was already in college going to Loyola Marymount in Los Angeles.

Andrew saw his children less and less during the proceeding years. He had taken up drinking and had grown bitter. Except for his search of the Sasquatch, his life had been wrecked, a dark pit that he tried to ignore through drink. And then six years ago, Sherrie had called him, a few years after her own divorce, and surprisingly wanted to spend time with him. It had given Andrew a fresh start. All that he had in his life was his quest, but now that his daughter was helping he couldn't even articulate how much he appreciated it and was relieved. Some of the regret that he had bundled up inside was finally gone. Andrew sighed as he thought of the past. He had to warn his daughter so she wouldn't come down here looking for him.

"A Martini would be nice right about now," he whispered and then with a loud grunt he forced himself up to his feet, his back protesting every inch of the way. Andrew stood hunched over and began rubbing his lower back. After a few minutes, the tight muscles relaxed enough for him to proceed. The cave's ceiling grew higher so he could stand up straight and take more pressure off of his back. He limped across the rocky floor, turned a corner and stopped, gasping loudly, his grey eyes growing wide with fear.

A tall, dark, man-like shape stood twenty feet away in the shadows of the tunnel in front of him; a raspy breathing could be heard. Andrew raised his flashlight, revealing an old Sasquatch covered in long white hair with many bald patches. It was tall and skinny. The Sasquatch raised its hands to protect its eyes from the light and then roared, a throaty, dry sound as if it had lost most of its voice. The wrinkled skin hung loose on its long limbs, revealing a skeleton-like figure. Its ribs could be seen through the skin. The Sasquatch swiped the air with its black claws as if it was trying to attack the light from his flashlight. Andrew noticed that a couple of its fingers were missing claws.

Andrew stood in place and stared at the beast for at least a minute taking in every detail. The Sasquatch stared back with black, curious eyes. "You're an old one," Andrew said in a loud, firm voice. "Kind of like me.

Are you the leader of this tribe ... the elder? Do the younger ones look to you for guidance or do they discard the old when they get weak? It looks like you haven't had much to eat in a long time." The Sasquatch grunted faintly and coughed.

"You must be the Grandfather of this lot my friend," Andrew said and clicked the safety off the dart gun, pointing it at the Sasquatch. "And you are in my way." Andrew stepped towards the Grandfather as it started growling a dry, raspy warning.

Chapter 15

Chad crawled next to Sherrie in the tight tunnel to examine the dead end as shrill screams and high-pitched roars grew louder behind them. Sherrie flashed her light back and cried, "They're coming." There was a bend in the tunnel about twenty feet behind them, so they would have little warning when the Sasquatch appeared. Chad pressed against the black, jagged rock searching for an opening, his eyes desperate for escape. The sounds of pursuit grew closer and louder. He pushed against the rock and it shook slightly.

"It's loose," Chad said, pointing his flashlight into a crack near the top. "It looks like the tunnel keeps going."

Sherrie turned back and shined her flashlight into another crack near the top of the four-foot tall tunnel. She peered into the crack for a few seconds. "Yes it does," she said, pushing against the boulder. "If we can move this damn rock." Both Chad and Sherrie braced themselves and pressed against the boulder that was blocking the tunnel. Their feet slipped several times as they tried to find leverage as the boulder began to rock. They pushed harder, the growling growing nearer. The boulder began to shift and then it suddenly rolled forward causing them both to fall on their stomachs. Chad sat up and shined his light, revealing an opening into a larger tunnel. The boulder had dropped down onto a ledge. Sherrie climbed out first, followed closely by Chad.

"We're in another lava tube," Sherrie said. "And about fifteen feet above the cave floor." The new lava tube was narrow, the roof about twenty-five feet from the cave floor. From what they could tell from their position, the cave sloped down to their right. The ledge that they were standing on continued in both directions for several feet before coming to an end. Discoloring in the sides of the walls revealed the flow marks from rivers of molten lava from centuries past. The rock along the walls and ledge was covered in sticky residue, which many people called cave slime. The air was cold and dank with moisture. Except for their flashlights, there were no other sources of light; the heavy darkness surrounding them, felt like a wall, ready to collapse in on them. Their flashlights did little to illuminate the cave, which seemed to absorb the light, giving them no indication of the extent or direction of the new tunnel. Behind them the apish squeals grew alarmingly louder as if they would be upon them at any second.

"We have to get down," Sherrie cried. "Hopefully there's a way out." She leaned over the ledge and dropped down until she was hanging by her hands and then she let go. She dropped several feet and fell back, landing hard on her backside.

"Are you okay?" Chad called from above.

Sherrie shook her head and stood up. "I hurt my hand."

Chad clicked the safety on his rifle and dropped it down the side. It made a clattering noise as it hit the cave floor. He put the flashlight in his pocket, climbed over the side, hung from the ledge and dropped to the floor, jamming his ankle and scraping his legs and arms. He jumped up, grabbed his rifle and looked at Sherrie. "Which way? Up or down?"

"Up," Sherrie said. "Hopefully it goes to the surface." Sherrie sprinted up the tunnel; the cave floor was relatively smooth with the occasional groove and hole to jump over. They hastened up the slope of the tunnel, the sounds muffled and the light faint in the overwhelming darkness making it very isolating. The tunnel narrowed for thirty feet and then opened up. Chad glanced at the ledges above them with wary eyes, his hands gripping his rifle ready to fire.

"Look," Sherrie said, pointing up ahead, where a point of light glowed in the distance moving towards them. "Help," Sherrie shouted, waving her hands in the dark.

The point of light stopped and the faint, almost ghost-like silhouette of a person was behind it. The light pointed up and flashed in their eyes and then to the ground again. They rushed over and found a young man in his mid-twenties with blond, short hair, wearing circular glasses, looking at them oddly as if he wasn't sure what to make of them. His eyes dropped down to Chad's rifle and then they grew wide with surprise as he stepped back, looking uncomfortable and nervous.

"We need help," Sherrie cried, stepping towards him.

The man took a step back. "What?" he asked in a heavy German accent.

"Where are we?" Sherrie asked and stepped closer. "Is there a way out?"

The man looked befuddled as if he didn't quiet understand what she was asking. His nervous eyes kept glancing at Chad's gun. "You're in the Ape Caves," he said, taking another step back.

"The Ape Caves?" Sherrie asked in shock, looking questioningly at Chad.

"Is this some kind of joke?" the German asked.

"No, no." Sherrie shook her head. "We're being chased. We have to get out of here. How far to the surface?"

"Who's chasing you?" The man took another step back and nearly tripped over a rock.

"Bigfoot," Chad said and glanced back at the blackness.

The man chuckled nervously and smirked. "You guys are freaks," he yelled and started off down the cave.

"Come back," Sherrie cried and rushed over to him and grabbed his shoulder. "You can't go that way. They're coming. I'm serious."

The man frowned at her and jerked free. "Get the hell away from me you freak," he yelled and started walking again.

"You're in danger," Sherrie shouted hysterically. "Come with us. You'll get killed if you go that way. Please listen to me. I'm not lying to you."

The man walked down the tunnel and quickly became a dark silhouette in the darkness before he vanished entirely as he turned a corner.

Sherrie rushed over to Chad. "We've got to go back and get him. He's going to die. We have to save him."

"No." Chad shook his head. "It's too dangerous."

"We have a gun," Sherrie cried, "and a knife." She pulled out her small, hunting knife and flashed it in front of his face.

"We are not going back. We can't force that guy to believe us. We have to get to the surface, find your father, call the authorities and get the hell out of here." Chad motioned Sherrie to follow him.

Sherrie remained in one place. "I just can't let someone die," she screamed. "We're not monsters."

"Listen Sherrie," Chad snapped. "We have to go. You don't understand. These creatures are ruthless. Our only chance to survive is to get as far from this place as possible … right now. We don't know how many of them are after us."

"No," Sherrie said. "I'm going back. I couldn't live with myself if I didn't. You don't have to go." Sherrie turned and started down the tunnel.

"Your father wouldn't approve," Chad called after her. "Don't be ridiculous." He watched in a mixture of surprise and anger as Sherrie moved down the slope. "Come back," he yelled as her silhouette grew darker and darker. "Fuck," he screamed and then the darkness swallowed Sherrie up until there was just a pinpoint of light from her flashlight that soon vanished around a bend in the cave. Chad remained in one place looking down the tunnel and then up the other direction, which lead to the exit and then back down. He gripped the rifle with white, trembling knuckles as he kept glancing back and forth with indecision. "Fuck it," he cursed at the top of his lungs as he turned and ran down the tunnel after Sherrie. "I'm going to regret this," he muttered.

The young German man moved quickly down the tunnel wanting to put as much distance between him and the crazy Americans as possible, hoping that they weren't following him. What had made him extremely nervous and apprehensive about the Americans was that one of them was carrying a rifle. "Why?" he thought. This was a national park and weapons weren't permitted. What were they trying to hunt anyways? There was nothing down here except for tourists and maybe a bat. The German continued down the tunnel flashing his light around, amazed at how cold it was down in the tunnels. "I should have brought a hat and gloves," he thought. It was first time he had been in the Ape Caves or any caves for that matter. He was going to the university in Seattle and had come down to explore the cave after a couple of friends had told him about their adventures in the Ape Caves last summer.

For Christmas break he was planning on flying down to Los Angeles to go to Disneyland, visit Hollywood and hopefully see some stars. He had never been there and was looking forward to the sunny weather. Although, Seattle's cold, rainy weather was comparable to his own hometown in Germany.

The German moved around a bend, as yells from the woman broke the silence behind him. "Crazy Americans," he said and stopped abruptly when something grunted, deep and viciously above him. His light flashed along a rocky ledge ten feet above him and then he gasped. A hulking, shadowy figure hunched over the ledge and stared down at him. The German froze, unsure if his mind was playing tricks on him and not comprehending what was above him. The creature hopped a few feet to its left on the ledge in quick, fluid movements. It opened its mouth revealing jagged teeth as it screamed, a piercing, apish monstrous sound. The German snapped out of his daze and stumbled back a couple feet. An adolescent leaped from the ledge with a horrid roar, slamming the German in the chest sending him crashing to the rocky floor. The German smacked his head against a rock, knocking him out cold.

Sherrie ran down the center of the tunnel keeping the flashlight on the ground ahead of her as she jumped down the uneven floor, avoiding potholes, dodging boulders and stepping down rock shelves. She called out at the top of her lungs, "Come back, come back," but her voice seemed to be absorbed by the darkness. "I can't let anyone else die because of these monsters," she thought. They had led the Sasquatch into the Ape Caves endangering the lives of anyone who happened to visit on this unlucky day.

Sherrie heard a muffled scream ahead, followed by monstrous shrieking. She went around a bend and stopped in her tracks, her eyes wide with terror. Two Sasquatch were kneeling over the German, biting into his flesh and gnawing on his arm. They were adolescents, five to six feet in height, weighing around two to three hundred pounds. The Sasquatch looked up, their black eyes glaring at her and glared at her as they snapped their teeth. Another Sasquatch on the ledge above growled and roared. It crawled across the ledge towards her in quick movements.

Sherrie gasped, turned and ran. The shrill screams of the Sasquatch filled the cave. Up ahead of her, Chad emerged from around a bend, just a silhouette behind a point of light in the encroaching black of the tunnel. "He's dead," Sherrie cried as she approached him. "Run … They're coming." They both sprinted up the passageway, despite the protest from their sore, scraped, bruised, aching bodies. "There's at least three of them," she said, gasping. "They were eating him."

Chad ran even faster. "Did they follow you?"

"I don't know," Sherrie cried. "I don't know anything."

They ran in cold silence with no sounds of pursuit, following the tunnel, which seemed never ending. Chad kept glancing back, gripping his rifle and making sure that the safety was clicked off. He was exhausted and his breathing haggard and shallow. His limbs felt numb and sluggish and a couple times he nearly tripped in a groove on the floor. Sherrie seemed no better off as she wheezed and gasped.

"How far to the exit?" Chad gasped.

"Not much longer," Sherrie said. "I've been down here many times. We're in the lower section of the Ape Caves, the easy part. It takes about an hour round trip walking."

As Chad ran, he thought of his trip in Canada, which returned to the forefront of his mind in horrifying detail. Many of the hunters that had been attacked at the Camp had been dragged into caves. Search parties found what was left of them, nothing but bones and a few pieces of clothing. The Sasquatch had feasted on the unfortunate men. Chad wondered if the caves in Canada were like the Ape Caves. Many of the hunters had never been found including Meredith. Chad had always wondered if Meredith had been dragged into the caves alive. He hoped that was not the case, praying that it had been quick and painless. Chad was determined to get out of the Ape Caves alive. Too many people had died in Canada including his father and best friend Shane, that he felt it was his duty and obligation to live and take revenge for them if possible. He was the only one left from that fatal trip.

The tunnel curved to the right and to their surprise, they found a group of people standing huddled together with flashlights talking among themselves. A young man, maybe 17 years old with a baseball cap on backwards, flashed his light in Chad's face and said. "Look, more people." All of the flashlights turned putting Chad and Sherrie in the spotlight.

Squinting and raising her hands to protect her eyes, Sherrie asked, her voice stricken with panic. "Where's the exit?"

The group of people all started talking loudly at once. The teenager with the baseball cap walked over to them. "I'm Billy. The exit is this way." The cave split into two tunnels, one going to the left and the other going to the right. Billy led them into the tunnel to the right that opened up into a tall, dark chamber-like room. Along the left wall was a steep, metal staircase. Sherrie rushed up the stairs, her boots clinking against the metal. Chad followed close behind and Billy walked up the stairs taking his time as if he was in no hurry. They reached the top of the metal platform and followed the tunnel to their left. They walked a few paces and stopped, faces aghast, shining their flashlights ahead into the darkness.

"This is the exit?" Sherrie asked in disbelief as her flashlight illuminated a giant mass of tree trunks and branches that had been stuffed into the sinkhole-like exit leading out into the forest. Dull, faint sunlight shined above them, in between small openings in the wall of trees. "There's suppose to be stone steps here that lead out of this cave," Sherrie said and walked to the wall of cracked tree trunks and branches blocking their way. Pine needles and fresh mud covered the cave floor around the trees.

"Me and a buddy had just gone into the cave when we heard this loud noise, a mix of screaming and wood snapping. We came back up here and saw the first tree crash down into the hole and then one after another. We heard all this grunting and growling, like apes or bears or something," Billy said. "My buddy and I freaked out and ran down the stairs to the lower level. A few others that were already in the cave joined up with us. We don't know what the hell is going on or what to do."

"The Sasquatch," Sherrie cried and rushed over to the trees searching for a way out.

"Sasquatch?" Billy asked.

"Bigfoot, whatever you want to call it. These monsters have blocked our way out." Chad shook his head in shock, desperation dripping from his voice. He looked in horror at the barrier of branches and tree trunks that blocked the exit and said, "We don't have much time."

Chapter 16

▼

Andrew limped slowly up the tunnel towards the Grandfather. He held the dart gun in his right hand with his finger on the trigger, aimed at the Sasquatch. The Grandfather, covered in long, white hair, growled in a dry, faint voice and with its long, skinny arms it swiped the air in threatening movements. Its black claws were broken and jagged, but still looked dangerous. Andrew approached cautiously, taking in as much detail as he could about the creature. The Grandfather was well over seven feet tall, but it hunched over as if its back had been hurt. Its saggy, skin drooped from its malnourished body.

"I'm not going to hurt you," Andrew promised in a gentle voice as he tried to make eye contact with it, in hopes of communicating some understanding. The Grandfather glared with black eyes and opened its mouth wide, revealing a mouth full of yellowish, black teeth, many of which were missing. It growled, raspy and low, and stood up to its full height in an imposing pose.

Andrew stopped about ten feet from the beast. "Are you going to let me pass? We can go our separate ways. You back down into the deep tunnels of your lair and me up to the surface where the sun shines. We have both lost loved ones today. The violence doesn't need to continue." Andrew sensed no comprehension in the Grandfather's harsh face or fierce eyes, but to his surprise, he did detect, underneath the rage, glimpses of fear and maybe some type of curiosity.

Andrew smiled and took a cautious step forward. The Grandfather reacted immediately; its black eyes narrowed upon him as it stepped to the center of the tunnel completely blocking his way. It began to make sharp, punctuated, apish grunts, squeals and clicking sounds as it gestured and pointed at Andrew.

"Are you trying to communicate with me? Is that your language? Fascinating." Andrew listened and stood steadfast, regretting he didn't have a camera or recorder so that he could analyze the sounds later. The Grandfather continued to make odd noises and gesture with its hands, but Andrew did not comprehend. "Let me pass my friend," Andrew said gently and smiled.

The Grandfather's raspy grunts and squeals grew louder as it gestured wildly with its arms and then it seemed to get frustrated. Suddenly, it kneeled down and picked up a rock the size of a baseball.

Andrew stepped back. "Let me pass," he said in a loud, stern voice, aiming the dart gun. The Grandfather raised his hand that held the rock and began making quick grunting noises. They each watched the other for several seconds as if trying to perceive each other's intentions.

"Maybe we're both scared and too bull headed to back down," Andrew whispered in the dark silence of the cave. All of the reports about the attack in Canada gave no indication that the Sasquatch had any type of fear. They had attacked a camp full of hunters and slaughtered them, hunting down the survivors with unrelenting ruthlessness. Were they more than just secretive creatures filled with rage? Did they have some primitive type of language? It appeared that they had a family structure. "If I could bring you back, study you, learn your language and possibly communicate with you, it would be a tremendous leap in science and world history."

Thoughts of Sherrie suddenly entered Andrew's mind. He had to warn his daughter not to come down into the caves. Once she was safe, he could focus on capturing a Sasquatch. He looked angrily at the Grandfather and said in a loud, forceful voice, "Let me pass. I do not want to hurt you."

The Grandfather raised the rock over its head and growled. Without hesitation, Andrew fired the dart gun, sticking the Sasquatch in the stomach. The Grandfather made a croaking sound, dropped the rock and looked down at its stomach with wide curious eyes, not comprehending what had just taken place. It pulled the dart out and looked up and glared at Andrew with black, bellicose eyes. It stepped forward and raised its clawed hands.

Andrew stepped back, dropped the dart gun and flashed the light in the Grandfather's eyes. Raising its hands to protect its eyes and squinting, the Grandfather stopped a moment, disoriented, giving Andrew time to unsheathe his knife. The Grandfather roared, a pathetic sound, its voice nearly gone and lumbered forward swinging one of its massive hands with sudden speed. Startled by its swift attack, Andrew tried to dodge, but the hand knocked the flashlight to the ground. Andrew nearly lost the knife too as he stumbled back losing his footing and falling against the side of the rock wall. The rasping Grandfather pressed forward, its long arms flailing wildly. Andrew braced his foot against a rock, clenched his jaw and pushed forward and smote the Grandfather in the stomach with his knife. The Grandfather screeched in pain and knocked Andrew to the rocky floor.

Andrew groaned and shook his head trying to keep focused as the Grandfather grabbed the hilt of the knife and pulled it out, howling in agony. Andrew crawled and scooted over the rocky floor to get away from the Grandfather. His bad knee flared as he knocked it against a rock. The Grandfather placed its hand over the bloody wound and began to moan as it threw vengeful looks in Andrew's direction. The flashlight was still shining and as the Grandfather stumbled about, it cast shadows on the cave wall which appeared as though some demon had entered the cave. The Grandfather suddenly collapsed to the ground and began whimpering loudly as it clutched the wound in its stomach with both hands.

With fresh bruises, a throbbing knee and aching joints, Andrew stood up with a loud groan and limped over to the flashlight and picked it up. He circled carefully around the Grandfather and mumbled, "I'm sorry my friend. I didn't want to hurt you. I hope it's not fatal." The knife was lying on top of a rock near the Grandfather, but he didn't dare retrieve it and chance being attacked again. "Goodbye," Andrew said and started limping up the tunnel as the cries of the Grandfather continued behind him. He walked around a bend in the tunnel and all went silent as if he was completely alone, enveloped in the darkness, his light doing little to illuminate his perimeter.

Andrew moved through the tunnel at a steady pace, shining the flashlight ahead, hoping not to run into any more Sasquatch, which he found humorous, since he had spent most of his life hoping to run into one of these creatures. Andrew limped over the rocky floor as his back began to stiffen again. The tunnel turned to the left. "Can't be too much longer," he thought as he walked around the corner and found the circular opening in the ceiling. The entrance to the tunnel above leading to the rock pile and the forest was six feet off the ground.

Andrew pointed his light up into the hole and a relieved smiled touched his face. "Almost there," he said and placed the flashlight up on the edge of the opening. He then gripped the slippery edge with both hands and tried pulling himself up, straining for several seconds. Unable to get a firm hold, he fell back down and rolled his ankle causing him to fall hard to the cave floor.

"Damn it," Andrew cursed as he struggled to stand up. His back flared in pain forcing him to sit down, grimacing. He began massaging his lower back focusing on the knots and tight muscles. The stiffness in his lower back continued unabated despite his best efforts. "I need a drink," he muttered and looked up at the opening where the flashlight shined on the edge.

Andrew frowned; he was cold, frustrated and annoyed that his body was giving out. He had been in great shape all of his life constantly hiking through all types of terrain from the deep forests of the Northwest, to secluded glens, through thick bracken, around meres, up and down hillsides, into boggy fens, through perilous canyons and to the tops of mountains. He had done this on a daily basis while others his age were sitting at home watching television for several hours each day. "I've always had my health," he thought. It was the only thing in his life that hadn't failed him until now. He had broken a bone only once in his life. He had just spent two weeks climbing around the Mount Hood area after a reported

Sasquatch sighting, which turned out to be a hoax. A couple of college kids had rented an ape costume and ran around the woods. They waited along the road and as a car approached, they would run into the woods. The people in the car would get just a glimpse of a hairy shape and report it. The secret had eventually gotten out as the kids blabbed and bragged about it on campus.

Hoaxes irked Andrew more than anything. It wasted his time and money traveling to investigate a joke, making him look like some crazy codger searching for something that people didn't think existed. Despite finding out it was a hoax, Andrew had decided to hike around Mount Hood and search for footprints. He had spent two weeks with Javier exploring the rugged territory, climbing up hills, descending steep slopes and never once did he hurt himself. After spending days around Mount Hood, Andrew found no hint of a real Sasquatch so he returned home to his rented house in Portland. Three days later, he had fallen off a ladder while cleaning the gutters and broke his right wrist and damaged his knee. It was the only time he had ever broken a bone. The wrist healed, but the knee didn't and slowly grew worse. Over the years he had spent a lot of money on surgeries and had to use the cane to support it.

And now he was trapped in a cave, his back hurt, his body bruised and scraped, his knee threatening to give out and his sprained ankle ached. Jose and Enrique were dead. The images of their mutilated bodies returned to his mind. He still couldn't believe it, like some nightmare from which he would soon wake up and everything would be back to normal. Unfortunately, nothing would be normal in his life again. His unrealistic view of the Sasquatch had been shattered and two of his co-workers, including Javier, a long time friend, were dead. And where was his daughter? "I have to get out of this damn cave and warn Sherrie," he muttered in the dark, trying to stand up, but his back flared and he fell back down. "At least Chad's with her," he thought. "Chad survived the massacre in Canada and will know what to do; especially if he got his hands on the rifle he was adamant about bringing. She's in good hands with him."

Andrew began to massage his lower back again with both of his hands as he planned his next move after he escaped the Sasquatch lair. He would return with many men, capture as many Sasquatch as possible and spend the rest of his life studying and trying to communicate with them. The Grandfather had spoken some primitive language and he wanted to learn it. It would be wondrous if he could speak to these creature. Questions swirled in his mind at the possibilities. Did they have some sort of oral tradition and history that they passed down from generation to generation? Did they have some sort of crude language? Did they produce any basic type of art? Perhaps Sasquatch and not humans had created some of the cave drawings that were discovered over the centuries he mused? Did they use tools? He had seen no evidence of it, except for the use of rocks, which they used trying to smash their opponents. "So much to learn," he whispered as he rubbed his back, loosening the knots and tightness.

After a few minutes, the muscles in his back relaxed enough for him to stand up. He sighed as he looked up at the opening where the flashlight sat shining on the edge. He reached up and felt for a sturdy place to grip. The rock was hard, rough, and cold with a grimy, slimy feel. He grabbed onto a small ridge in the rock and started pulling himself up. Groaning loudly, he managed to get one elbow up before he slipped and dropped to the floor. "Damn it to hell," he yelled in frustration. He took the flashlight and shined it along the cave floor until he found a loose rock. He picked it up carefully as his back strained and then placed it under the opening. He slowly gathered more rocks, taking his time so not to hurt his back again, until he had a pile on the floor.

Andrew stepped on the pile of rocks bracing himself with his hands against the cave wall. He placed the flashlight up in the opening. The rocks gave him an extra foot so he wouldn't have to pull himself up so far. He reached into the opening, gripped a groove and pulled, heaving himself up until both elbows were on the edge. He waited a moment, taking deep breaths, his feet dangling, and then shifted his weight and inched his arms forward until he dragged his whole body up into the upper tunnel.

"I did it," he said breathing hard and resting a moment. The upper tunnel was only three or four feet tall so he would have to crawl. He flashed the light down the narrow tunnel and started to crawl. "Not much longer," he muttered. The tunnel twisted and turned with a slight incline.

Several minutes later, the muffled sounds of rain pouring grew louder. He turned another corner and dull, gray light illuminated the tunnel ahead. Andrew smiled as he crawled out of the tunnel mouth to find himself under the branches of a Western Hemlock tree with rain pouring overhead. He sat under the tree relieved and happy, next to the secret Sasquatch trail leading into the forest. "I have to find my daughter," he said as he rubbed his back, breathing in the fresh air of the forest.

Chapter 17

▼

"We have to get out of here," Sherrie yelled, rushing over to the wall of trees stuffed into the sinkhole-like entrance to the Ape Caves, blocking their way out. Twisted and cracked tree trunks and branches were scattered everywhere covering the ground. Pine needles, fresh mud and foliage were stacked on the base of the trees as if they had been ripped up from the forest floor and thrown into the hole.

Chad followed close behind with a desperate look on his face. "Maybe we can climb out."

"I already tried," Billy said.

Sherrie shook some of the branches and looked up toward the muted, gray light shining through small openings in the barrier. She climbed up a tree trunk, pushing through the heavy branches and made it halfway before she reached a dead end. "It's almost solid," she cried trying to push her way through, but to no avail. She grabbed another branch and nearly fell in the process, her foot slipping on the slick bark. She dangled from the tree branch for a moment, before pulling herself up to a second tree. She spent a minute probing for an opening and with much effort was only able to climb up another foot before the branches became too dense.

Chad struggled up another tree trunk on the opposite side, but only managed to get a few feet off the ground before the solid wall of branches stopped him. Escape was within reach and being able to see the gray light of the cloudy sky made it even worse. The sunlight meant freedom and eventual safety if they could get out of the forest and back to the town of Cougar. Even there, he still wouldn't feel safe, until he returned to Longview and the police were alerted of the danger. He breathed in the fresh pine-scented air coming from the surface. It was so refreshing compared to the dank, stale air of the cave. He circled around a thick branch only to be stopped by several smaller branches that had been jammed together. Unable to climb any higher, he tried another direction, but debris blocked his way.

"I told you I already tried," Billy said, looking up in their direction.

Chad climbed down and asked, "What now? Those Bigfoot will come after us once they finish with the German guy. They won't stop with him believe me. They are probably on their way now."

Sherrie jumped from a branch and landed on the cave floor. She stood and looked up with frustration at all of the trees blocking the exit. "We don't have time to try to get out this way. We would need several chain saws."

"There's another exit," Billy said. "And what do you mean Bigfoot?"

Sherrie glared at him for a moment and then turned her attention to Chad. "It will take about two hours to reach the upper exit. I've been through the cave several times. It's a little more difficult than the lower cave, but with what we've been through today, it will be a piece of cake."

"I don't see any other alternative," Chad said, wiping off his rifle with his shirt. "Let's do it."

They left the barrier of trees, the fresh air and the glimpses of daylight behind and descended the metal staircase into the lower chamber, where the other three were waiting with worried looks on their faces.

"Listen up everyone," Sherrie said in a loud voice. "My name is Sherrie and this is Chad. We don't have much time. You may find this hard to believe but there are Sasquatch in this cave. They slaughtered a man down in the lower cave, blocked the entrance and right now are coming this way. If they find us, they'll kill us."

A heavy set, rough-looking lady in her mid forties, wearing a flannel and jeans, said with an angry, distrusting scowl, "You sure in hell can't be serious."

"Is this a joke?" asked the angry woman's friend who was shorter, mid thirties and wore the same type of flannel shirt.

"It's not a joke," Chad said. "The Bigfoot are coming and we've got to get out of here. We're hiking to the upper entrance. I suggest you come with us."

"Steve and I will go with you," Billy said and flashed his light on his friend, another teenager with a baseball cap on backwards.

"Yep," Steve said in a deep voice and spit on the floor, his lower lip full of chew.

"What about you two?" Sherrie asked the two women dressed in flannels. "What are your names?"

"I'm Danita," said the older lady who still had a mean-looking scowl on her face Her defiant eyes looked suspiciously at them behind her glasses.

"Noel," the younger flannel lady said curtly.

"I don't believe your damn story about a Sasquatch, but we were planning to hike through the upper cave anyway," Danita said with contempt as her scowl lines creased deeper on her face.

"Is this some kind of reality TV prank?" Noel asked.

"No," Sherrie snapped, walking over to the cave wall and shining a light on a sign that was attached with an arrow pointing to their left:

← =========
Upper Cave
Difficult walking
1 1/2 miles to upper entrance
Return trail on surface

"Let's go," Chad said as he glanced at everyone's shadowy faces. They had already spent far too much time in one place, which could be deadly when dealing with the Sasquatch. The only way to beat them Chad realized was to keep moving.

A loud, screeching roar filled the cave behind them. Everyone turned as dark shapes appeared out of the shadows and several hairy, clawed hands grabbed Steve, who had been standing in the back, and pulled the teenager into the darkness. Steve cried out and then went silent. It happened so fast that everyone stood in one place, aghast, mouths agape with shock. Danita and Noel looked at each other in terror and fled the other way towards the upper cave. Billy started to run in the direction of the Sasquatch to help his friend, when he stopped in his tracks. His flashlight revealed a grotesque, hairy creature hunched over Steve, biting into his friend's chest. The Sasquatch turned and glared with its black, rage-filled eyes and chomped its jagged teeth before making a loud, monstrous roar.

Billy gasped and darted back after Danita and Noel. Sherrie and Chad hesitated for only a moment and chased after the others. All the exhaustion they had felt, fell to the wayside and with renewed vigor they ran. They turned the corner and all went silent as if the walls themselves absorbed all sound, except for their ragged breathing. They hurried over the cave floor, which was relatively smooth with random ridges and occasional potholes. Danita and Noel were ahead of them, their flashlights bobbing up and down in the black of the cave and then they vanished as they turned another corner. Billy sprinted ahead and turned the same corner, catching up to Danita and Noel seconds later. Chad ran with terrifying images in his mind of hairy hands grabbing him from behind. He gripped the rifle and kept glancing back as he ran faster and then he tripped in a groove in the floor. He stumbled forward and caught himself from falling, but he had slowed considerably. He stood up and glanced back afraid of what he might see.

"Come on," Sherrie yelled ahead of him, her voice sounding distant in the black of the cave.

Chad squeezed his rifle and flashlight and sprinted to catch up, his breathing hard and fast. Sherrie turned the corner and all ahead of him became pitch black. At that moment, Chad was completely isolated and started to panic. He glanced behind him several times, but saw nothing in the dark except for the cave walls that towered up ten feet on each side. Chad rushed around the corner and to his relief he found the others huddled together talking worriedly amongst themselves. They all flashed their lights on him at once.

"We have to get out of here," Noel screamed.

"We will," Danita yelled back.

"Let's keep going," Billy said, his voice cracking with fear and his desperate eyes brimming with panic. "They might be following us."

"Let's go," Noel screamed.

"Are you okay," Sherrie asked Chad once he reached them.

Chad nodded. "We can't stop. Come on."

All of them moved up the tunnel, which narrowed to about ten feet across. The clunk and scrapes of their hiking boots and heavy breathing was all that could be heard as they rushed through the deep, black of the cave. Minutes later, the passage opened up into a massive chamber ninety feet across and thirty to forty feet tall. A giant pile of boulders made up of broken pieces of basalt filled the center of the room.

"This is called the Big Room," Sherrie said as they entered. "We'll have to climb over the rock pile to get to the other side."

Without hesitation, Billy rushed forward, hopping up the first rock and then to the second in one fluid movement, climbing quickly up the rock pile. Danita and Noel lumbered over to the right side of the rock pile and started up, while Chad and Sherrie climbed up the left side. Almost immediately, Chad stepped on a rock and slipped, falling down to his knees, dropping the rifle as he braced himself by grabbing onto another rock.

"Watch it," Sherrie warned and shined her flashlight down to help him see.

Chad reached for his rifle and pulled it out from between two sharp rocks. He stood up and started climbing with more caution. Danita and Noel were having a difficult time traversing the boulders. Not as limber as the others, they moved slowly, finding the rocks sharp and slippery. Noel stepped on the pointed ridge of a boulder, her foot slipped and she fell hitting her right leg hard as the flashlight she held shattered against the rock.

"My light," she yelled in panic. "My flashlight."

Danita, stopped, turned around and shined her flashlight down. "Are you okay?"

"No," Noel screamed in the dark picking up the smashed flashlight and then clicking the on and off switch several times to no avail. "It doesn't work," she yelled. The bulb had been shattered. Noel threw the flashlight and doubled over, grabbing her leg and moaning. "I think I twisted my ankle."

Danita moved down the rocks back to Noel. "We'll use my flashlight. I should've brought an extra one."

"I'm scared," Noel cried as Danita helped her to her feet. "We have to get out of here. I want to go home. I should've never come here. I don't want to die."

"Well get out of here," Danita assured. "Here, I'll shine the light for you. I will climb up a rock and then help you up. Come on."

"No way," Noel cried. "I don't want to go last. I want the flashlight."

"To hell with that," Danita yelled back in a husky, mean voice. "You broke yours. Now calm down. I'll shine the light ahead so you can go first, now let's go. Hurry up!"

A loud shrieking roar filled the Big Room.

"Oh shit," Chad said as he turned around shining his flashlight back towards the sound.

"They're here," Sherrie screamed as her light revealed a Sasquatch staring up at her and then putting its clawed hands over its eyes. Other dark shapes emerged from the shadows, grunting and growling. "Hurry," Sherrie yelled to the others. Danita and Noel were about half way to the top of the rock pile. Chad and Sherrie were at the top and Billy was already climbing down the other side. Noel screamed and scrambled clumsily up a boulder, banging her knee and scraping her shin. Danita moved right behind her trying to shine the light for both of them.

"Sherrie," Chad yelled. "Give me some light." He set his flashlight down and stood up. He aimed his rifle as he tried to balance on the uneven tops of two jagged boulders. Sherrie shined her light down at the bottom of the rock pile where the Sasquatch were approaching. Chad fired, the gunshot booming in the room. The Sasquatch screeched, loud and shrill, and then scattered into the black shadows. Chad fired again blindly hoping to clip one.

"There's one," Sherrie yelled and shined her light on a short, squat Sasquatch, which was racing across the cavern floor towards the rock pile. Chad fired, but missed. The beast ran, low to the ground, jumping over a boulder and out of sight. The other Sasquatch spread out and began to advance upon the rock pile from various directions. "Run," Sherrie said. "They're going to get us."

Chad stepped to another boulder, picked up his flashlight and started to descend the other side of the rock pile. Danita and Noel had climbed to the top as the first Sasquatch reached the base of the rock pile. Noel screamed and slipped down a boulder.

"Faster," Danita yelled at her. "Hurry."

Everyone stumbled down the rock pile with new bruises and scrapes. Billy had already reached the bottom and fled the Big Room, vanishing from sight. Chad and Sherrie reached the bottom moments later.

"Hurry," Sherrie screamed to Danita and Noel who were making their way down. The first Sasquatch reached the top of the rock pile and roared, making high-pitched shrieks. Chad fired his rifle hoping the sound would scare them off and give them time to escape. Danita and Noel reached the bottom and all of them rushed out of the Big Room through a much narrower tunnel, as the monstrous, frenzied roars grew louder as more Sasquatch started down the rock pile after them.

Chapter 18

Chad, Sherrie, Danita and Noel rushed through the tunnel as the roars faded and became silent. The cold, quiet darkness of the cave enveloped everything giving them no hint of what was behind or ahead of them. Billy was nowhere in sight having sprinted ahead of everyone. Noel sobbed as she ran next to Danita, whose scowl grew nastier and angrier. Chad and Sherrie stayed close together, both of them exhausted physically and mentally. Sherrie was not only scared and worried for herself, but also for her father, wondering where he was, hoping that he had escaped the caves alive. The mutilated corpses of Javier and Enrique kept coming back into her mind making her feel sick. Not until she reached safety would she let the tears flow. She hoped her father had found another exit out of the caves. She couldn't and wouldn't let herself think that something bad had happened to him. Her father was intelligent and if anybody could find a way out of these damn caves it would be him. The sickness in her stomach grew worse as she thought about her father. She had to get out to safety and find him. Sherrie ran faster, pushing her body to the limit.

Chad moved through the tunnel in an almost zombie-like state, thinking of little except forcing his tired body to keep moving. He ached all over and his hands were numb as they gripped the rifle and flashlight. He was thankful that Sherrie was with him and her presence was giving him the courage to continue. Thoughts of his father and the others who had died in Canada entered his mind. He clenched his teeth and ran with more determination. "I'm going to make it out of here Dad," he promised.

The ceiling of the tunnel lowered to the point that they had to hunch over as they ran to avoid hitting their heads. They were forced to slow down considerably, which worried Chad as he continually looked back behind them at the solid blackness of the cave, thinking that the Sasquatch would emerge at any moment. The ceiling continued to get lower until they had to get on their hands and knees to crawl.

"Is this a dead end?" Noel asked in between loud sobs. "Did we go the wrong way?"

"No," Sherrie said. "This is the right way. It opens up again in a little bit."

"I don't trust her," Noel said loudly to Danita. "Those monsters were after them, not us. They brought them here."

"Shut up," Sherrie yelled and started to crawl down the tunnel taking the lead, followed closely by Chad. The cave floor was hard and sharp, punishing their knees and hands. Chad found it difficult to crawl while holding a rifle and a flashlight. Danita came next, lumbering and panting and Noel crawled behind her in darkness without a flashlight.

Danita turned to Noel, "Don't worry about them. We'll sue their asses off as soon as we get out of this God-forsaken cave."

Noel frowned, wiping the sweat out of her eyes. "Those freaks are gonna pay."

Danita cursed loudly and grimaced when she bumped her knee. She shook her head and glared at Sherrie and Chad who were ahead of her. She looked back at Noel who had a frightened expression on her pale face. "Hurry," she said. "Everything will be all right."

Noel started to crawl faster after the others. The black ceiling of the cave, which was only a few inches above them, looked almost alien, covered with tiny stagalites and spotted with white cave fungus. Their flashlights made shadowy patterns continually moving and changing.

"I don't see Billy," Sherrie said as she shined her light ahead revealing the low ceiling of the cave close to the rocky floor. It looked like a mouth that was about to chomp down upon them. Beyond the reach of her flashlight was complete and utter darkness.

"What?" Chad yelled from behind. Sherrie's voice had sounded faint and muffled even though she was just a few feet ahead of him.

Sherrie turned her head. "I don't see Billy."

"He'll turn up. Keep going," Chad said, clenching his teeth as a sharp rock gashed his knee. The cave spread out to their left and right, while it curved one direction and then another. The only constant was that the cave continued to get dangerously lower. Chad pointed his flashlight in front of him, but saw no opening up ahead. "Are you sure this is the right way?" He asked loudly as the feeling that the cave was about to crush him grew stronger.

"Yes," Sherrie yelled back. "Trust me."

The ceiling dropped a few more inches until it was impossible to crawl anymore, instead they had to lie completely flat on their stomachs and pull themselves over the cave floor. Chad took several deep breaths, shining his light ahead in hopes of seeing an opening to escape the suffocating darkness. "Don't panic," he thought, trying to calm his mind, as he pulled himself over the cold, damp, hard cave floor. He glanced behind him and saw the one distant light from Danita and Noel. Sherrie appeared to be doing the best out of all of them, moving at a steady pace. Chad focused on Sherrie, following behind her, trying to keep his fearful thoughts at bay. He had to trust that she knew the way out. "The ceiling is getting even lower," he thought on the verge of panic as stalactites scraped his back. "What if I get stuck?" His breathing was ragged and shallow. Shining his light, ahead hoping to see an opening, he saw no escape as the ceiling seemed to close in upon him. He pulled himself another foot ahead, his shoulder blades hitting the ceiling. Behind him, Noel screamed. Chad looked back, but all he could see was the shadowy silhouettes of Danita and Noel on their stomachs near the one flashlight.

Danita who was a few feet ahead of Noel, turned and asked, "What's wrong?"

"The monsters are here," Noel screamed, crawling quickly towards Danita.

Dark, hairy shapes moved silently over the cave floor towards them. Once they were spotted, shrieks and howls broke the quiet as the Sasquatch rushed forward on their stomachs, navigating through the confined space with ease. Noel screamed as a Sasquatch reached her in seconds and seized her ankle with its powerful hand. She kicked desperately as she was yanked back and dragged screaming into the darkness.

"Noel," Danita cried as she struggled to turn her body around in the confined space to help her friend. By the time she had turned around, Noel had already vanished into the wall of black. "Noel," Danita shouted as she flashed her light back and forth, unable to spot her friend. Suddenly, her eyes grew wide as a Sasquatch emerged out of the shadows to her right, glaring at her with feral, black eyes. It pulled itself forward on its stomach with its muscular, hairy arms, its claws making a clicking sound against the rocky floor. The creature moved quickly and would be upon her in seconds.

Danita reacted instantly, flinging her flashlight with all her might at the approaching creature. The flashlight slammed into the Sasquatch's face, causing it to screech in surprise, stop and cover its eyes from the light. Danita turned around, her body scraping against the cave floor as she pulled herself towards the light in the distance, which she guessed was Chad's flashlight. Despite Danita's large size, she moved quickly bumping her back against the ceiling as she heaved her body across the floor. By that time, Chad had turned and was lying on his stomach, aiming his rifle in Danita's direction. Sherrie laid next to him shining her flashlight toward her.

"Hurry Danita," Sherrie yelled. "Over here."

The Sasquatch that had nearly caught Danita, knocked the flashlight away with one of its large fists, sending it clattering across the floor before shattering, plunging that area of the cave into complete darkness. The Sasquatch shrieked an apish, high-pitched yell and charged forward after Danita, pulling itself effortlessly with its muscular arms.

"Shoot it," Sherrie said. "It's going to get her."

Chad aimed and fired, the gunshot making a thunderous boom echoing throughout the confined space. An instant later, the Sasquatch screamed in an almost human-like voice, but much more savage and filled with agony. It stopped for just a moment as it shook its whole body, and continued moving forward after Danita.

"I think you clipped its leg," Sherrie cried. "It's still coming."

Chad steadied the rifle finding it hard to aim in the dark. The Bigfoot was a black shape blending into the darkness. Sherrie's light was only able to light part of its body. Chad pulled the trigger followed by a click. He pulled the trigger again to yet another click. "I'm out of bullets," he cried, frantically placing the rifle down. He rolled over onto his back so he could get the ammo out of his front pockets. Danita continued slowly towards them, huffing and crying out. The Sasquatch growled louder in anticipation of a kill as it neared Danita.

Danita screamed as the grunting and growling grew closer behind her. She tried to go faster rubbing her stomach raw on the rock floor and bumping her head on the low ceiling. She came within five feet of Chad and Sherrie when she was suddenly jerked to a stop. Danita screamed, her eyes growing wide in terror, as the Sasquatch grabbed her ankle and began dragging her back. Even though Danita was heavy-set and strong, she could do nothing against the overwhelming strength of the Sasquatch. She kicked and struggled as her fingers tried to find something to grasp as they were scraped against the cave floor.

Chad fished out a handful of shells from his pocket, rolled over onto his stomach and reloaded as quick as his trembling hands could move. Danita kicked the Sasquatch in the face hard enough that the Sasquatch loosened its grip on her, giving her a chance to break free of the hairy hand. Chad aimed at the Sasquatch and fired. The bullet punctured the creature's left shoulder and it wailed loudly. Chad shot again as the Sasquatch shuffled back into the darkness behind Danita, out of the line of fire.

Sherrie grabbed Danita's bloody hand. "Come on."

Danita looked at her with bulging, terror-filled eyes, her face was pale and dripping with sweat and tears, and said nothing. All three of them turned at once and frantically began pulling themselves on their stomachs through the cave as the roars of the Sasquatch filled the darkness behind them.

"More are coming. How much farther?" Chad asked, unable to see any opening.

"Not long," Sherrie yelled as she moved over the rough surface. Occasionally a low point in the ceiling would poke their backs. Chad was too scared to feel claustrophobic. The high-pitched howls grew louder and closer reminding him of three years before in Canada. The Bigfoot howls had come from every direction in the forest moments before they had killed his friend Shane and slaughtered thirty people at Camp Elizabeth.

"A light," Sherrie cried, pointing ahead of them. She began pulling herself toward the light followed closely by Danita. Chad, reluctantly, was last as he kept glancing back ready to turn and fire if the Sasquatch suddenly gained on them.

"Sherrie," Billy called in front of them. "Hurry."

Sherrie reached the light a few moments later and to her relief crawled out from under the low ceiling into a tunnel that opened up to ten feet in height. Billy grabbed her hand and helped her to her feet, his eyes wide with fear.

"I thought they got you. I didn't know if I should wait or keep going," Billy said in a panic looking as if he was about to bolt down the tunnel.

Danita was the next to emerge and it took both Billy and Sherrie to help her stand up. Chad appeared seconds later and stood up, quickly stepping away from the entrance to the low tunnel as images of hairy hands grabbing his ankles and pulling him back in flooded his mind.

"Where's Noel?" Billy asked.

"They killed her," Danita said in an angry voice. "Those fucking monsters killed her."

"I'm so sorry," Sherrie said and tried to give her a hug, but Danita pushed her away.

Billy stepped away from them and glanced up the tunnel. "Are they coming?"

"Yes … of course they're coming … they're always coming … they won't stop," Chad said angrily. "I hope to God we don't have to crawl again. They nearly got us in there."

"We don't," Sherrie said. "That was the lowest the cave gets."

"Good, now lets go." Chad motioned for everyone to start moving.

Sherrie walked over to Billy and put her hand on his shoulder. "Are you okay?"

Billy shook his head, his skin pale in the dim light. "They killed Steve. He was my best friend."

Sherrie tried to smile and squeezed his shoulder, at a loss for words, as they started up the tunnel. Billy scrambled ahead of everybody and led the way. The tunnel was narrow and the deep grooves in the ground were difficult to navigate over without tripping. Sherrie went next, followed by Danita and then Chad taking up the rear of the group. Almost immediately, Danita tripped and fell forward, knocking Sherrie over as well. Chad rushed up to them and helped them to their feet.

"I need a flashlight," Danita said as she wrinkled her face in anger. "I can't see a damn thing."

"We don't have an extra one," Sherrie said.

"Give me yours then," Danita snapped, trying to grab it.

Sherrie stepped back. "No way."

"You and Chad can share," Danita yelled and tried grabbing it again.

"Chad needs his for the rifle. If he can't see what he's shooting at we'll be defenseless." Sherrie took another step away from Danita.

"He didn't do fucking shit when they killed Noel," Danita shouted, glowering at both of them.

Billy walked over. "I have an extra one. It's not very big, but it's all I have." Billy pulled out a flashlight not much larger then a pen and handed it to Danita, who flipped it on and flashed it around. The flashlight seemed to appease her and she started walking again without another word.

Chad glanced back and shined his flashlight on the black walls of the caves. "They'll be coming after us," he thought. "They won't relent until we're all dead." Filled with apprehension and impending doom, he rushed after the others.

Chapter 19

▼

Cool forest air filled Andrew's lungs as he massaged his tight back, thankful that he had escaped the Sasquatch lair. He sat down under the branches of a pine tree, next to the rock pile where the cave mouth stood open, a black gaping hole with dangers and secrets hidden in its depth. The rain poured overhead pattering loudly against the rocks next to him. The thick branches protected him from the brunt of the rain, but occasionally a big drop of water would fall from a branch and splash on him. He rather enjoyed the rain at the moment. It made him feel alive and anything was better than the dank, musty air of the cave enveloped in perpetual darkness and hunted by Sasquatch that would feed on him as soon as they captured him.

Andrew sighed and stopped massaging his sore back. He crawled out from under the trees and found the backpack that Javier had left behind. Quickly unzipping the pack, he pulled out a hunting knife with a six-inch blade, which he placed in the leather sheath attached to his belt and continued rummaging through the bag. He grabbed a flare gun with three flares and loaded one of the cartridges into the gun and put the other two in his pocket. A relieved smile momentarily touched his face as he felt somewhat safer armed, although he wished he had his hunting rifle and a handgun.

"This will have to do," he said quietly taking out his battered cell phone, which was scraped all over and had a large crack in the casing. The damaged, he concluded, had occurred when he had been crawling over the basalt fleeing the Mother or when the Grandfather had knocked him to the ground. He pressed the power button and in a few seconds the cell phone surprisingly lit up, except for the display screen, which flickered. He immediately dialed Sherrie's number. "Pick up honey," he said quietly, but after a few rings it went to voice mail. "Sherrie, it's your father. Enrique and Javier are dead. The Sasquatch killed them in the cave. There is a tunnel in the rock pile that leads to an unexplored cave system. It's their home. I've found the Sasquatch lair. Do not go down there. It is too dangerous. We will have to return with many armed men. Please call me immediately when you get this. I am returning to the van."

Andrew dialed Chad's phone but it also went to voice mail. "Chad. I've found the Sasquatch lair. They killed Enrique and Javier. Call me as soon as you get this." Andrew then called Donald but it too went to voice mail. "Donald, where are you? Why aren't you answering? Enrique and Javier are dead. I found the Sasquatch lair. We need help. Call me ASAP."

Andrew ended the call and said, "Why doesn't anyone answer their damn phone?" He stood up as the rain beat down hard against his hat and jacket. He put the phone into his coat pocket and started hiking back through the woods. Escaping the cave had given him a second wind and he moved quickly through the trees over the rocky terrain, excited at his discovery despite the loss of two of his comrades, not to mention his bad knee, weak ankle and sore body. He would mourn his friends later and promised that they would be known as heroes to the world. "I won't forget either of you," he said quietly as he hiked up a slope. His limp began to grow as his bad knee ached and with each step he grimaced in pain, but he kept going. "I wish I had my cane." The cane had been given to him as gift from one of his fans. Andrew had been a guest speaker at a Sasquatch conference in Seattle twelve years ago and after his speech a man from Tacoma, who had carved the fine detail in the cane, had presented it to him during the autograph signing. The man, named Willy, owned a gift shop in Tacoma, Washington. He was an avid believer in the Sasquatch and had followed Andrew's career for years. Andrew had used the cane ever since. It was detailed with a Sasquatch head and along the side were images of the Sasquatch walking through the woods.

"When I have time, I'll have to make a visit to his shop and have him make me a new one," Andrew thought. The future was rushing fast upon him. His dreams of finding the Sasquatch had now been realized and his life would never be the same again. He now had to organize a team, capture a live specimen, find the dead ones and thoroughly explore the cave system. Studying them would consume the rest of his life. He would also have to find time for the endless interviews from the media, presentations, and documentaries and of course he would write a detailed book. "Books, actually," he whispered. "I'll write a series of books."

Andrew reached the top of a ridge and walked into a line of trees. "How will I find the time? Life is too damn short. If only I had found the Sasquatch earlier. I could've already spent decades researching them, learning to communicate with them instead of being ridiculed for most of my life. The majority of people believed that I have wasted my time on some stupid fairy tale, but now my life has finally been validated. The attack in Canada proved that there were Sasquatch, but I shall actually bring in a specimen." A smug smile appeared on his lips for a moment and then his back tightened up in hard knots, his wrinkled face, creasing deeply in pain.

Andrew moved through the thick undergrowth despite his aches and emerged into a clearing. Ahead of him stood the Dead Woods, a wall of gray skeleton-like trees, cracked and broken, without needles. The bare branches shook in the wind as heavy rain fell in torrents. Many of the trees were black from a fire that must have burned through the area during a dry summer. There was long grass and foilage growing on the rocky ground. Andrew had learned that the Dead Woods had been created by a combination of a heavy ash fall from one of the mountain's eruptions, fire and disease. The trees became dry tinder in the hot summers, so fires started easily causing even more devastation as the years pass. Andrew walked through the clearing avoiding the rock outcroppings, which he had no desire to climb over and then entered the Dead Woods, examining the gray trunks as he walked by them. The bare branches gave little protection from the rain overhead and the ground was muddy and black so he had to walk slowly to make sure his bad knee didn't give out.

A branch snapped to his left. Andrew stopped and looked in the direction, where several dead tree trunks, long grass, and a boulder stood in a cluster in the heavy rain. He wiped the water from his eyes and raised the flare gun. The rain chattered fiercely in every direction making it hard to hear anything else. He lowered the gun, looking behind him and gasped startled at what he saw. He raised the flare gun and pointed it at a dark shape. For several seconds he stared, his hand trembling, and then he sighed with relief realizing the man-like figure was the remains of a tree, its branches twisted out like grotesque arms. Andrew gritted his teeth and continued forward, stepping through the thick grass into a mud puddle. His boot sank up to his ankle and he nearly lurched forward, but he caught his balance. He pulled his foot out making a slurping, popping sound and trudged through ten feet of thick mud before he reached a firm layer of rocky ground. He moved around the tree trunks and rocks glancing anxiously at the dark shapes in the rain.

Andrew reached a fast rushing creek, swelled with rainwater from the last couple weeks. He followed it a ways until he found a stump in the center of the creek, which he used to step over the water. He reached the other side and walked up a muddy slope stopping as he scanned the perimeter of dead trees surrounding him. He pulled out his phone and called Sherrie, but it went to voicemail again. This time he didn't leave a message.

Suddenly, ahead of him, at least thirty yards away, something moved behind a tree. It happened so fast; he only caught a quick glimpse of movement. Andrew stared for several minutes at a thicket of dead trees. "Maybe I'm growing paranoid," Andrew whispered looking behind him. Dead trees were on all sides of him, gray and black in the rain. He clenched his teeth and with grim determination started walking again, veering to the right, avoiding the trees where he had seen movement. He passed by the thicket of trees and saw nothing on the other side. "I must have been imagining things."

As he neared the end of the Dead Woods, his foot slipped and he fell to the ground into a mud puddle. "Dang blasted," he yelled, struggling to his feet. He wiped the flare gun as best he could with his drier shirt underneath his coat. The rain continued to pour overhead in a constant rumble. He found a moss covered log, which he sat on to catch his breath. His entire body was sore, aching and exhausted. "I thought I was in pretty good shape," he said as he glanced around at the dead trees. He tried calling Donald and Chad but no one answered again. "Where the hell is everyone?" he thought, growing more anxious as feelings of foreboding settled upon him. Donald had always answered his phone, especially since that was his job to keep in communication with all the team members, not to mention he was usually in the van with all of the equipment.

After a few more minutes, he stood up and started walking slower than before, his tight back and bad knee giving him too much trouble. A branch snapped behind him. Andrew turned and raised the flare gun in his trembling, wrinkled hand. Dead trees stood in front of him, branches creaking in the wind.

"I know you're out there," Andrew yelled in a deep, powerful voice. "Show yourself." He swung around, his eyes searching the trees, rocks and tall grass. Leaves crunched in the opposite direction. Andrew twirled around and pointed the flare gun. "I do not fear you," Andrew called out and slowly turned the other way not sure if he was surrounded. There were so many places that a Sasquatch could hide he thought. "I will not harm you," Andrew shouted and then waited several moments as the rain rumbled all around, the gray clouds growing darker.

With the flare gun gripped tightly in his right hand, he continued walking again hoping to reach the van and the others. He would return with reinforcements and put the odds in his favor. He walked around a tree and ahead were two stumps, gnarled together. As if from a nightmare, a loud, high-pitched, shrill cry brimming with madness and rage filled the Dead Woods as a Sasquatch seven feet in height stepped out from behind a tree only twenty-five feet away. Its black eyes zeroed in on Andrew as its mouth opened revealing jagged, yellow fangs. It raised its thick, muscular arms, claws outstretched and with a deep, monstrous roar, the Sasquatch stepped towards Andrew.

Chapter 20

Chad, Sherrie, Danita and Billy had already climbed over two more rock piles since leaving the Big Room when the tunnel opened up wider with fallen pieces of basalt piled in the center. Billy was the first to climb over, followed by Sherrie and then Danita, who progressed slowly, dragging her hurt ankle. Chad followed Danita as he kept checking behind him preparing for the inevitable. He climbed over the boulders with aching feet and hands numb from the cold of the cave. Physically exhausted and emotionally drained, pure terror and the desire to survive kept him going. He knew the Bigfoot too well. These nightmarish monsters would viciously hunt them down one by one appearing out of nowhere, ambushing them and then vanishing to attack again.

Sherrie climbed over the rock pile with a fierce determination as she worried about her Father. She had to escape the cave and find him. She couldn't bear to think that he was lost somewhere down in the caves alone. "I will find you Daddy," she whispered to herself. "You're going to be all right." They had spent the last several years working together, which Sherrie had enjoyed immensely. She was thankful for making up for lost time, since she had rarely seen her father after the divorce. Her mother had kept him away as best as she could, always talking bad about him. Sherrie always hated when her mother did that, and had tried defending him on countless occasions. Sherrie had rebelled, moved out of the house a few weeks after graduating from high school and had married her high school sweetheart, which turned out to be a mistake. They had been too young and immature and after four years they called it quits. She hung out in Portland for a couple years working as bartender and then she went back to school and graduated from Portland State with a degree in history. Her Father had shown up for graduation and had taken her out to a nice dinner in downtown Portland. At the dinner Sherrie asked her father if he needed any help. After the initial surprise, her father had said yes, with a smile and joy in his eyes, which she had rarely seen. Originally, Sherrie was only going to work for her Father for a few months until she found a real job, but she had enjoyed it so much that it turned into years. And now their dream of finding a Sasquatch had turned into a nightmare with two of her coworkers dead, her father missing, and she was running for her life from those dreaded monsters.

The next section of the cave was composed of reddish rock, which Chad glanced at briefly and kept walking as the cave floor narrowed. The walls leaned inwards with grooves along them with gray and black rock and white spots of fungus covering large sections. The floor had an incline so that they were always walking up a slight slope.

"This fucking sucks," Danita said loudly and bent over, rubbing her ankle where the Sasquatch had grabbed her. It was bruised, tender and already starting to swell. The pant leg was ripped and shredded.

"You okay?" Sherrie asked.

"Fuck no," Danita yelled with an angry scowl. "My best friend is dead."

"I'm sorry," Sherrie said.

"Fuck off," Danita snapped and slowly stood up. "Let's just get out of this damn cave." Danita pushed passed Sherrie and walked after Billy who had just turned a bend in the cave and vanished from sight. Sherrie rolled her eyes and shook her head as Chad shrugged his shoulders.

"Ungrateful bitch," Sherrie mumbled.

Chad patted Sherrie on the shoulder. "Don't let it get to you. We have bigger problems to worry about."

"I'm not," Sherrie said and walked ahead of Chad. They moved around a bend in the cave and a slight breeze started blowing cold air.

"Are we almost to the end?" Chad asked, his face filling with excitement.

"Not even close," Sherrie said. "There's wind in the cave. I don't know the scientific explanation, but I've been down here many times and it can get pretty gusty. Something about how the hot air rises and the cooler air sinks creating the wind."

"Strange," Chad said. They were underground in the dark and there was wind.

The tunnel grew narrower until the cave floor was about ten feet across. The breeze died down suddenly once they turned a corner. The ground became uneven and treacherous with lots of loose rocks, potholes and deep grooves. They had to navigate through the tunnel slowly. Danita was having a hard time and would periodically let off some steam and curse using every four-letter word in her vocabulary. Drops of water splashed ahead of them as the ground became wet. A shallow pool of water, only a few inches deep, filled one section of the cave. Chad stepped on the rocks avoiding the deeper spots and moved passed the pool to the drier area.

Chad thought about his father. They hadn't spent much time together in the last few years of his father's life. Chad had moved to Los Angeles to pursue his dream of becoming a screenwriter. He regretted not making more of an effort to spend time with him. Chad had been too busy partying in Los Angeles, while getting more frustrated with his writing. "I'm just glad that we got to spend the last couple days of his life together," Chad thought as the image of the Sasquatch jumping up from the ferns, seizing his father, snapping his neck and then flinging his body in an instant of blurred motion, flashed through his mind. "It happened so fast," Chad thought. "If only I had seen it in time and shot the fucker." He looked at the cave floor ahead pushing the worries and regrets away for now, knowing that they would return. He would go insane if he dwelled on it. The last three years had been full of mental anguish. "And now this," Chad thought and shook his head in disbelief. "How could this happen to me twice?"

They reached another rock pile, smaller then the others. Billy had already climbed over it by the time the others had arrived. "Hurry," he yelled, his voice faint in the darkness.

"How much longer is this stupid, damn cave?" Danita cursed angrily.

"We still have a good ways to go," Sherrie said.

"That's not what I wanted to hear," Danita snapped. "I hope those monsters have stopped following us." She stepped up on a boulder, bracing herself with her good ankle.

"I hope so too," Sherrie said as she climbed up a rock.

Danita straddled her legs over a boulder and groaned as she slid her leg off, stepping on a rock that shifted sending her slipping. She fell forward trying to catch her balance, but she slipped and tumbled to the rock floor. She grabbed her ankle and cried out. "It hurts."

Chad and Sherrie rushed over to help.

"Damn it to hell," Danita cursed loudly. "I need help up." Chad grabbed Danita's hands and pulled her to her feet. She glared at him and started walking, limping badly. They moved through the cave at an even slower pace.

Chad sighed angrily and kept glancing back down the dark tunnel. "We're going too slow."

Danita stumbled and nearly tripped again. She leaned one hand against the wall trying to brace herself as she walked.

"Billy," Chad yelled at the teenager who was in the lead.

Billy rushed back looking questioningly at Chad.

"Can you help Danita?" Chad asked.

"Sure," Billy said glancing worriedly behind them. Danita put her arm around Billy's shoulder for support and was able to walk faster. They continued forward in the cave, which never seemed to end. All of them moved quietly, too tired and scared to talk. Sherrie glanced back; her eyes caught movement, a shadow stepping into the darkness behind a bend in the cave. She gasped and raised her flashlight, revealing nothing but a rock wall. "I saw something," she yelled.

Chad turned around and aimed his rifle and flashlight. "Where?"

"It was standing over there, then moved around the corner." Sherrie stepped back.

"Are you sure?" Chad asked and yelled, "Danita and Billy keep going." Without a word, they moved faster down the cave. Chad fought back the desire to flee. He took several deep breaths as he shined his flashlight. He rifle was raised and pointed with his finger on the trigger. He listened but the cave was silent, dark and cold. "Ok Sherrie," Chad said quietly. "Let's go. Keep the light shining behind us."

"I'll try," Sherrie said as they started walking sideways so that they could look in both directions. The cave narrowed until it was about ten feet across. They moved as quickly as possible until they caught up to Danita and Billy. All of them hurried through the cave worried and scared, each to their own thoughts. Danita frowned, while Billy's fearful eyes scanned the tunnel ahead. Sherrie was somber and determined. Chad was tense and kept looking back, his hands gripping the rifle. The tunnel opened up and in front of them was another rock pile that they would have to climb over.

"Not another one," Danita said wearily. Luckily the rock pile wasn't too big and with the help of Billy, they made it over rather quickly. Chad and Sherrie followed. The walk felt like hours as they moved through the tunnel, always moving up hill through narrow passageways, climbing over boulders in the cold black. The tunnel narrowed again and then came to a stop with an eight-foot wall blocking their way. At the top of the wall was a black opening big enough for a crawl space.

"How are we going get over this?" Danita asked.

"It's the lava fall," Sherrie said. "We have to climb it to get out of here."

"I'll go first," Billy said and let go of Danita. He started to climb, finding small grooves in the wall for his fingers and feet. He put his flashlight in his pocket. The others shined their flashlights to help him see. Billy climbed the rest of the way up struggling near the top until he pulled himself over. At the top of the lava fall, the crawl space was only four feet tall, enough room for him to sit. "Who's next?" Billy asked as he pulled the flashlight out of his pocket and shined it down on the others.

"Me," Danita said with a deep scowl and pushed to the front. "I'm going to need help."

"Okay, let's do this quick," Chad said and placed his rifle down. "Come on Sherrie."

Danita limped over to the wall and reached up finding a groove to put her thick fingers in to pull herself up. Chad and Sherrie bent down and lifted her legs. Danita rocked back and fourth trying to find another handhold. Billy reached down and grabbed her hand.

"Hurry," Chad said, groaning as he glanced back at the black shadows behind them.

Danita grabbed Billy's hand and nearly pulled him off the ledge. He braced himself and started pulling. For the next several seconds Danita struggled madly, cursing loudly until she managed to crawl over the top.

"Thank God," Sherrie said.

Chad grabbed his rifle and said to Sherrie. "You go next."

Sherrie climbed the lava fall quickly and effortlessly. Chad shined his flashlight behind him revealing the damp gray and black walls of the cave. He started to panic as he realized he was now at the bottom of the lava fall by himself. If the Sasquatch attacked now, he wouldn't have a chance.

"Come on Chad," Sherrie called down. "Give me your gun."

Chad held up the rifle and handed it to Sherrie and started to climb. His hands were numb and sore, finding it hard to get a good grip. He finally managed to climb halfway up when Sherrie helped him over the ledge. They were all at the top of the lava fall, sitting together in the low hanging crawlspace.

"Thanks," Chad whispered.

"No, thank you." Sherrie gave him a quick kiss on the lips.

"For what?" Chad asked, smiling.

"Staying level headed through all of this," she said and grabbed his cold hand and massaged it. "There were a couple times I nearly lost it, so thanks."

"Well I've been through this before," Chad said, squeezing Sherrie's hand back. "Panic equals death so we have to keep our wits."

"I'm taking you out for dinner after we get out of here," Sherrie said. "Somewhere nice in Portland. I know a lot of great places. Sound good?"

"I'd love that," Chad said, "As long as it is warm."

"Hey lovebirds," Danita said. "I need to rest here for a moment. I don't know how much longer I'll be able to walk on this ankle."

"Okay," Chad said. "Just for a couple minutes. Were somewhat protected up here. Sherrie can you post lookout. If something comes I want to be ready with the rifle."

Shining her light back down the way they came, she looked worriedly at Chad. "I need to find my father."

Chad nodded. "We will find him. I promise you. He might already be on the surface calling for help and looking for us."

"I hope so," Sherrie said, forcing back the tears.

"Anyone got any food," Danita asked.

"I have some jerky and a bottle of water," Billy said and pulled out a plastic bag from his coat. They all feasted on the jerky as Chad held the rifle with numb, scraped hands scanning the darkness behind them, while Sherrie shined her flashlight down the tunnel.

Chapter 21

"I think my ankle is broken," Danita cried out. "Owwwwwwwww ... shit."

"You're going to have to tough it out and walk on it," Chad said as he glanced briefly over at her. He was perched at the top of the lava fall next to Sherrie keeping post. They had rested for ten long minutes and he was anxious to get started before the Sasquatch caught them. They hadn't seen one in a while and there was part of him, hoping that they had given up the hunt and had returned to their lair. He knew it was foolhardy to think that way, but he prayed that it was true. They were all tired and battered and he didn't know how much more they could take. Billy seemed to have the most energy and was tapping his foot anxious to get going. He didn't know what to do about Danita, who was slowing them down. He couldn't just leave her although the thought had crossed his mind. She had been a bitch towards them, but Chad guessed he couldn't fault her considering the circumstances. Her best friend had been killed and Danita had been nearly dragged to her death by a Bigfoot.

"I don't know if I can walk anymore," Danita whined, wincing in pain as she touched her ankle.

"We can't carry you," Sherrie said.

"So, you'll just leave me behind like you did to Noel," Danita snapped as her angry scowl returned, her face creased with deep lines.

"We did no such thing," Sherrie shot back.

Danita's eyes beaded up with disdain and she took a deep breath before she yelled, "You brought the monsters to us and they killed Billy's friend Steve and then they killed my best friend in the whole world. My little darling Noel didn't do anything to deserve to die. You could've helped me try to save her, but you left us behind."

"It was too late. We would've all been killed if we had stayed," Chad yelled.

"You don't know that," Danita yelled back. "I shouldn't have gone on this damn trip. Noel didn't want to go. She said it was too cold and rainy. We should've just walked our dog in Capital Park like we usually do. We've lived together for eight years now. She was the world to me and now she's gone. Fuck this place," Danita screamed. "Fuck those things ... those Bigfoot."

"Sasquatch," Sherrie corrected her out of habit.

"Whatever the fuck they are," Danita yelled. "Noel, my baby, is gone and I don't give a shit about anything."

"Do you think the Sasquatch are still following us?" Billy asked nervously, uncomfortable with everyone screaming at each other.

"Yes," Chad said. "We've got to keep moving. They won't stop hunting us until we're out of this cave and miles away from this area. Even then I won't feel safe until I'm back in Longview."

"Give me a couple more minutes," Danita said as she touched her ankle and moaned. Her knee was scrapped and caked with blood. Her hands were rubbed raw and her face had scrapes and bruises all over it. Her chin was bleeding where she had hit the rock floor as the Sasquatch yanked her back.

"A couple more minutes and then we leave even if you have to hop the rest of the way," Chad replied.

"Shut up," Danita said and screwed her face with contempt and disgust. "Why didn't you try shooting those things when they grabbed Noel?"

"I did," Chad said thru his clenched teeth.

"Where did these things come from?" Billy asked.

Sherrie, who had been shining her flashlight down the lava fall turned around to answer. "We discovered a hidden cave system that they use as their lair. They've probably been living in those tunnels for centuries. It's connected to the Ape Caves by a small passage up on a ledge, hidden by a rock. Two of the people I work with were killed and my Father is missing. He went down into the caves before me and Chad and we haven't seen him since." Sherrie glared at Danita. "So you're not the only one who has lost someone today. We all have."

"Whatever," Danita quipped and then turned to Billy and asked, "Any more jerky left?"

"It's all gone," Billy replied. "I have more in my car ... if we get there."

"You know that it was Noel's 32nd birthday last week," Danita said with a sigh and wiped her eyes. "I took her on the ferry to Bainbridge Island for lunch. We spent the whole day walking around the gift shops. It was so much fun. We decided to come here on a whim. We were going to stay with some of our friends in Portland for a couple nights. Oh God ... they don't even know what happened to her yet ... no one does." Danita wiped the tears from her face. "Her birthday was so much fun. I bought her a pretty leather bracelet which she wore today ... oh, it's on her now ... wherever they took her. Oh my ... she's out there now in the dark and cold surrounded by those monsters."

"Danita," Chad cut in. "Do you think you can walk?"

"I don't know. How much farther is it?"

"We still have a ways to go," Sherrie said, "but I would say were over half way, close to three quarters of the way. Once we get out of the cave we still have a two mile hike down the hill to the parking lot."

"Fuck," Danita said. "I'm fucked."

"We'll make it," Chad said. "All of us."

"I think we should go now," Billy said. "I don't want those things to get us."

"Okay," Chad "Let's get ..."

A loud roar exploded right next to them as dark, hairy arms grabbed Chad's leg. Chad cried out in surprise and turned to see a beastly face glaring at him from only a couple feet away. The Bigfoot had jumped up the lava fall when they had been distracted by Danita's conversation. The Bigfoot began to slide down the lava fall, pulling Chad with it. Struggling,

Chad fell over the side as Sherrie cried out trying to grab him, but he slipped out of her grasping hands. Danita yelled and Billy gasped, backing quickly away from the ledge. Luckily for Chad, he fell on top of the Sasquatch, breaking much of his fall, before he tumbled to the rocky floor. The Sasquatch jumped up and stood above him as it screeched. It was an adolescent, a little over five feet tall, thick and muscular and weighed close to three hundred pounds. Chad was on his back, his flashlight and rifle on the ground next to him. The Sasquatch raised it fists ready to strike.

"Chad," Sherrie screamed and flung her flashlight down at the Sasquatch with all of her might, sending it crashing onto its head. The Sasquatch glanced up and roared at Sherrie. Chad reached for his rifle, but the Sasquatch reacted instantly and grabbed his shoulder. Sherrie yelled at the top of her lungs, pulled out her knife and jumped off the ledge landing on top of the Sasquatch, knocking it to the ground. She slipped off the Sasquatch, stood up, raised the knife over her head with both hands, her eyes wide with fear and rage, and then she stabbed the beast deep in the back. The Sasquatch wailed in agony, jumped up and knocked Sherrie back with a swing of its arm. Sherrie stabbed the Sasquatch again, slicing it across the forearm. The Sasquatch struck back with its other arm, knocking Sherrie off her feet.

Chad picked up his rifle, stood up and fired at close range. The bullet slammed into the Sasquatch's lower back. "Get away from her," Chad commanded in a voice full of seething anger and authority. He fired a second time striking the beast in the gut as it turned towards him. The Sasquatch stumbled back and collapsed on the floor.

Sherrie struggled to her feet battered and bruised with the bloody knife still gripped in her trembling hand. She picked up Chad's flashlight and shined it down the tunnel. Two other growling Sasquatch appeared, making deep guttural noises. Sherrie immediate flung her knife, missing the closest Sasquatch by inches as the blade clattered against the wall. The Sasquatch seemed to hesitate as if not sure what course of action to take. They were adolescents like the one that had attacked them.

"Back off," Chad shouted and fired his rifle, the gunfire exploding in the cave. The bullet struck the wall next to the Sasquatch. The creatures backed off as Chad fired a second time and then they leaped out of sight around the corner of the cave as he fired a third and fourth time. The rifle clicked as he pulled the trigger again. "I'm out of bullets," Chad said and dropped the gun. "We've got to get out of here."

"I lost my knife." Sherrie scrambled up the lava fall and as she reached for the top, she slipped, but Chad caught her and pushed her the rest of the way up. "Hurry," Chad said. "I scared them off, but that won't last long."

Sherrie reached for the top of the ledge and found a groove to pull her body up. Adrenaline pumping, Chad climbed the wall after her, despite the protests from his bruised body and numb fingers. He reached for the top and Sherrie pulled him the rest of the way.

"They are young and inexperienced, scared of the gunfire. We lucked out. If they had all attacked at once or if adults had been with them we wouldn't have survived," Chad said as they crawled down the four foot tall tunnel that opened up enough so they could stand up. They found Billy helping Danita down the tunnel, moving slowly, both of them struggling.

"Are you guys okay?" Billy asked.

"Yes," Sherrie said as they caught up to them. "Chad killed one, but there are at least two more."

"And I ran out of bullets," Chad said. "We have to move fast. We're unarmed except for my knife." His hand touched the handle of Vengeance for reassurance, making sure it was still in its sheath.

"Shit," Danita said and started moving faster despite her hurt ankle. The four of them rushed up the tunnel constantly, glancing back, hoping they weren't being pursued and wondering when the cave would end.

Chapter 22

▼

"Stay back," Andrew commanded loudly. "I do not want to hurt you. Go back to your cave." The Sasquatch stood twenty-five feet away, a giant dark silhouette in the rain. It's black eyes filling with aggression as it uncurled its long, hairy fingers revealing sharp, jagged claws. It started growling, deep and low at first, growing louder as the seconds went by.

"Back off," Andrew said in a powerful voice, masking his fear. "Go home." His right hand gripped the flare gun, his finger resting on the trigger. His bad knee began to ache with pressure as he stood in one place on the uneven ground. The muscles in his lower back also began to stiffen, but Andrew remained still putting on the appearance of strength. He could show no sign of weakness in the presence of such a creature. He slowly raised the flare gun and aimed it at the beast. The Sasquatch reacted to Andrew's movement and made fierce warning roar.

"Leave me be," Andrew yelled waving the gun. "Back off."

The black eyes of the Sasquatch grew wide as it hunched down and suddenly charged, barreling forward, taking long, quick strides. Andrew gasped, aimed the flare gun and fired, sending the projectile slicing through the rain, exploding against the Sasquatch's upper chest, consuming it in flames. The Sasquatch stumbled back and screamed in agony as the flames spread over its body. Andrew watched as the Sasquatch flailed its arms trying to put out the flames. It cries of agony were horrific and human sounding. It bolted away in into the dead trees; its screams piercing thru the rumble of the pounding rain.

"Sorry old boy," Andrew said. "I didn't want to do that." He loaded the flare gun with another cartridge and started walking again. He emerged from the Dead Woods into a grassy field with boulders jutting up from the wet, muddy ground. He moved over the slippery earth as best he could, eager to get back to the van, worried that he hadn't heard back from Sherrie, Donald or Chad. Was that the only Sasquatch lurking above ground or were there others he wondered? His rational mind tried to reason why the Sasquatch had become so aggressive. In Chad's case in Canada, a hunter had shot and killed one of their young, but they had done no such thing this time.

"They're starving," Andrew muttered as he wiped the rain off his face. The deer virus had savaged the animal population all around Mount Saint Helens. "Starvation makes any animal more aggressive. It changes their behavior," he thought as he walked around a crumbled rock. "We also intruded into their home, their secret lair that had been undiscovered until now. I can't blame them," Andrew thought. "They're just trying to protect their home."

Andrew limped through a line of trees and found the muddy Ape Cave trail that led back to the parking lot. "Fear also," he thought. "The old one, the grandfather, had fear in its eyes. Fear can also be the root of aggression. Destroy what you fear and all will be better." The trail curved down a steep slope. Andrew moved slowly stepping in the mud, bracing himself on the slippery rocks. He reached the bottom without falling and stepped through an ankle-deep mud puddle. The trail turned left and went down another hill.

"I will capture them," he said quietly. "I will feed them, study them and communicate with them. I'll have some sort of preserve where they can walk outdoors in a woods surrounded by a great fence, monitored at all times." When he reached the bottom of the slope the trail weaved around the trees on flat ground for a distance. He pulled out his phone to check for messages but no one had called. He thought of calling Stephen Denmin to tell him of his discovery, but first he had to find his daughter. He dialed her, but it went to voicemail. "Where are you Sherrie?" he whispered and limped faster over the muddy trail as the rain beat against his wet clothes.

"I fear something bad has happened," he said as the trail opened up into a grassy clearing. Deep mud puddles filled the path through the clearing. He stepped through the water anxious to get back to the van, where it was dry and warm. He loved the outdoors, but his body had taken a beating and was chilled to his very core. Once through the clearing the trail moved up a slight hill and dropped down into the woods.

"I wonder if the Grandfather survived the attack," he thought. He had left the old Sasquatch in the cave bleeding from a knife wound. Would it die? Was it strong enough to heal its famished body? He hoped so. He doubted the Sasquatch he had burned with a flare would survive.

Never in his wildest dreams or thoughts did he ever think he could harm a Sasquatch. He had quite possibly killed two Sasquatch in one day. Always a major advocate in protecting these rare endangered animals; Andrew had always endorsed any law that protected the Sasquatch from hunters. His team never carried weapons. Their mission had always been to capture one to prove that they existed and to study them. He never thought that they were deadly, only misunderstood, even after all that had happened to Chad in Canada.

And now all of his beliefs and ideas had been shattered. "Jose and Enrique were killed because of our intrusion into their home," Andrew said as unbidden feelings of guilt settled in the back of his mind. "I most likely killed their leader, the Grandfather. I wonder how old the Grandfather was? How long do they live? Was it decades old or centuries? What a shame." Andrew moved underneath a thick cluster of trees protecting him from the heavy rain. "What a damn shame," he said out loud. "And what about the one I shot with the flare gun? It was younger and stronger than the Grandfather, but could it survive such burns? Did I blind it? They must be hardy beasts, but I still don't think it could have survived the flames." Andrew stopped suddenly and looked up.

A tree had been knocked over, splintered near the base and dragged off. Branches and needles littered the trail. "What is going on?" he whispered as he moved farther down the trail and found another freshly created stump with sharp splinters of light colored wood sticking out of it. He walked over to the stump and touched the top feeling the softer wet wood inside the bark. "It can't be them," he said, glancing fearfully around. Another tree had been ripped out of the ground further down the trail. Branches, leaves, needles and undergrowth had been trampled everywhere.

"Good Lord," he whispered when he saw the all too familiar giant footprints in the mud. He kneeled down and touched one of the prints, guessing it was about 16 inches long. "The Sasquatch," he said and stood up, his gray eyes filling with dread. He limped along the path stepping on the broken branches and finding more footprints. He reached an area where six trees and been knocked down and snapped up from the ground leaving nothing but splintered trunks.

"The Ape Caves," he said and followed a bend in the trail to find the entrance to the Ape Caves jammed with tree trunks. The Sasquatch had stuffed the trees into the sinkhole creating a barrier he realized in shock and horror. With wide, nervous eyes, he walked over and touched one of the trunks that was sticking out amazed that anything could lift such a great weight. "What power," he whispered with awe and wonder. "What kind of rage is driving them?"

He glanced warily around and tried calling his daughter, Chad and finally Donald, but no one answered. He continued down the trail with his flare gun gripped in his white, knuckled hand. Panic touched his eyes as tried to put together the day's events that led to this unleashing.

Andrew reached the parking lot and stopped in his tracks. "Lord have mercy," he muttered finding the destruction ahead almost unbelievable. Every car in the lot including his own green van had been overturned with the windows smashed and the sides dented in as if sledgehammers had demolished them. He stared for several seconds trying to comprehend what had happened, almost not believing what his eyes told him to be true. His eyes were drawn to the center of the parking lot where a body lay in a pool of red. Andrew limped over as he glanced back and forth in terror. Would they attack again? Were they waiting for him? Would they try to get revenge?

As Andrew approached the corpse, his mouth dropped open in shock and recognition. The body had been mauled, most of the flesh had been chewed off of it, bones had been broken, but despite all of this, Andrew knew for certain it was Donald. He kneeled down as disgust and anger filled his face. He recognized his friend's clothing, shoes and the silver ring that was on what was left of his finger.

"They killed you," Andrew cried, aghast. "I'm sorry Donald. I never thought something like this would ever happen. I'm so sorry my friend." Tears streamed down Andrew's wrinkled, pale face, mixing with the rain. "I won't forget you Donald ... The world will remember you." He groaned and stood up, wobbling on his feet feeling faint. "Where's my daughter?" he asked with sudden urgency as the rain pelted loudly against the asphalt that covered the parking lot. "Sherrie," he yelled, gazing in desperation at the line of dark trees that surrounded the parking lot. "Sherrie where are you?"

He limped over to the overturned van dreading what he might find. The back door had been ripped off and lay several feet from the vehicle. He peered into the back and sighed with relief finding it empty. "Thank the Lord," he said and pulled out his phone. "You're fast my little Sherrie. No one could ever catch you when you were growing up. I could never catch you, your sister could never catch you and neither could the neighborhood kids. Those beasts wouldn't have gotten you either. No one can catch you." He dialed Sherrie's number and it went to voicemail. "Call me Sherrie ... it's your father, please call." Andrew hung up and as the tears rolled down his face, he started back towards the Ape Cave trail determined to find his daughter.

Chapter 23

"My ankle," Danita cried out as she slipped on a loose rock and would have fallen if not for Billy who managed to hold onto her. She steadied herself and stopped for a moment and frowned, glancing about the narrow cave. "I have to slow down."

"Keep going," Chad snapped from behind her. He was next to Sherrie who held the flashlight. "If they catch up to us, we won't have a chance."

"I'm trying," Danita yelled back and hopped on her good foot for a few seconds before limping again. She groaned each time she stepped on her wounded foot. "I don't want to die," she muttered. "You guys better not leave me like you did Noel."

"We won't leave you," Sherrie assured, although part of her wanted to leave everyone behind so she could sprint ahead and search for her father. It angered her that he was missing; she needed to know where he was as soon as possible. It was eating her up inside that he could be lost somewhere, alone in one of these hellish caves. Her patience and resolve were nearing its end. Her face grew sullen and more determined. "I'll find you Father," she kept thinking to herself.

Danita leaned heavily on Billy for support and whispered into his ear. "Promise me Billy, you won't leave me. I don't trust the others. These liars brought the monsters to us."

"I'm not leaving anyone," Billy said, his voice devoid of any confidence. He grunted as he tried to support Danita's heavy weight.

"You're a good one," Danita whispered. "We both lost someone today. Steve seemed like a good guy."

"He was," Billy said. "We've been friends since the seventh grade."

"Noel and I have been best friends for years. We were always there for each other through the good times and the bad, through relationships, through every damn thing and now I'm going to be alone. I don't have many friends Billy."

"You'll find some new ones," Billy offered quietly as he nearly stumbled because of Danita's clumsy steps.

"I don't want new friends," Danita said with a scowl, her voice growing louder. "I want my Noel. How could this happen? Bigfoot isn't supposed to be real. It's just a story, a myth, bad late night television."

"They found some in Canada," Billy reminded her.

Danita turned and looked suspiciously at Chad. "Yes, I thought you looked familiar. You're the guy that survived the Bigfoot attack in Canada. Everyone was killed but you somehow survived. How so?"

"Pure luck." Chad shook his head and gave Danita a frustrated glare.

"Bullshit," Danita snapped, her face screwing with contempt and rage. She pointed an accusing finger at him. "You conveniently survived when all the others were murdered and now you brought those damn monsters with you. They're killing us one by one. That's your plan isn't it?"

"What?" Chad asked with an incredulous look.

"Isn't it?" Danita demanded in a loud accusing voice.

"Shut up," Sherrie yelled. "I've had enough of you."

Danita continued her rant, "We're all going to die except for Chad and then he'll walk out of here a hero, making money off our deaths. You're in cahoots with the Bigfoot!"

"You're one crazy lady," Chad yelled. "You need to keep quiet now. Your loud mouth is going to draw all of the Bigfoot to us. Shut up."

Danita wiped her eyes and cried out in agony as she stepped on her bad ankle. The tunnel narrowed to about six feet across. They had to step up onto ledges and move around broken boulders. Danita's pathetic pace slowed their progress considerably.

"I don't want to die," Danita muttered quietly to Billy. "Promise me that you'll protect me."

"You won't die, just keep going and be quiet," Billy said in frustration.

Sherrie, who for the most part had been quiet for this leg of the journey, suddenly looked up and touched Chad on the shoulder. "We haven't found my father yet."

Chad nodded and shook his head. "Maybe he found another way out."

Sherrie squeezed Chad's shoulder as she flashed the light ahead so both of them could see. "I just want this nightmare to end."

Chad stopped. "Sherrie, shine the light behind us." The flashlight revealed nothing, but the cave walls they had just passed, which turned left around a bend. They listened and looked for a moment, and then Chad turned back around. "I thought I heard something." They started walking again. "I don't want to get caught down here. We have to make it to the surface."

"Did they find us?" Danita asked loudly. "Did they find us?"

"No," Chad yelled back. "Keep quiet."

"Don't tell me what to do." Danita tripped, taking Billy with her. Both of them fell to the ground. Billy jumped up immediately.

"Don't leave me Billy," she cried as Billy struggled to help her to her feet. After much effort she was able to stand again. "How much fucking longer?" she screamed.

"Not much longer," Sherrie said. "Keep going Danita and shut up."

They turned a corner and a sudden gust of wind hit them, blowing and whistling through the cave. It was much stronger than the breeze they had felt earlier. Everyone looked at each other questioningly.

"Are we at the end?" Danita asked.

"No, but we're getting close," Sherrie said. They hiked through the cave as the wind moaned and then it stopped almost immediately as they turned another corner. The air became still as if the wind had just been in their imagination. The walls narrowed to about five feet across, twisting and turning.

"Sunlight," Billy yelled excitedly back to the others and ran ahead, leaving Danita to fend for herself. Sherrie and Chad followed Billy around the bend in the cave and up ahead beautiful, gray sunlight poured down from above illuminating a section of the cave. They moved along the passageway and caught up to Billy who was looking up into the light.

Above them was an opening in the ceiling, a big hole in the ground that led up to the surface. They could see the dark green branches of pine trees swaying in the wind overhead. Rain fell, sprinkling their faces. Chad had never felt or seen anything so good. He took deep breaths of the fresh, forest air. Along the cave wall where the sunlight hit, moss and other small plants grew. There were long sticks against the wall, broken branches that had fallen into the hole. The surface was about twenty-five feet above them. They would have to scale a steep wall to escape the cave.

"Is this the way out?" Danita asked angrily as she caught up to the rest of them. "I can't climb this. Where the hell are you taking us?"

"This isn't the exit." Sherrie said. "This is the skylight. People have gotten hurt trying to climb out this way. There's warnings saying not to attempt it."

"Then where is the fucking exit," Danita snapped and glowered at her with eyes bursting with disdain.

"Not much longer," Sherrie said and frowned back at her. "Maybe another twenty minutes."

"I'm going to try to climb out," Billy said in a burst of excitement and moved over to the wall. "I can climb it."

"Don't go," Danita begged. "Stay with me. Don't leave me with those two."

"I'll call for help when I get to the top. I have my cell phone." Billy smiled and pulled out his phone to show everyone, before he stuffed it back into his jacket.

"Ok," Sherrie nodded. "Good idea."

"We should stay together," Chad said and glanced back at the way they came.

"Yes," Danita agreed and grabbed Billy's sholder. "Stay together. Junto in Spanish means together. I've been practicing my Spanish because Noel and I were thinking about going to Cancun. Junto, Junto, Junto."

"We need help," Sherrie said. "We need the police. We don't have any weapons. The sooner we get help, the better."

"Okay." Chad nodded and looked at Billy. "We don't have time to argue. Be careful Billy."

"I will," Billy said, his eyes gleaming. "Wish me luck."

The first half of the wall was the steepest, while the upper half was more concave with ledges. About six feet up the wall was a groove a few inches deep. "Help me up," Billy said as he grabbed the groove and pulled himself up. The others steadied Billy as he strained to find finger holes to grip. He clambered up until he was able to stand up on the groove. His toes were jammed into the groove as he held on to a rock knob on the wall. He nearly slipped, but he finally braced himself enough to stand up on the narrow ledge, which was six feet off the ground.

"Piece of cake," Billy said looked up. The next groove in the rock was about a foot out of reach. He would have to jump up to grab it. If he missed or slipped, he would fall all the way down to the rock floor. "Catch me if I fall," Billy said nervously. He looked up and took several deep breaths. He jumped up with a loud grunt and grabbed the ledge. His fingers slipped, but held as his feet dangled trying to find a hold. He looked up and found the next ledge only a foot higher. He heaved himself up and grabbed the next rock with his left hand, pulling himself up. His foot found a bulge protruding a few inches from the wall big enough to brace himself. He glanced down at the others. The cave floor was twelve feet below him.

"Almost there," Sherrie cheered. "Go for it."

"Call the police," Danita yelled.

"I'll get help. Don't worry," Billy called back, looked up and started climbing the rest of the way, which was much easier with wider ledges. Billy moved with swift, agile movements and everyone had relieved smiles on their faces.

"If the police arrive with guns, we might actually have a chance," Chad thought and felt renewed hope.

As Billy neared the top, just a couple feet from the surface, he suddenly stopped and gasped. Towering above him was a giant Sasquatch, staring down at him with black, rage-filled eyes. The Father, over eight feet tall, opened its mouth filled with jagged teeth and roared ferociously. It dropped quickly to its knees and reached for Billy with its black, clawed hand.

Chapter 24

▼

Billy let go of the ledge he was hanging from and dropped down, but the massive, hairy hand grabbed his right arm, stopping his fall. The hand squeezed and Billy cried out in fear and pain. He kicked off the side of the wall, dangling in mid-air, helpless like a child's doll. The others below him yelled, but the only sound Billy heard was the deep, monstrous growl of the Father as it started pulling him up.

"No," Billy cried shaking and kicking his feet, trying to break free, but the monster's grip was like steel. Billy was suddenly yanked up several feet out of the hole, and placed face to face with the Father. Billy's wide, terror-filled eyes gazed in horror at the Father's beastly appearance. The Father's heavy breath, hot and stinky, blew over Billy as it examined its prey. Its dark eyes squinted as it stared at Billy's pale, petrified face, finding only weakness in the pathetic, small thing. The Father growled, displeased and furious, opening its mouth filled with sharp teeth, before biting Billy's neck, ripping his head off. The Father flung the body into the trees and looked down into the hole.

Chad gasped and Sherrie bolted into the shadows of the tunnel, leaving the light of the skylight behind. Chad followed trying not to trip since he didn't have a flashlight. Danita limped after them surprisingly fast, keeping pace.

The Father turned around as three other Sasquatch emerged from the trees dragging Billy's body. The Father made quick grunting noises and pointed into the forest. The others grunted back in reply and disappeared into the undergrowth, carrying Billy's body. The father peered down into the skylight with fierce, dark eyes. With a snarl of rage it jumped into the hole, landing hard and stumbling down to its knees. It stood up as madness and blood lust burned in its black eyes. The father bellowed with a growing fury as if the pit of hell had opened. It sniffed a moment, its nostrils flaring, and then charged up the tunnel after its prey.

In the cold tunnel the roar sounded faint to Danita, Chad and Sherrie.

"I heard it," Danita cried, her face cringing in pain as she stepped on her bad foot. She barreled up the tunnel despite the pain. "It's coming."

"Hurry," Sherrie yelled and briefly glanced back at Danita who was lagging behind. "The exit is not much farther."

"Don't you leave me," Danita cried, panic brimming her voice.

Chad ran alongside Sherrie, up the constant incline of the cave, dodging over potholes, deep grooves and boulders, as they stepped up onto rock ledges. A loud high-pitched shrill, pierced the quiet of the cave.

Danita screamed. "It's here," she yelled, limping as fast as she possibly could go with her damaged ankle. Sudden growling erupted as a massive dark shape emerged from the shadows and rushed up behind her. The Father tackled Danita sending her slamming to the ground, flat on her stomach, pinned by the creature's massive weight. She struggled to turn and fight back, but the force of the creature was overpowering. The Father roared and snapped Danita's neck with its thick, long fingers. It shook Danita hard to make sure she was dead and then it stood up, its eyes wild with anger and the excitement of the hunt. The Father spotted the rest of its prey and charged after them.

"It got Danita," Sherrie screamed. They both sprinted around a bend in the tunnel and to their relief a faint light appeared to the left.

"The exit," Sherrie cried and ran for the light. A ladder bolted into the side of a curved wall led up to an opening that was just big enough for one person to pass through at a time. Sherrie dropped her flashlight and started up the ladder. Chad was right at her heels as she strained up the rungs, her adrenaline pumping. Chad glanced back and saw the Father, the biggest

Sasquatch he had ever seen, like a giant black shadow, growing closer as it charged towards them.

"Hurry," Chad cried as Sherrie reached the top and moved through the opening to the surface. The Father reached the base of the ladder and jumped up, its clawed hands striking the ladder next to Chad's foot. Chad jumped up dodging the hand, scrambling up the remainder of the ladder. Sherrie grabbed his hand and pulled him through the opening. They found themselves at the bottom of a rock pit, rain still pouring from the dark, gray, windy sky.

"Come on," Sherrie yelled stepping through a deep mud puddle and up the gravel pathway just as a giant, hairy arm lurched out of the hole and missed Chad's legs by inches. They climbed out of the rock pit as the Sasquatch roared, pushing its way slowly through the narrow opening. They ran down the muddy Ape Cave trail, which led through the forest, both of them gasping, winded, exhausted, cold and numb. Chad followed behind Sherrie, his legs sluggish as he ran. Only fear drove his tired body. Behind them, a shrill, blistering shrieking pierced the air. Chad ran even faster down the steep trail. His foot suddenly slid out from underneath him in the slick mud and he fell to the ground tumbling down the path several feet. Covered in mud, Chad popped up and ran after Sherrie who hadn't even noticed that he had fallen. He glanced briefly behind him up the trail but there was no sign of the Sasquatch. The rain lashed down upon them with a growing intensity; the dark, gray sky grew black as dusk started to settle over the forest.

The trail was about to drop down a steep hill when Sherrie suddenly stopped in her tracks and raised her hand in warning. She twirled and put her fingers to her lips for silence. Chad ran over to her, breathing hard, unable to catch his breath. Sherrie pointed down the hill where a second Sasquatch stood by the trail looking in the opposite direction before it walked into the undergrowth. Sherrie motioned for Chad to follow her as she rushed off the trail into the trees. Chad followed pushing through thick foliage and ducking under the boughs of pine trees. They climbed over the branches of a tall bush and moved down the slope. They jogged as quickly as possible snapping branches and crunching foliage, the rain thundering everywhere concealing the noise.

They continued through the woods always moving downhill. Chad followed silently focusing on Sherrie's back. She knew the area well and he trusted her. Chad had no idea where she was going, but at the moment he didn't care as long as it was away from the Ape Caves and Bigfoot. They crossed over a fast rushing creek that came up to their knees and then down another slope where the ground started to level off. A layer of centuries old, rocky basalt covered the forest floor ahead of them. The rock was slick from the rain and the bright green moss that covered it. Sherrie slowed down after she slipped on a rock and scrapped her knee. They moved over the mossy rock around the trees as Chad kept glancing back. Luckily, there was no sign of pursuit.

Suddenly, Sherrie's cell phone rang, loud and clear. Sherrie stopped, startled for a moment, and then pulled it out of her pocket. "Daddy," she cried. "I didn't know what happened ... yes ... yes ... Chad's with me. Listen ... the Sasquatch are everywhere. They tried to kill us. Meet us at the Trail of Two forests and call the police. I love you," Sherrie put the phone in her pocket, her face overflowing with relief and excitement. "He's alive," she said and wiped a tear from her eye. "He already called the police and is going to meet us. Hurry," Sherrie said and renewed vigor as she moved faster through the undergrowth.

Behind them, they heard the loud cracking and snapping of branches, followed by a powerful roar, which made them both, stiffen in fear.

"Run," Sherrie cried as the Father burst thought the undergrowth, a giant, dark shape in the rain and failing light day. The father growled fiercely, its black eyes growing wide with malevolence and a focused intensity as it spotted its prey. It charged, taking long strides, its weight pounding hard against the ground.

Sherrie and Chad fled over the slick rocks at a frantic pace. Sherrie jumped over a circular hole in the ground that was about two feet deep. Chad raced around the hole and tried to keep up with Sherrie, who rushed through bracken of ferns and dodged another hole in the ground. "Forest of holes," she muttered remembering that was the name her father had given the area when she was a child. Before the divorce, he had taken the whole family sight seeing, one summer weekend and Sherrie always remembered the name. She had run around pointing out as many of the holes as possible. Her older sister had stayed with her mother near the car, but her father had kept up with Sherrie and they had explored the area on a sunny which had seemed to last forever. It was a memory she had always cherished with her father and now that she had grown up they had been doing the same thing, exploring forests around the country in search of the Sasquatch, which they had unfortunately found. With determination, she ran faster towards the Trail of Two Forests, which was in the center of the forest of holes.

Chad barely kept up with Sherrie and nearly slipped into one of the holes in the ground. Chad remembered Sherrie telling him about the Trail of Two forests. Lava had flowed through the area two thousand years ago, burning the trees, but leaving casts of some of the trees in the ground. Many of the tree casts were only a couple feet deep filled in with dirt and debris, while others were ten to twenty feet deep. Some of the trees had fallen over creating tunnels as the lava covered them. So molds of the ancient forest were preserved in the rocky basalt, while the new forest grew on top of it, hence the name of the Trail of Two Forests.

They climbed up a rock outcropping, leaping over to the muddy ground on the other side. They jumped over two more holes in rapid succession. The mossy layer of rock was difficult to navigate as they ran for their lives. They emerged from under the branches of a pine tree and in front of them was a wooden plank walkway for sightseers to use to observe the tree casts in the rocky ground. The walkway was built a couple feet above the ground so not to damage the delicate moss-covered forest floor. Sherrie rushed over to the walkway, jumping onto it as the Father exploded out of a thicket of bushes nearby, closing the distance between them. Chad climbed up after Sherrie and ran down the walkway. The Father reached wooden structure moments later and smashed through the railing. It followed them, its heavy steps making the whole wooden structure shake and creak.

"Here," Sherrie cried and jumped down off the walkway to a tree mold that went down into the ground about six feet. There was a ladder attached to the rocky side, but Sherrie didn't bother to use it and jumped into the hole. She crawled into what was once the inside of a tree that had been lying on the ground when the lava had enveloped it and then she vanished from sight. She had entered "The Crawl," the highlight of the Trail of Two Forests. Several trees had been lying on the ground when the lava flowed over them creating a maze of short tunnels.

Chad jumped into the hole just as the Father reached for him. He leaped down into the tunnel when the Father swiped its claws, missing his foot by an inch. The circular tunnel was about three feet tall. They were inside the remains of an ancient tree. The basalt surface of the tree cast was rough, patterned after the bark that had once covered the tree. Chad crawled down the tunnel for ten feet and caught up to Sherrie who sat holding her knees close to her chest as the Father roared above them.

"What now?" Chad asked, gasping for breath.

"We wait here until the police arrive," she said quietly, grabbing Chad's hand.

Chad unsheathed Vengeance and handed it to Sherrie. "Keep it," he whispered.

Sherrie nodded and took the knife. Chad squeezed her other hand and kissed her lightly on the lips as they sat hunched over in the narrow tree cast listening to the Father's rage and heavy footsteps that shook the ground above them.

Chapter 25

Trapped in "The Crawl," Chad and Sherrie held each other, both of them stiffening each time the ground boomed, sending tremors through the rocky cave. Bits of dirt and chips of the cracked basalt dropped from the ceiling. The rain rumbled and dripped into the entrance where the gray light of dusk grew darker. Chad hugged Sherrie, each of them fighting back panic. They were alone in the dark tunnel weaponless except for Vengeance and all that they could depend on were each other. They were also cold, wet, muddy and exhausted, physically, mentally and emotionally. Sherrie's face grew more distressed with each passing moment as she thought about her Father.

"He's on his way," she thought worriedly and pulled out her cell phone to warn him not to come to their location, but she received no reception underground.

The Father roared furiously and the ground shook with a heavy impact. Sherrie grabbed Chad's right hand and started rubbing it as she kept glancing back and forth down the tunnel, her tired eyes, wide and fearful.

Sherrie leaned over to Chad and whispered, "Are we still on for dinner?"

Chad looked at her for a moment as if not comprehending. "What?"

"Remember, dinner … you and me." Sherrie shook his hand that she was holding as a faint smile touched her lips.

Chad nodded. "Yes."

Suddenly, the Father dropped down the six-foot hole and reached into the narrow tunnel. Chad and Sherrie scrambled back, moving deeper into the tree cast, which continued for another twenty feet before it opened up to the surface. The Father clawed at them unable to fit into the small crawl space. About halfway down the tunnel, Sherrie stopped and crawled left into a connecting tunnel, the entrance concealed by the darkness. They sat at the junction of the two tunnels as the Father pushed in, unable to reach them. It was too big to crawl into the ancient remains of the tree.

"Where the hell are the police?" Chad said. "They should be here by now."

"It shouldn't be much longer," Sherrie whispered as she glanced up the connecting tunnel to the surface.

Frustrated and lashing out in fury, the Father roared at them, snapping its teeth. It backed out of the tunnel and jumped out of the hole. The ground thumped above them and then the Father's hand reached into the opposite side of the tunnel through the smaller opening. Both Sherrie and Chad tensed, even though the hand was at least ten feet away.

"It can't get us here," Sherrie whispered.

"I hope you're right," Chad said still amazed at the size of the Sasquatch. He had seen many in his days, but none compared to this behemoth. The only other one that was anywhere close in size was the Sasquatch that had killed Jay in Canada. It had ambushed them right before they reached the cabin they had been looking for hoping to get help. The Sasquatch had been tall, covered in scars, with a lot of gray hair. It was mean and fierce looking and had chased Chad through the forest after it killed Jay. Chad had tried escaping by climbing up a tree, but the Sasquatch followed and would have killed him if it hadn't been for Meredith shooting the beast several times. "Thank you Meredith," Chad whispered at the thought. The Sasquatch that was attacking them now was even bigger than the one Meredith had killed in Canada.

"Where does the second tunnel go?" Chad was unable to see down it since Sherrie sat near the entrance.

"It's a twenty foot crawl to the surface."

"At least we have a few exits. It gives us more of a chance," Chad said quietly. They had the main entrance, the smaller opening at the end of the first tree cast and now another exit at the end of the second tunnel.

Suddenly the ground began to shake above them as pieces of dirt and rock fell to the cave floor. Chad scooted closer to Sherrie, both of them looked anxiously at each other. The smaller opening to the first tunnel suddenly went dark as piles of dirt and rock tumbled in.

"It's trapping us in here," Chad said.

"Should we go out the second tunnel?" Sherrie glanced about desperately. The exit to the second tunnel suddenly turned black as a stump was stuffed into it.

"Shit," Sherrie cursed. "The only way out now is the way we came in."

"We'll just wait here for the police," Chad said thankful that light was still coming from the main entrance since they had no flashlights. The tunnel had grown considerably darker now that the other two tunnel mouths had been closed. They heard footsteps and growling again.

"What's it doing?" Sherrie asked as fear lined her voice.

"Stay calm." Chad gripped her hand.

Sherrie took deep, slow breaths as she glanced around the dark tunnel fighting back feelings of claustrophobia. "Just a few more minutes," she said quietly, "Until help arrives." Loud pounding thumped against the ground above as the whole cave began to vibrate, chunks of rock and dirt fell from the ceiling.

"Leave us alone," Sherrie screamed, but the pounding continued, heavier and louder. "It's not giving up until it gets us."

"It can't reach us in here," Chad said as he braced himself against the side of the cave, watching pieces of debris break off the ceiling and fall to the cave floor.

"Should we try to run for it," Sherrie whispered.

"No." Chad shook his head. "That's exactly what it wants us to do. It left one opening for us to try to escape. It's trying to scare us out of the cave and into its clawed hands."

"It's doing a pretty damn good job," Sherrie said.

"Let's just keep our cool and wait. It can't get us." Chad squeezed Sherrie's hand.

Suddenly, the whole ceiling began to shake and rattle as more rock chips broke off, pelting them. Chad held his hand up to protect his face. "Owwww," Chad said as a large chunk of basalt bounced off his back. The shaking continued and then an entire section of the cave collapsed to the right of them in a loud, cracking rumble. Sherrie followed Chad crawling down the tunnel closer to the entrance as the cave collapsed behind them.

"It's forcing us to the entrance," Sherrie yelled.

The entire tunnel rattled with each heavy thump as the frenzied growling continued above them. The ceiling collapsed again, burying Sherrie in dirt and rock. Light shining from above appeared as the rock cracked open. A monstrous roar of triumph erupted when two giant hands grabbed Sherrie by the legs.

"Chad," Sherrie screamed as it was dragging her backwards. The beast tried to pull her body through the newly formed opening. Chad grabbed Sherrie's hand tightly, ignoring the falling debris. More of the ceiling collapsed pelting Chad, covering him with rock and dirt. He lost his grip on Sherrie as she was yanked up and out of the hole screaming at the top of her lungs.

Chad forced himself up coughing and spitting up dirt as he pushed shattered basalt off of him. He scrambled through the rubble and out to the entrance. He climbed up the six-foot ladder to find the Father standing on the walkway nearby strangling Sherrie who gripped Vengeance in her hand. She stabbed the Sasquatch with all of her strength, sticking the blade deep into the monster's upper left arm. The Father cried out and growled angrily as it squeezed Sherrie, her bones cracking and then it flung her against the side of a tree, her body making a loud snapping sound.

"Sherrie," Chad cried as he climbed up onto the platform. He picked up chunk of basalt and threw it at the Father hitting the beast in the chest, doing little damage. The Father glared at Chad with bulging, black eyes as it slowly pulled out Vengeance from its arm and flung it into the undergrowth. Chad grabbed a thick stick on the ground the size of a baseball bat. He knew he wouldn't be able to outrun the monster. He raised the stick and yelled, "Fuck you," as the Father approached, black claws outstretched ready to strike.

Chapter 26

Chad continued cursing and yelling as the Father approached to kill him. There was a clarity that settled upon him as time slowed down, knowing that the end was near. Images of all the other Sasquatch he had seen touched his mind all at once starting with the very first one, an adolescent that Shane had shot, found dead in the middle of tall ferns. After that, there was the one that had tracked them back to their camp, that Chad had seen standing by the fire pit, moments before it attacked. That same monster killed his father the next day. There was the Sasquatch that had stepped from behind a tree next to the river and killed his best friend Shane. Chad had been crossing the river and all he could do was watch helplessly. Right after that, several Sasquatch emerged from the woods next to the riverbank. Chad had escaped by taking the raft down the river. He met up with Jay and Meredith and they headed for a cabin, praying that they weren't being followed. They had almost made it when the gray, scarred beast ambushed Jay. Luckily, Meredith had killed it. The images of dark, hairy shadows of a horde of Sasquatch that attacked the cabin flickered through his mind. Chad had escaped on a boat to the middle of a lake. Some of the Sasquatch had swum out to kill him, but Stephen Denmin had arrived on a plane just in time. It was the last time he thought he would ever see a Sasquatch and now three years later he had seen many more.

Chad yelled angrily and flung the stick he had been carrying through the air, but the Father was quick and knocked it out of the way with one strike of its clawed hand. Chad jumped off the platform and lunged for another stick on the ground, which was water logged and heavy. The Father broke the railing and jumped to the ground after him. Chad madly swung the stick back and forth yelling at the top of his lungs. The Father didn't hesitate and moved closer with no fear in its vicious eyes. Chad charged and snapped the stick over the Father's raised arm. He slipped on a rock and fell to the ground as Father towered over him like some giant behemoth roaring loudly and raising its claws to strike.

Suddenly, the Father's entire back exploded into a ball of flames. It cried out and raised its head in agony as the fire spread and began to devour it. The Father turned and roared.

"Go to hell my friend," Andrew called out as he pointed the flare gun. The Father charged, its fiery back creating moving shadows in the dark forest as dusk was upon them. Andrew calmly lowered the gun, loaded the last cartridge, then aimed and fired when the Father was only ten feet away. The flare exploded into the Father's chest knocking it back as it screamed and fell to the ground. It rolled around trying to put out the flames that continued to spread over its entire body as it moaned and squealed. Andrew dropped the gun and limped over to Chad. "Where's Sherrie?" he asked, his worried gray eyes glancing around the perimeter.

Chad stood up and ran over to Sherrie's broken body as police sirens whistled in the distance.

"Oh Lord, No!" Andrew gasped, dropping down on his knees next to Sherrie's body. Her neck had been broken and arm had been snapped in two pieces, pulled out of its socket. There was no life in her body. "No," Andrew muttered, "Not my daughter."

Chad felt for a pulse but the body was lifeless. "I'm so sorry," Chad said. "It grabbed her and threw her against the tree. I tried to hold on to her, but it was so strong."

The sirens grew louder as the Father rolled on the ground wailing loudly. It moaned for a moment and then went quiet.

Andrew felt for any breath or pulse in his daughter. "No," he yelled again, his voice cracking with agony. "Not my baby. I'm so sorry," he said as he held her lifeless hand. Tears began to roll down his weathered face.

"Andrew," Chad cried out, pointing.

Three Sasquatch had emerged from the undergrowth and rushed over to the Father. They dropped to the ground and began sniffing the burnt corpse of the Father for several seconds. They raised their heads and made groaning, weeping sounds. The biggest of the three, a young adult male, glared at them with black, hard eyes and began growling in a low threatening tone before it stood up. The other two lifted the Father's smoldering corpse and carried it into the trees, vanishing from sight. The eldest stared at Andrew and Chad and swiped its claws through the air in warning, before it turned and followed the others, disappearing into the dark shadows of the undergrowth.

Chad and Andrew sat next to Sherrie's body, both of them in tears, exhausted and cold. They stayed by her body until the police arrived.

EPILOGUE

Chad walked through the lobby of a 5-star hotel in downtown Seattle. It was late in the evening and the lobby was relatively quiet with only a couple people checking in, a family returning from a night out and two girls leaving to go to a club. Chad walked towards the hotel bar. He had spent the last few hours at a Sasquatch conference, which was filled with news media, scientists and the curious. Andrew had been the guest speaker discussing the latest findings and participating in a long Q&A session. Chad had been asked to speak, but he had declined. He didn't like to talk in front of large groups or be in the spotlight, especially when it had to do with Bigfoot. There were too many painful memories associated with those loathsome creatures. They had taken away so many people from Chad's life including his Father, best friend Shane and now Sherrie. Andrew on the other hand, despite his loss, thrived at these events and Chad had been impressed by his lively presentation and insight.

It had been a long three months since the Ape Cave Horror, which many people in the media had dubbed it. Chad had attended too many funerals, Enrique's, Javier's, Billy's, Donald's and finally Sherrie's, which had been the hardest to sit through, especially when Andrew broke into sobs. It also didn't help when in the middle of the funeral Andrew's ex-wife accused him of getting their daughter killed. She had yelled and cussed him out. It had been very uncomfortable for all. Sherrie's sister didn't even come up to her Father; instead she sat next to her mother and ignored him. Getting through the grief and trauma had been hard enough for Chad, while he was constantly under a media barrage wanting interviews and information. Chad lost track of the number of interviews he had given. There were countless phone calls, emails and talent agents wanting to set up book deals, buy the movie rights, exclusive contracts and on and on. If that wasn't enough, there were the common people in day-to-day life that would approach him asking questions about the tragedy. All this he had expected since it had happened the first time he had crossed paths with Bigfoot in Canada.

What surprised Chad this time was the backlash from some quarters. Many animal rights groups were up in arms demanding new legislation to protect the Sasquatch. Both Chad and Andrew had been called murderers by some and many wanted to press charges and throw them in jail. There was such a furor that Chad sometimes thought life was much simpler when he was in the woods fleeing the Sasquatch.

"No wonder they've hidden from mankind all these years," Chad thought as he walked through the lobby.

During the last three months, thrill seekers, hunters, government agencies and other organizations swarmed the Mount St. Helens area, trying to catch a live specimen. The cave system the Sasquatch had lived in was thoroughly explored. They found no living Sasquatch, but they did find a chamber with dozens of Sasquatch skeletons in various states of decomposition. It was hard evidence that these creatures did indeed exist. Scientists were in a frenzy studying the skeletons coming up with various theories.

The biggest catch was the discovery of the dead Sasquatch near the rock pile. It had been the one Andrew had shot with the flare gun in the Dead Woods. Its face and body had been burned, but somehow it had managed to reach the rock pile. It must have wandered blindly about trying to find the tunnel when it had died only a short distance from the entrance. There were already calls to try to clone the creature taking blood and DNA samples. Some were worried that this new species would soon become extinct.

Chad walked into the hotel bar and glanced around the dimly lit room at all of the tables. In the back, Andrew sat in a deep booth sipping a drink. Chad noticed Andrew's new cane with the carved head of a Sasquatch, leaning against the seat.

"Chad," Andrew said and waved him over.

"Great presentation." Chad said as he sat down at the booth.

"Thank you." Andrew smiled briefly, as his blood-shot, tired eyes gazed warmly at him. Andrew looked exhausted and pale, having gotten little rest in the last three months. He had thrown himself into his work trying to do as much as possible, which Chad assumed was his way of keeping his mind off his daughter's death. Andrew had gone back into the caves exploring them with the police. He was also in the center of all of the research that was being done on the Sasquatch skeletons. All of this and of course the speaking engagements, television appearances and interviews. Chad wondered when he was going to slow down and get some rest. He could see a deep sadness in Andrew's eyes and his face was stricken with guilt. Andrew curled his hand around the vodka martini and finished it, signaling the waitress over. "Another martini and one for my friend," Andrew said to the blonde waitress. "And lots of olives."

Chad noticed that Andrew had been drinking heavily since Sherrie's death. Whenever they met, Andrew almost always had a drink close at hand.

"I've been thinking about the Sasquatch," Andrew mused as the emotions faded from his face, replaced with his usual stern expression. "No bodies have been found except for the one I shot with the flare gun in the Dead Woods. I'm not including the dozens of skeletons found in the funeral chamber. The Father, Mother and Grandfather were all killed but where did they take the bodies? Where are they hiding? How many are left? Let me preface, that I'm not sure if the Grandfather died. I did stab it, but it was alive when I left it bleeding on the ground. It may still be alive. They are a sturdy race of creatures. But the question is where did they go?"

Chad shrugged his shoulders. "I have no idea."

"Well I'll tell you," Andrew said with a gleam in his eyes. "They are hiding in some other tunnel yet to be discovered, another lava tube or hole in the ground. They are scared, desperate, leaderless and hungry. The elders of their tribe are gone and with them go their experience and wisdom. They must've carried the recent dead with them to be buried in a nearby cave. Maybe they keep their dead close by as some sort of primitive superstition or as a sense of comfort that the deceased are still watching over them. As for their numbers, I would say five to ten are left. We saw three of them carry the father's body into the trees and you said that at least three adolescents pursued you through the Ape Caves, one of which was killed, possibly two. There was the one that attacked you in Lava Canyon that has never been found. That's at least five and there were probably one or two stragglers we never saw."

The waitress brought the vodka martinis. Chad took a sip finding it very strong and salty.

Andrew took a deep drink and smacked his lips together. He sighed and rested his head back on the booth. "Have you made a decision?"

Chad put down his drink. "That's why I wanted to see you tonight. I have thought about it for sometime and I want to join up with you and get your outfit running again. I've been wandering aimlessly for the last three years and the best way to deal with the pain the Sasquatch have caused me is to confront it. I want these beasts hunted down, killed or at the very least captured and put away where they can't harm anyone again. I also want to do this for Sherrie. I really liked her in the short time that we spent together and she taught me to never give up. I think she would be happy to know that I was working with her father. I'd be honored to work with you."

"Very good," Andrew said and then took another drink of the martini. "Stephen Denmin is going to fully fund my operation. To be frank Chad, I've lost everyone. It will just be you and me to begin with; we'll hire more as needed."

Chad nodded and smiled. "As I've told you before, Sherrie talked very highly of you the short time that I was with her and she was very proud of you."

Andrew grimaced and for a moment his eyes teared up before a firm, determined expression settled over his face. He took a long drink of the martini. "Thank you," he said sadly.

"I have one condition," Chad said with a smirk.

"Which is?" Andrew asked.

Chad grinned and said, "I'll join you as long as I can take a gun with me … many guns."

"Agreed." Andrew chuckled, raising his martini glass. "Cheers."

"Cheers." Chad said as they clinked their glasses together, guaranteeing that a perilous future awaited them.

AUTHOR'S NOTE

If you've made it this far, then that means you've escaped the Ape Caves alive. I hope you didn't get hurt and everyone in your party survived. What did you think? Will you ever go into the caves again?

Unfortunately, I have some bad news for you. The danger isn't over yet. You still have to go on a journey … a deadly one.

"Meredith's Journey" takes place a few days after the events in "The Unleashing." Meredith was last seen being pulled through the kitchen window of cabin by a Bigfoot. Her body was never found. Did she die or did something worse happen? You're about to find out.

I hope you didn't leave your flashlight in the Ape Caves, because you're going to need it. Remember to be careful, be quiet and don't draw attention to yourself and just maybe, you'll survive the journey. Good luck!

MEREDITH'S JOURNEY

The sound of guttural, grunting noises woke Meredith from her light, restless sleep. She opened her eyes to darkness and breathed in the foul odor. It wasn't Frank grunting and farting next to her she realized in utter horror. Her Frank, her husband of twenty-two years was dead, killed by the bear men or Bigfoot or whatever the hell they were. One of them was next to her now; its heavy, hairy arm was resting over her stomach. She was lying on her back on rocky ground that was poking into her. She closed her eyes tight, clenching her teeth and forcing back the tears.

"Be strong, be strong be strong," she repeated rapidly in her mind. She could feel the chest of the Bigfoot pressed into her as it breathed in and out, grunting and snoring. "Help me Lord, help me Lord, help me Lord," she prayed over and over again. How long had it been since her abduction? Would help come? Where were these bear men taking her?

She didn't have a clue, guessing it had been days, maybe weeks since they had captured her. It had been one never-ending journey through darkness, whether they were in some tunnel or moving through the forest in the middle of the night. She had lost all track of time and hadn't seen daylight in what might as well have been an eternity.

Everything had happened so fast. The Bigfoot had appeared out of nowhere and attacked Camp Elizabeth. She had been cooking lunch in the cabin, when one of these freakish monsters had knocked down the door and killed Frank in a matter of seconds. It would have killed her too if it hadn't been for a hunter named Jay who shot the beast in the back.

"I hope you're in heaven Frank," Meredith thought with desperation. They hadn't gone to church much, mostly twice a year, only on Christmas and Easter, but they were believers. Meredith still had a copy of her Mother's bible on the bed stand in her bedroom in Longview, Washington. It was scribbled throughout with red notes that her Mother had written every Sunday in the church pew listening to the Pastor. Meredith and Frank on the other hand, liked to sleep in and Sunday was their day to relax, watching television, ordering pizza and on sunny days barbecuing, so church had always been the last thing on their minds. "It should've been the first," she thought. "Maybe the good Lord would've spared us from this horror."

The Bigfoot pressed up against her, coughing loudly and clearing its throat. Meredith shuddered a moment and then tried to remain completely still so as not to wake it. Who knew what it would do once it woke? Her thoughts returned to Jay, the young man who had saved her. He had just gotten engaged to a young lady that probably didn't even know he was dead yet. A giant, gray, scar-covered Bigfoot had killed Jay shortly after the initial attack. It had ambushed him from behind a tree. It was an awful image that constantly replayed in her mind. "Thank God I killed that one," Meredith thought. She had used all her ammo filling that nasty beast with lead until it dropped down to the ground dead. Meredith still had Jay's engagement ring in her pocket. She had retrieved it from his body with the intent of giving it to his fiancé.

"Those demons killed close to thirty people," she thought with revulsion and sadness. Frank and her had managed Camp Elizabeth for several years. It was only a plane ride north of Vancouver, BC. Thirty hunters, mostly from Longview, had flown up to the Camp for their annual hunting trip. They had all been slaughtered, grown men, who were experienced hunters and armed with rifles. The thought was bewildering to Meredith. The Bigfoot had quickly and easily wiped them all out, after emerging from the tree line, like a wall of death, and swarming the camp in minutes.

From that terrifying moment onwards, Meredith had found no escape or relief. A young man named Chad had survived the attack, and both of them, with Jay, fled through the woods to another cabin by a lake. Unfortunately, Jay had been killed shortly before they reached the cabin, where they met a woman named Claire. They had called Claire's husband for help, who promised to fly to the cabin and rescue them. Meredith even had a chance to call her son Andy in Portland and inform him of his Father's death. That had been one of the hardest things she had ever done.

Everything had seemed to be getting better and escape from their nightmare was in their reach, when suddenly it all turned bad. They had just finished dinner when Meredith volunteered to do the dishes. She had walked to the kitchen and moments later a grotesque face had appeared in the window above the sink. Before she could even react, giant hands had exploded through the glass grabbing her and pulling her through the window. She had been knocked unconscious. When she woke up much later, Meredith had found herself in a cave on top of a heap of dead bodies, many of them hunters and close friends from Camp Elizabeth. It had been chaotic as the Bigfoot rushed around in an almost panic-like state, making alarmed cries. Some of them had been feasting on her friends; while others were howling, screeching and grunting, sounding confused and possibly scared. Other Bigfoot had been holding their wailing children. This confusion had continued until the leader, a tall, powerful looking bear man roared and all went silent. The leader had started making grunting and clicking sounds gesturing wildly with its hands. A short while later, all of the Bigfoot left their lair, taking the bodies and moving down a deep tunnel. Meredith guessed that the Bigfoot knew that they were in deep shit and that more humans would be on their way to hunt them down. She had fainted and woke up again finding herself being carried down a dark passageway by one of the Bigfoot. It had been one of the scariest moments in her life.

The Bigfoot sleeping next to Meredith shifted its weight and its arm slipped off of her. It was still breathing in a slow rhythmic pace so Meredith assumed it was asleep. She opened her eyes slowly and let them adjust to the darkness. It wasn't completely black this time she realized. There was a source of light coming from somewhere. Which Bigfoot was next to her? She already knew the answer, but she had to look. It took her several minutes to build up the courage to move her head to the right to see if Igor was lying next to her.

She grimaced and shuddered when she saw the beast so close to her body. Igor was always sleeping next to her and carrying her whenever they traveled at night. Igor had even saved her life at one point when she had first been captured. Three Bigfoot had surrounded her to feed. The other hunters had all been eaten, their corpses discarded along the way in the tunnels and caverns. She was next.

They had begun nipping at her when Igor snatched her away and roared at the others, knocking them back with its fists. The others had seemed scared and scattered into the dark. From that moment on, Igor had rarely left her side. She had named this Bigfoot Igor because of its disfigured appearance. Igor had a hunched back and not much of a neck. A big growth, resembling a giant tumor, grew on its back and shoulder. It also had some blisters on its left cheek the size of marbles. It was disgusting and Meredith had to turn her eyes when Igor scratched its face. Despite its disfigurement, it seemed strong and could fend for itself.

Meredith shifted her head slightly to the left, her eyes growing wide in surprise and awe. Across the cave, light emanated from the tunnel mouth. "It must lead to the surface," she thought with a nugget of hope. Her body had been battered, cut and starved and she didn't know how much longer she could persevere on this forced journey. She had to escape and reunite with her son. He had already lost his Father and didn't need another parent to die. She wondered what had happened to Chad and Claire. Had they survived? Did they make it back to civilization? She prayed that they were safe and sound. A bleak, terrifying thought slid across her mind like a snake. What if the Bigfoot had captured them too? What if they were in the same position, held captive in some cave by these fucking monsters? She hoped not. The Bigfoot had killed Chad's Father and friends. They had gone through so much trying to survive and escape. It was a dismal thought to think that none of them had escaped so she brushed it from her mind.

Meredith turned her head further left to get a better visual as she breathed quietly trying not to make a sound. In between her and the tunnel opening, where the light shined, were dozens of sleeping Bigfoot lying on the floor. A couple sat near the tunnel looking as if they were posting watch. She would have no chance to even make it halfway across the room. Dismayed by the sight, her heart grew heavy as hopelessness settled upon her mind.

The Bigfoot had been on the move for days, never staying in one place long. They had abandoned their lair and journeyed through tunnel after tunnel. They were fleeing she had come to realize. They were intelligent enough to know that after the attack against Camp Elizabeth, more humans would come sweeping the area, searching for them. It was the only explanation for why the Bigfoot were fleeing Meredith thought, which renewed her hope a little. She was sure there were rescue teams, police and maybe the military combing every inch of the forest.

If Chad and Claire had survived, they would have told the authorities that she had been taken. There was no way the Bigfoot could escape, although there was some lingering doubt in the back of her mind. They had hidden from mankind for all of recorded history. "They must have some smarts," she thought forcing back the utter hopelessness that threatened to consume her.

"Be strong, be strong, be strong," she repeated again in her mind. "I am going to get the hell out of here," she promised herself.

Igor broke into a loud burst of coughing for a few seconds and then quieted down, but its breathing grew quicker and shallower.

Meredith slowly turned her head to the right and gasped. Igor was lying on its side staring at her with its black eyes. It grunted loudly and pulled Meredith closer. She shuddered and started to whimper quietly as Igor began to grab at her curly hair rubbing it between its thick fingers. It had played with her hair several times now. Meredith kept quiet even though Igor pulled too hard on occasion.

"Help me Lord, help me Lord, help me Lord," she kept repeating as Igor spent several minutes feeling her curly hair. It then pulled her closer and licked her forehead leaving a wet mark of salvia dripping down her face. She could feel its hot, stinky breath blowing against her skin. Igor grabbed her left hand and pulled it close to its face as its hairy fingers touched the diamond on her wedding ring as if intrigued by it.

Frank had bought the ring in Portland for her after they had gotten married in Reno after a drunken night. It hadn't been the most romantic wedding, but she was glad that they had gotten hitched. They were made for each other and had been a perfect match despite their constant bickering and arguing over the years. Underneath all of the bullshit, they had loved each other.

Igor wiggled the ring and tried pulling it off but it wouldn't budge. It growled quietly and pushed her hand away as if frustrated. It rested its head on the ground and pulled Meredith closer before falling back asleep.

"I wish I had a gun," Meredith thought as she lay helplessly next to Igor feeling so alone. When would help come? Were they even searching for her? She tried remembering the Lord's Prayer but couldn't find the words, something about the valley of the shadow of death. "The cave of death," she thought.

At some point she fell asleep and dreamed she was back in Longview with Frank at their home watching movies, but unfortunately it turned into a nightmare when Bigfoot knocked down their front door and attacked.

She woke to the clamor of apish grunts and growls as the other Bigfoot began to rise. Igor sat up and yawned. Meredith looked across the chamber and found the tunnel that led to the surface was completely black. "It must be night," she thought, feeling discouraged.

A deep, heavy grunting voice rose over the others as if it was barking orders. Meredith recognized the deep, hard voice as that of the leader. All others deferred to the giant Bigfoot and grew quiet to listen. A few minutes later, Igor picked her up and carried her over its hunched back. They began their nightly walk. There were Bigfoot all around her and as they started off, all of them grew quiet.

They emerged from the cave into the forest. Meredith filled her lungs with the fresh, pine-scented air. It was such a sweet smell to Meredith and much better than the stink of dozens of Bigfoot mixed with the stale air of a cave. Whenever they were outside the Bigfoot became completely silent making little noise except for their quiet steps through the undergrowth.

Meredith twisted her body and looked up to see the countless, bright stars flickering above the branches in the night sky. It was such a beautiful sight and gave her some sense of comfort. When they were above ground she felt better knowing that someone may spot them. There would be no chance of being discovered when she was deep underground.

The Bigfoot walked for over an hour avoiding clearings and staying underneath the canopy of trees. Meredith wondered what direction they were going. They stopped at a fast rushing stream chattering loudly in the quiet of the night. The Bigfoot knelt down all at the same time and began drinking. Igor placed Meredith gently on the bank of the stream, dropped on all fours, and began taking big gulps. Meredith put her hand in the cold water and splashed it on her face wiping off the grime and dried blood from the cuts she had received along the way. She then cupped water in her hands and began drinking, giving relief to her dry, sore throat. She drank more and more. It would be the last time she would be able to drink until the next night. It was a pattern, she noticed, to stop by a stream or lake once every night, usually near the beginning of the hike.

As if receiving a signal, which Meredith didn't recognize or hear, they all stopped drinking at once and stood up. Igor picked her up and followed the others into the trees. Meredith hung over Igor's hunched back in a daze, her back aching and weak knees throbbing as she focused on her breathing trying to remain calm. Igor's muscles tensed and relaxed in a rhythmic motion as it walked while its hair brushed against her body with each step. Meredith glanced at the two Bigfoot walking behind them. They were old, covered in gray hair, sagging skin and frail looking. She wondered how many were in the group, but had no idea. They were spread out at night in the forest and during the day she couldn't tell in the dark of the cave.

She glowered at the old ones wishing that they would drop down and die. She wished they all would die. If only she had a grenade or a machine gun. She would make them pay for what they had done she thought. "If only," the words lingered in her mind. "If only a million different things would've happened, but there was no use in wishing. It won't help my situation."

Crickets or some other type of insect chirped in the night. It was a peaceful sound. She concentrated on the crickets to pass the time, thinking it must be nice for the insects to be free and sing through the night.

At one point, they began to hike up hill, which was uncomfortable for Meredith as Igor made jarring movements and stumbled a couple of times. They emerged from a tree line onto an open rocky ridge. Meredith looked up and saw the black sky filled with bright, numberless stars. She also saw the moon, three quarters full. It was the first time she had seen it in so many nights. The sky had been cloudy for the last few days, but tonight it was clear, so there was much more light. As they walked along the ridge, Meredith saw a dark, forest-covered valley below them with a river rumbling in the distance somewhere in the shadows below, but she couldn't see it. Hills and mountains were standing in every direction, blending into the night sky.

Meredith just wished she could see some hint of civilization like the bright lights of a town or even a lone house, but there was nothing except wilderness. They followed along the ridge for a distance and then up a steep slope before moving descending again. It had been nice for Meredith to be out in the open. They entered an area of rocky ground with trees spread thin with less undergrowth. They continued along the hill at the higher elevation for a while and then went downhill for a short way before ascending a rough slope.

A child Bigfoot, maybe five feet tall, began jumping around and making loud squealing noises until an adult rushed over, growled and hit the child across the face sending it to the ground. The child immediately went silent and made no more noise for the rest of the night.

Finally, they stopped near a rock outcropping and a steep cliff face. Up ahead, a Bigfoot climbed up the cliff and vanished. It returned a short while later and made grunting noises and clicking sounds to the leader, who responded back with deep grunts. By this time, the eastern sky started turning from black to a dark gray.

"The sun will be rising soon," she thought, hoping that they would still be outside when dawn arrived. To feel the sun's warmth and see the world in the light would be a blessing. Her whole existence since her abduction had been spent in darkness.

The Bigfoot at the front of the line climbed up the rock and vanished into the shadows. Others followed until it was their turn. Meredith gripped the hair on Igor's humped back trying to brace herself as it climbed up the rock. Luckily, Meredith didn't fall or bang her legs against the rock and they were at the top in a few seconds. They reached the cliff wall where a black, gaping cave mouth appeared. Meredith managed to glimpse the eastern sky once more before they entered the cave and found that the horizon had turned from a dark gray to a light gray. The sun would be rising shortly she realized with dismay knowing that she would miss it.

Once inside the cave, they walked down a tunnel and passed by Bigfoot sitting down along the walls. The Bigfoot grew loud again, grunting, clicking and making growling noises obviously communicating with each other. Igor found an open spot and placed Meredith down by the wall and then it sat next to her. Meredith felt exhausted, having eaten little but a few roots Igor had given her. Most of the time her stomach had been upset, but she felt ravenous at the moment. She needed to eat and gain strength back, which she would need if she ever found a chance to escape.

Igor put its heavy hand on top of her head and began pawing through her hair. She wanted to yell at the top of her lungs, "Leave me alone," but she kept quiet too scared of the consequences. Whatever the reason, Igor had taken a liking to her. If the monster hadn't, Meredith knew she would've been killed by now. They most likely would've eaten her like all the others. She let Igor caress her hair knowing that the beast could turn on her and probably would at some point. For now she had to use Igor to her advantage and hopefully find a way to escape, although its touch disgusted her.

The cave entrance lit up with morning daylight allowing Meredith to see her surroundings. Bigfoot were all around her sitting in the tunnel, some were already lying down sleeping. It was a horrific sight as occasionally one of them would glare at her with black eyes blistering with insolence and hate. One of the adults flashed its teeth at her and growled. Igor reacted immediately and growled back, swiping its claws in the air. The adult moved down the cave away from them.

"I'm an unwanted stranger in their midst," Meredith thought fearfully.

Sudden commotion began at the entrance of the cave as several Bigfoot entered carrying the freshly killed carcasses of deer and another held two fish in its clawed hands. Eager shrieks and excited squeals filled the cave as many of the Bigfoot moved towards the entrance to feast. Igor stood up and pushed through the crowd returning with handfuls of flesh that it was stuffing in its mouth. It handed Meredith a chunk.

Meredith took the slimy wet piece of flesh, which was still warm. She couldn't tell what part of the deer she held in her hands, but she knew it wasn't the fish. Igor chomped his portion, consuming it quickly. She was so hungry. "If I don't eat, I'll die," she thought as she looked at the piece of raw meat, which still had hairy skin on one side of it. "At least its was just killed." She lifted the piece to her face and sniffed unable to smell anything except the stink of the Bigfoot. That was all she had smelled for days being surrounded by dozens of them in cramped caves. They all stunk, but she was growing use to it. She squeezed the flesh prodding and probing it, feeling no bones and concluding that it was mostly muscle with little fat.

"If I have to do this to survive so I can escape and see my son again, I will," she thought and bit into the meat forcing herself to chew and swallow it. The meat was wet and coarse, hard to swallow until she chewed it several times. It wasn't so bad that she couldn't tolerate it, so she took another bite and chewed. She continued the process until she was done. She threw the bits of hair-covered skin to the ground.

After the feast, the Bigfoot settled down and began to rest. Meredith started to drift off, exhausted physically, emotionally and mentally. Tears filled her eyes before she finally fell asleep.

Sometime later she woke up in pain, her stomach churning as sweat beaded on her forehead. Igor was snoring next to her. She glanced down the tunnel at the entrance where daylight still shined like a beacon calling for her to escape. Her stomach felt like it was twisting as it made a loud gurgling sound. She hunched over and suddenly threw up, heaving raw venison from her stomach in a stream, splattering the cave floor. She gasped for air and spit up more with a momentary reprieve before she barfed again, this time mostly a dry heave except for bile and salvia. Igor snored through it and after a while she felt better although her stomach still ached. She lay down on the rocky floor and began to cry. About an hour later she threw up again.

That evening when they left the cave, she was thankful that Igor carried her, since she felt weak and sick to her stomach. As they moved through the forest she wondered how she would escape. She had bad knees, wasn't in shape and her strength was quickly draining. How could she possibly escape? That question floated in her mind until she somehow fell asleep on top of Igor's hunched back as the beast walked through the forest.

The group of Bigfoot found another cave hours later. Igor brought Meredith a handful of blackberries, a few acorns and a couple roots. She ate the berries first. The sweet taste was a delight. She licked her lips trying to savor every taste. The nuts were next and felt good to eat even though her stomach was still slightly upset. She was ravenous and had to eat. The nuts were something solid that filled her up a little. The roots she wasn't sure about, but ate them anyways. The outside was rough and the inside was crunchy and wet with a bland taste, kind of like a cucumber. No matter, it filled her stomach and she felt much better afterwards. Igor watched her eat and when she was finished, the creature began playing with her hair for a few minutes. She wanted to slap its hands off and yell at it to leave her alone, but she didn't dare. Igor seemed to grow bored with her hair after a while and pulled her left hand near its face and touched the diamond on her wedding ring. Igor squeezed the ring and tried to gently pull it off. When it didn't budge, Igor dropped her hand and grunted in frustration.

At that moment, she decided she would try to escape during the coming night. She had no choice, unsure how much more she could take and not trusting Igor. The beast could turn on her at any moment. She had to see her son again. Who knew what he thought at the moment? His father was dead and his mother was missing.

Meredith dozed off on the sharp, rocky ground of the cave as Igor's massive shape laid next to her. Its body pressed in on her as its thick, heavy arm pulled her close. Meredith trembled at Igor's touch. The beast stunk and its chest rubbed against her back. It scared her to have this monster, the same kind who killed her husband, so close. Igor licked the back of her neck with its leathery, wet tongue and squeezed her breast. Meredith cringed and forced herself to remain still. Igor grunted a couple times and then fell asleep. Meredith drifted in and out of a half sleep plagued with nightmares of being chased through the woods by Igor and all the others.

Meredith woke to the loud grunts and clicking noises of the leader as it barked orders to the others. Igor sat up and cleared its throat and spit on the ground. It stretched its arms and touched Meredith's hair a moment. The other Bigfoot all around began to rise and get ready for the night's journey. Meredith stood up and groaned as she put pressure on her left knee, finding it swollen and throbbing. She prayed it would hold up, especially if she found an opportunity to escape.

Igor rose to its feet as the Bigfoot started a procession out of the cave. Meredith cringed as Igor stared at her for a minute in the dark of the cave with cold, black eyes that gave no hint of humanity. Meredith backed away trying to keep her wits and resolve. The eye narrowed and grew beastly. She gasped quietly trying to remain strong. Igor grunted and seized her in a quick motion, picking her up and putting her over its shoulder. Meredith winced as her face pressed into Igor's thick back lump.

"Be strong," she thought. "I must escape."

They proceeded out of the cave and into the cool, fresh night air of the forest. They walked down a hill winding in and out of the trees. Two female Bigfoot with saggy breasts walked behind Igor. Meredith glanced at them as they ignored her, keeping their heads down in silence. Behind the females, walked an adolescent that kept looking at her curiously.

In the distance the sound of a river rumbled in the valley below them. Occasionally the sound of fluttering wings from a bat or some night bird would start and fade quickly. They reached level ground and crossed through a clearing giving Meredith a chance to gaze up at the night sky, which wasn't as bright as the night before because of the clouds that floated over them. Many bright stars were still visible which made Meredith feel good and gave her a little joy. She liked the stars and for some reason they gave her hope, little bits of light in a world of darkness.

They crossed the clearing quickly and entered the cover of trees. A short while later, the procession stopped at the banks of a dark mountain lake. Igor placed Meredith down and began to lap up the water like all the others. Meredith placed her hands in the cold water, tempted to jump in and start swimming. Would the Bigfoot pursue her? Could they swim? She remembered Chad saying that they had crossed a river to attack Camp Elizabeth. She wasn't a strong swimmer either, but the thought of escape at that moment was pleasant.

She cupped the cool lake water and began drinking as the Bigfoot around made slurping and splashing noises. Even though the water was cold, she wished she could wade in just to get clean and get the stink off of her. She hadn't showered for days and was covered in dirt and dried blood. Her clothes were ripped and tattered. She must look like a mess. The leader made a single screeching noise and all the Bigfoot stopped drinking and stood up. Meredith struggled to her feet as her left knee threatened to explode if she put too much weight on it. She didn't have to worry since Igor picked her up immediately and flung her over his hunched back. The bump on his back was boney with lots of fat padding it.

The line of Bigfoot moved away from the mountain lake and back into the cover of the trees as Meredith's thoughts turned to Frank. She had been cooking them hamburgers when a Bigfoot knocked down the cabin door. It was upon Frank so quickly that he didn't even have time to stand up from the dining room table. Her brow furrowed at the thought as her anger boiled to the surface. She wanted to strike out and make them pay. "They killed my Frank," she thought.

Igor stopped abruptly. Other Bigfoot in the line also came to a sudden halt and looked up. This perplexed Meredith, who had heard no signal from the leader for them to stop. She gazed up at the night sky and saw stars flickering through the branches of the trees and then she heard it, a quiet hum in the distance. The other Bigfoot glanced at each other, some even making quiet, worried grunts. The hum grew louder and closer overhead and then she recognized it.

"A plane," she whispered, shifting her body so she could look up easier without completely straining her neck. "A plane," she gasped in excitement.

A Bigfoot, possibly the leader made one loud screech and the rest of them immediately became silent and dropped to the ground. Many vanished into the dark shadows of the undergrowth. Igor placed Meredith on the ground and pulled her into a crop of tall ferns. Igor sat down and forced Meredith to sit on its lap. Meredith struggled to break free, until Igor yanked her back and gave a low growl of warning. Meredith yielded, but pushed back some of the ferns so she could have a clearer view of the sky. The hum grew to a loud buzz.

Igor breathed quick and heavy, looking up into the sky with wide, fierce eyes, tinged with fear. Meredith could feel its chest expand and contract against her. Its hot, stinky breath blew against the back of her neck and head. The buzzing grew even louder. It was the most wonderful noise Meredith had ever heard. Her heart began to race.

"It's flying low to the ground," she thought excitedly. "Maybe they're looking for me."

Suddenly the plane roared overhead in a quick blur of motion, its lights briefly illuminating their hiding place. Igor tensed in fright and pulled Meredith back. She struggled to break free, but didn't have the strength against such a powerful foe. The buzzing quickly became a low hum again. Meredith's head dropped and her eyes filled with tears that began to slide down her dirty face. "No," she whispered. "Come back."

Anger began to build, deep inside her. She would do anything to escape. The longer she was held captive the harder it would be to escape. She wasn't getting any stronger and who knew how much longer Igor would keep her. The beast could grow angry or hungry and eat her for all she knew. They waited for several minutes until the faint hum vanished completely. It was disheartening, but also it renewed her will to try to escape. She was scared, but that would have to be brushed away. It was the first sign of civilization she had seen since the Bigfoot had pulled her through that window.

"Lord help me," she prayed. "Give me a chance. Let someone find me. Thank you."

The Bigfoot emerged from their hiding places all at once. It was a scary sight seeing all these tall, dark shadowy figures appear from the undergrowth standing all around her. Igor stood up and flipped Meredith over its shoulder. The Bigfoot began to walk, but this time their pace was faster as if hurrying to the next resting place and safety. Meredith kept replaying the image of the airplane flying overhead in her mind.

Frank had been a pilot and part of his job was to fly the hunters back and forth from Camp Elizabeth. There had been many times when Meredith and Frank had taken day trips flying around the area sightseeing and exploring the beautiful mountainous regions with green lakes, deep valleys and treetops of the forests carpeting the rugged terrain. It had been a breath-taking sight, but little did she know that the wilderness they had flown over so many times contained such terror. "Beasts from hell," she thought. If only her and Frank were in a plane right now, flying away from these monsters. It was a pleasant thought, but Frank was dead and creatures that shouldn't even exist had captured her.

The Bigfoot procession moved along the slope of a hill overlooking a broad valley. The cloudy sky hid the moon making it darker then the night before. Meredith glimpsed a dark lake in the valley and wasn't sure if it was the same one that they had drank out of at the start of the night. A Bigfoot ahead of them made a quick shrill, apish scream. Igor halted immediately, glancing around in a panic, looking up in the sky. Other Bigfoot started making quiet grunts of confusion. A whooshing buzz began in the distance, different than the airplane.

All of a sudden, across the valley, a helicopter rose from behind the hill, its bright spotlight shining down on the tops of the trees. The Bigfoot reacted immediately and rushed for cover. Some hid behind trees while others lay flat on the ground blending in with the foliage. Pulling Meredith with it, Igor jumped behind a rotten log, which had ferns and other plants, which could be used as cover. The helicopter flew over the treetops of the hill across the valley moving slowly as the spotlight moved back and forth on the ground in a methodic manner.

"They're looking for me," Meredith thought. "They're looking for me."

The whoosh of the helicopter's propellers filled the valley. Meredith realized that this was her chance. Without thought, She stood up, lunged over the rotten log and started running to the open ground of the slope.

"HELP ME," Meredith screamed with every last bit of air in her lungs. "HELLLLLLLLPPP," she shouted with all of her might waving her arms back and forth. The helicopter proceeded along the distant hill, the spotlight far from her position.

Igor jumped up and chased after her, growling angrily. Despite her bad knee, Meredith ran as the heavy thumps of Igor's footsteps grew closer and louder.

"HELP ME," she screamed. "HELPPPPPPP."

Igor tackled her to the ground. Meredith fought back viciously, hitting, and trying to gouge out its eyes with her fingernails, while screaming for help the entire time. Igor roared hard and deep, flashing its jagged teeth and slamming her in the head with its fist knocking her unconscious.

It was sometime before Meredith woke up drifting in and out of a dream state and a black nothingness. Her dreams were of the helicopter flying overhead and of a plane landing with Frank at the controls waving for her to jump in so they could fly to safety. Meredith ran for the plane, but Igor caught her every time. The image of Igor towering over her would always appear and then the dream would end.

She slowly drifted into consciousness in stages, feeling a cold sensation through her body. The pain in her head grew into focus until it became an overpowering migraine, as if a drill was being pushed into her forehead. Her nose was clogged and it was hard for her to breathe, one nasal passageway was completely closed. She realized she was lying on her side on the rocky ground. She felt something big and hairy behind her, breathing deeply. She knew exactly what it was and opened her eyes to complete darkness. She turned slightly and felt Igor's hairy chest. They were in some cave sleeping, the helicopter long gone.

"Tonight," she thought. "I will escape tonight." The helicopter and plane were probably searching the area for her and other possible survivors that may have escaped the massacre at Camp Elizabeth. She was positive that the whole forest around the camp was filled with rescue teams, police and reporters not to mention others who would see this as an opportunity to bag them a Bigfoot and become rich and famous. The further these monsters took her away from the Camp, the less chance there was of someone finding her.

"Tonight," she thought. "It has to be tonight." She touched her face finding it covered in crusted, dry blood. Her nose felt like it had been broken. One nostril was completely closed. "I must look horrid," she thought and then a sudden feeling of sadness hit her, realizing she was completely alone. No one was here to help her. "Be strong," she thought.

Igor woke up later and began caressing her hair with its heavy rough hands. It licked the back of her neck several times and squeezed her right breast. Meredith cringed at the touch as she plotted her escape. The beast grabbed her left hand and began touching her wedding ring, pressing down on the diamond as if it liked the hard surface. It pulled her hand close to its face and licked the back of her hand three times and then put it down.

The leader screeched an order from somewhere in the darkness of the cave and the Bigfoot began to rise around her.

"This is it," Meredith whispered in a dry, hoarse voice. They left the cave and followed the line of Bigfoot moving quickly, much faster than previous nights. They moved downhill into the deep forest. Meredith kept glancing up at the sky and listening for any sign of a helicopter or plane.

Her chance came about three hours into their walk. Igor placed her down and walked a few feet away and squatted in some ferns to take a shit. The adult Bigfoot right behind them walked by quickly without a second look. An old white haired Bigfoot was lumbering towards them, its head down as it navigated slowly around the uneven ground.

Meredith clenched her teeth and ran from the line of Bigfoot into the trees. The ground dropped sharply and Meredith fell almost immediately, rolling through the brush for several feet. She struggled up and almost fell again because of her bad knee, but she braced her hands against a tree for a moment and continued.

Igor gave a high-pitched, punctuated shriek. Meredith ran faster, barreling through the undergrowth as fast as she could, her only thought was that of reaching her son. She burst out of the branches of a bush into a rocky clearing. It was a cloudless sky allowing the stars to shine bright giving her enough light to move around the rocks without tripping.

"Help me Lord, help me Lord," she prayed as a Bigfoot stepped from behind a rock and growled raising its claws to strike. It wasn't Igor, but another adult, mean and ugly, without the hunched back and much taller. Even at night Meredith could see a deep, pinkish, thick scar that covered one side of its chest. Without hesitation, she yelled defiantly, dropping to the ground and grabbing a loose rock. She flung it at the advancing beast with all of her might. The rock bounced off its shoulder before it was upon her swiping with claws that would have lopped off her head if her bad knee hadn't given out at that moment causing her to fall to the ground.

The Bigfoot missed and was preparing to strike again when Igor jumped from the top of a boulder and knocked the other Bigfoot down, hacking and slashing with its claws. A vicious battle ensued, both monsters growling and roaring until the taller one, broke off the fight and moved away, flashing its teeth defiantly before disappearing in the tree line. In the meantime, Meredith had crawled several feet away. She tried to stand, but her left knee gave out and she crashed to the ground. She crawled faster, determination lining her desperate face.

Igor turned around and glared at Meredith with blistering, black eyes. It roared and rushed over to her. It snapped its teeth in front of her face and flashed its black claws. Salvia spit out of its mouth as it roared spraying her face. It raised its claws over Meredith's head preparing to strike a deadly blow when Meredith pulled out Jay's engagement ring from her pocket.

"Here, take it," she cried and offered it in the palm of her hand. Igor stopped in mid strike breathing deeply and growling. It stared at the ring for several seconds and then lowered it claws. "Take it … it's all yours," Meredith said. Igor kneeled and snatched the ring from her hand. It examined the ring, squeezing the silver in its fingers for several minutes as Meredith watched, petrified, unsure of what to do.

There was no way she could outrun Igor with or without her swollen knee. Igor tried putting on the ring, but it wouldn't fit. Igor finally managed to shove the ring a quarter of the way down on its left pinky. The Sasquatch's expression turned less hostile as it looked at Meredith and then at its new ring. Igor licked Meredith's forehead and then picked her up, flipping her over its shoulder. It began to jog through the forest to catch up with the others.

"I will try again tomorrow night," she whispered with all of the determination she could muster.

Tomorrow night arrived and the leader screeched its orders and the Bigfoot began to rise. Igor finished playing with her hair and then picked her up. This time, the Bigfoot didn't head for the exit; instead they began to descend into the cave.

"What?" Meredith whispered, glancing nervously about in the dark in a worried panic, searching for the entrance to the cave that was across the chamber. Igor turned a corner and they were enveloped in pitch-black darkness. They continued walking through the tunnel. Igor moved slowly touching the cave wall for guidance.

About an hour into their journey, Meredith knew deep within her heart that they wouldn't be going to the surface that night and her chance to escape was gone.

"Tomorrow," she whispered trying to keep her wits. "I'll escape tomorrow."

Tomorrow came and they never surfaced into the forest, instead they walked through black, narrow tunnels and wide caverns, filled with cold, stale air. Four sleeping cycles later, Meredith's resolve was crumbling quickly and what little hope of escape she had managed to keep was nearly extinguished. They were still deep in some tunnel system and she knew no help would find her in the depths of the earth. Each day, she was getting farther away from Camp Elizabeth and the search parties. Igor picked her up and grunted a moment before taking her down the passageway.

"I will escape, I will escape, I will escape," Meredith whispered as the dark of the cave swallowed her whole.

978-0-595-48376-1
0-595-48376-3

Printed in the United States
109309LV00003B/260/A